The Daisy Chain Reaction

Book One

A.C. Nightingale

Book 1 of 2 in The Daisy Chain Duo

Publisher of Record: Indie Author Revolution

ISBN: 978-1-968700-85-0

Cover Design & Art: Nina Wegert https://theburntpencilart.square.site/

To my husband Will, thank you for not letting me give up on my dreams. Even when it felt impossible you refused to let me give up on myself and I will forever be grateful for all of the experiences I have been able to have from becoming an author. I couldn't do all that I do without you by my side. **You're my smelly cheeseburger for life.**

To my sister, Nina, thank you for your tireless work to bring my covers and visions to life. **We are Rose and Violet forever.** You're my built in best friend and the reason I have kept pushing through all these years.

To my sister, Kay, thank you for showing me that family doesn't mean we share the same blood. I wouldn't change anything that happened in my life for fear that I wouldn't have the privilege to know you and have you as my adopted sister. **I wouldn't have Joy without you, and without Joy the story just wouldn't be the same.**

The Trauma Troopers: my lifeline, my best friends, the reason I get up every morning. No yeeting unless you want to enact the pact.

Momo, Beep, Lizzie, Fives, Bubby, Bean, Kong, and Zilla.

The Indie Author Revolution: When one of us rises, we all rise together. Totally worth the spleen sacrifice.

"Tell them I loved you right up til' the end,
Tell them to love you was everything I am,
Darling, I won't let you fade, from here."

-Vincent Lima, End of Eurydice

ASL Terms Explained

FISH: Done, Finished.

VEE VEE: Good to know.

TRAIN GONE SORRY: "You missed the boat."

KISS FIST: To love something, but not in a romantic way.

TRUE BIZ: For real. Seriously.

CHAMP: The best of the best.

258: Very Interesting.

Communication that is SIM-COMMED (ASL & Spoken English simultaneously will be in this font.

Communication that is "voice-off" Signed Language will be in bold.

As a Hard-of-Hearing author, my goal is to showcase my Deaf characters and their experiences. Stories can challenge stereotypes and promote inclusion. Learning even a handful of signs can create meaningful connections between Deaf and hearing people. These small efforts can spark big changes in how we interact and connect. **I hope you love Violet as much as I do.**

CONTENTS

Stepping into the Mews & Brews Cat Cafe, my BBFL, *Best Barista For Life*, hands my usual, an Apple Spice Chai Latte, over the counter. It's still steaming, and I wrap my fingers around it, enjoying the warmth.

"What do we have for snacks today?" He snaps his fingers before exclaiming, "We've got a perfect match for your yoozh today. Care to try an Apple Pie Scone with Clotted Cream?"

"Do you even have to ask?" I tease as he hands the pastry to me.

With my little treats in hand, I settle into my favorite corner table. The noise of the coffee shop blends into a comforting backdrop. It's a little piece of home amidst the chaos of New York City.

Recently, I was promoted to Columnist for The Manhattan Beacon, and thankfully, I got to keep the luxury of working remotely. I started at the bottom as an Editorial Assistant and have worked my way up the ladder, slowly but surely. It isn't the highest-paying gig, but it has kept me on the path to where I want to be. Getting to work in my dream field makes all of the sacrifices I've made worth it. The extra perks, like the daily food and drink allowance, help too.

I pull out my laptop and sift through leads for this week's *Health & Wellness Trends*. It's not glamorous and is only a tiny feature in bi-weekly articles, but it's my foot in the door.

I've always loved writing. In high school, I was on the school paper, and my desire grew through my college journalism classes. Every article, every lead, is a step toward that big break I've been dreaming of.

As I work, I pull out my phone and press Violet's number for a video call.

She answers almost immediately, her face smeared with paint. I wave to get her attention, which is hard when she's lost in her art.

"Hey, Violet!" I sign to her.

I wave at the screen, signing a casual greeting. Violet looks exhausted, but she brightens when she sees me.

"What's up?" she signs back, wiping her forehead, leaving a streak of pink paint in its trail.

"Mrs. Wong is making Peking Duck tonight. She said it'll be ready at 6," I sign.

I tilt my head slightly, knowing she's got a soft spot for the dish. I can tell she's already drooling at the idea.

"Do you want me to pick you up?" I motion.

"Yes, please. I do not want to drive. Mama's drinking tonight!" she replies.

I chuckle. **"You deserve it! And I was thinking we could go back to your house after dinner. I'm sure Mei is dying to see your new house."**

"Yeah, sounds good. I'll force Cam to do some cleaning," she signs with a wink.

"Put that boy to work!" I gesture emphatically, and we both laugh. **"I'll pick you up around 5:30, okay?"**

"Okay, see you then."

After ending the video call, I send a quick text to let Mei know about going back to Vi's house after dinner. I can't believe we are all going to be together after so long.

I look at my watch, wishing that time would speed up, but it doesn't.

For the next few hours, I busy myself with the various work assignments that are littering my inbox. Even though there are many tasks on my to-do list, I am grateful that today's work has not been too labor-intensive.

I wrap up my work, check the time, and shut down my laptop with a decisive click. I have enough time to run home and take a quick nap before dinner.

Once I'm back at home, I practically throw myself onto the bed. As soon as my head hits the pillow, I shut my eyes, and I am out.

I jolt awake, drenched in sweat. I glance at my reflection in my Art Deco mirror - I'm a mess. I'm sporting sleep lines that make me look like I've been wrestling with a pillow all afternoon. That nap was CHAMP.

I've got about thirty minutes before I need to head out, so I shake off the sleepiness and get to work.

I brush out my rose-colored hair until it's smooth and flowing, touch up my makeup to bring back that fresh-faced glow, and slip into my favorite outfit: a pair of black ripped skinny jeans, a vintage Nirvana tee that's seen better days - but calling it *vintage* gives it a few more years of wear - and my lucky leather jacket that adds just the right edge. I finish off the look with my combat boots, and I'm officially ready to see my girls.

I head over to Violet's, an excited buzz filling my abdomen.

Violet is sitting on the front stoop when I pull up. She looks more put together than I've seen her in a while. **"Looking good!"** I sign to her as she slips into the passenger seat.

She scoffs. **"Yeah, right. I have 3 mystery stains on my shirt, and my hair is a mess,"** she signs defeatedly.

Violet pulls the visor mirror down and throws her hair up into a messy ponytail as I drive to our destination.

She looks at me with an expression that clearly says *good enough.*

I park, and we walk up to the restaurant. Violet turns to me and signs, **"I can't believe Mei is back. It feels like it's been forever."**

"I know!" I sign excitedly.

We give a knowing look and race each other to the door.

The noise and clamor of the place always feel calming, like a chaotic symphony I've grown accustomed to. I see Mei's vivid red hair through the kitchen window.

Her parents used to force her to wear a black wig while working at the restaurant, but no one has ever been able to tell Mei what to do. I love that about her. We've been friends since the day we were born, and I've never seen her get pushed around once.

Violet and I sneak up to the kitchen door, and I push it open an inch. "THE SERVICE HERE IS TERRIBLE!" I yell into the kitchen, trying to stifle my laughter.

There's a clatter of dishes and an excited shriek coming from within. Moments later, the swinging door flies open, and the three of us are locked in a long-awaited embrace. I hadn't entirely realized how much I missed us being together.

We stand hugging until Mrs. Wong shoos us out from behind the counter. "Employees only! Mei is officially off duty!" she yells as she's pushing us out.

Mei quickly interprets for Violet, and we burst into a fit of laughter.

We slide into our usual booth that's hidden in the back. We fit in comfortably like we have since we were small children.

Mei's parents don't waste any time, and soon enough, our table is overflowing with steaming baskets of duck, crispy spring rolls, and all the mouthwatering dishes that make this place legendary.

We dig in immediately, and our conversation flows like we have never been separated for any amount of time.

We talk about everything and nothing, the good, the bad, and the ugly. For a few hours, the world outside doesn't matter, just three friends, a mountain of delectable dishes, and the kind of bond that makes every bite a little bit sweeter.

As we finish eating, Mei's eyes catch Violet's hair. She smirks. **"Violet, when was the last time you dyed your hair? The purple is gone!"**

Violet rolls her eyes but laughs, a familiar light in her gaze. **"Life has been so busy. My roots haven't been a priority."**

We exchange knowing glances. The idea hits all of us at seemingly the same time.

"Should we have a hair dyeing party, like old times?" I suggest. They both nod eagerly.

After dinner, we pile into my car, the excitement bubbling over as we head to the hair supply store. It's a throwback to simpler times, and we all relish the thought of unwinding together.

After picking out the perfect shades of rose pink, violet purple, and a vivid plum red, we decide to go to Violet's house to get the job done. It might seem like a cliché, dyeing our hair to match our names, but it's something we've done since high school. Did we get made fun of in school for our choices? Absolutely. Did we care? *Absolutely not.* Through all of life's ups and downs, the three of us have stayed consistent.

On the way to Violet's house, I flick on the overhead light, rummaging through the glove compartment for a familiar CD labeled *Violet's Beats.*

When I finally find it, I flash it around the car like I just discovered a lost treasure before sliding it into the player.

These early 2000s to 2010s tracks with solid bass aren't exactly what I'd call masterpieces, but they've got one key feature: Violet can feel the beat when the volume's loud enough.

Her favorite song, *Black and Yellow,* comes on, and I crank it up to full blast, and the three of us laugh as we try to sign along to the lyrics. Trust me, it's more complicated than you think when you're driving and can barely remember half the words, even if most of them are in the title.

If I knew then what I know now, I would've forced myself to cling to every fleeting detail of that night. I wish I had realized that it was the last time I'd ever experience a sense of normalcy. I wish I had made the most of every second with my girls, not just letting the moments slip by.

I wish I'd told them I loved them more often, not taking their presence for granted. I wish I had understood the significance of that night, how it would be the last echo of our untroubled laughter before everything changed. I wish...

Black and yellow. Black and yellow.

1

CHAPTER ONE

My mornings always start the same way: the soft chime of the coffee shop door and the familiar scent of fresh coffee and baked goods.

At 7:15 AM, as if by clockwork, Sam hands me my Apple Spice Chai Latte. I never deviate, and today is no exception. Routine is everything, especially when I've got work breathing down my neck.

All is going to plan until I turn away from Sam, and my smile drops immediately. Someone is sitting in my booth. The one I occupy every single morning. The one by the window. The booth is practically molded to fit only me. I can't even think straight if I'm not in my seat.

A dark-haired brute, head down, scrolling through his phone like he owns the place, sits comfortably in my booth.

My chest tightens, and I feel like my day is already slipping out of my control.

I shake my head, gather my strength, and stride over, tapping on the table to get his attention. "Hey, I'm sorry, but you're in my seat." My tone is sharp because I am not in the mood to play nice. "I sit here every morning. I've got a lot of work to do, so if you don't mind... I need you to move."

I can't sugarcoat this. If I don't get that seat, the day is shot, and today's project will be taken down with it. That's a risk I'm not willing to take.

The man looks up, and for a second, I'm completely flustered. His chiseled jaw and kind green eyes are not what I expected, and I can tell he is thoroughly amused by this whole situation.

He smiles, a little too confident for my liking, and leans back in my chair. "Well, I wouldn't want to ruin your workday," he says, teasing as he slides out of my booth, grabbing his coffee. "I'd be happy to oblige."

He bows. Like actually bows. I can't help but roll my eyes at the exaggerated show of it all. "Name's Thorne, by the way. What's yours?"

I hesitate, caught off guard by this man towering over me. "Rose," I say quickly as I set my things on the table. I'm so ready to just move along with my day if only this guy would buzz off. But instead, he just lingers there with a goofy smile that I'd just love to smack right off his face.

"I'd say 'it's been a pleasure,' but it's not actually enjoyable to stick your hand in a rosebush. You know, with the thorns and all. I can tell you are a little prickly. Something tells me you could easily rip me to shreds."

The audacity. "Only when I need to be," I shoot back, trying to maintain my composure.

"Good to know," he replies, leaning against the edge of my table.

He's even more attractive up close, and I can't seem to look him directly in the eye.

"But seriously, what's a beautiful girl like you doing eating alone? This place is a gold mine for great conversation."

I raise an eyebrow, trying to keep my cool. "I came here for the coffee, not the company. Besides, I'm too busy to take on a mining side hustle."

"Busy, huh?" He tilts his head, studying me like I'm a puzzle he's eager to solve. "I would be happy to bring the gold mine to you."

I roll my eyes, though a smile fights its way to my lips. "I appreciate the offer, but I really don't need the distraction right now. My life is exciting enough without adding a cheesy flirt to the mix."

"Me? A flirt? Never," he teases, his gaze never leaving mine. "Cheesy? Always. You can't blame a guy for trying to make some friendly conversation. But now that I know you're a regular, maybe I'll come see you again when you're less 'busy.'"

He winks.

I roll my eyes again, fighting a smile. "Good luck with that. I think you'll find I have been eternally buried six feet under in work assignments."

"I always loved the idea of trying to become a graverobber," he says, leaning in just a fraction closer. "Guess I'll have to go home and polish up my good shovel. See you around, Rose."

I watch him finally leave my table, and I find I am irritated and intrigued by this strange man. I got next to no sleep last night thanks to a delightful little nightmare about dying in the emergency room, and now this." Great start to the day, Rose," I mutter, shaking my head.

I barely have time to manage my own life, let alone add some self-absorbed lover boy like him into the mix. It takes everything I have to ignore him chatting up the new barista with that same cocky grin. *What a flirt.*

I pull out my notebook, determined to violently drown the remnants of our interaction.

As soon as I'm settled in, Dolly Purrton, a white Persian kitten, hops into my lap. She's only three weeks old, and I'm already in love. I swear one day I'll adopt her, but for now, Sam keeps her here just for our morning snuggles.

I take a minute to dote on Dolly, and then I open my laptop, ready to dive into my day.

The familiar ping of incoming emails greets me, but I get a knot in my stomach when I see eighteen bold subject lines all screaming "URGENT." Every single one is from the team, of course. They are scrambling for a break in the latest feature, and naturally, they need it now.

There's an Italian deli in Bensonhurst, Brooklyn, a true neighborhood gem. It's been around for over seventy years in the same storefront. It's a place where you can feel the history, but with the original owner in hospice, his grandson is on the verge of having to close the doors for good.

A family restaurant is a legacy - precisely the kind that pulls at a reader's heartstrings. As an Associate Editor / Researcher, it's up to me to dig into their past, trace it all the way back to Italy, if I can, and craft an entirely unforgettable packet of information. *No pressure, right?*

I dive in, scrolling through old articles, searching archives and town records, and making phone calls to anyone who could be considered a lead. I'm lining up interviews, setting appointments with family members, neighbors, happy restaurant customers - anyone who can give me the history to bring this story to life.

For reasons I cannot explain, I catch myself looking up from my screen every once in a while to glance toward Thorne. And every time he's already watching me, that same smile is still plastered on his stupid face. I feel my cheeks heat, and I immediately return my attention to the task at hand. I don't have time for distractions. *Not today.* Not ever, really.

Time always slips away when I'm deep in my research, and today is no different. I get lost in the shuffle of piecing together the deli's history like a puzzle, one phone call at a time. It's my rhythm.

A tap on the table snaps me out of my trance.

I glance up, and Thorne is leaning against the booth with a teasing grin. "Ground control to Major Rose." He chuckles. "Didn't mean to pull you out of your work zone, but it was like you didn't even know that the rest of the world existed."

I'm annoyed at how easily he catches me off guard. He makes some offhand comment about how he'll "see me around," and with another mock bow, he's gone just as quickly as he appeared.

I try to shake off the interruption, returning to my work, but I can't help feeling upset with myself. I liked the attention, even if it was just a little. I was almost tempted to invite him to sit with me for a little while. Which is ridiculous.

I don't have time for this - least of all, some smooth-talking stranger who has nothing to do with the story I'm trying to crack. Still, I catch myself replaying the moment in my head before forcing myself to focus again.

I can't focus. I have a killer headache, and I'm starving.

I head to the counter, stomach growling, and order a sandwich. I joke with Sam about brain food, and he tells me he'll bring it to my table.

It arrives, not glamorous, but it'll do the job.

I eat hurried bites between phone calls, fingers flying across my keyboard as I keep at my work.

Hours pass in a blur of articles, interviews, and digging through the deli's long, layered history.

When I finally look up, the cafe is darker and emptier. Only then do I notice Dolly Purrton curled up, fast asleep beside me.

With a satisfied breath, I type up the last bit of info and send everything to the team. I know I did well today. This story will have the heart they are looking for.

I pack up my things, taking a moment to snuggle with Dolly before I go. "Thanks for keeping me company, girl," I whisper, giving her a scratch behind the ears before heading out the door.

On the walk home, I pull out my phone and press Mei's number.

"Hey, Mei," I say with an awkward laugh. "I think I might've met the man of my dreams today, and all I said to him was, 'Move, you're in my spot.'"

"The man of your dreams, huh?" Prodding for more details.

"I don't know." I sigh. "What I do know is that I've never met a more conceited or more attractive man in my entire life."

I launch into the whole story with Mei, telling her how I marched right up to the guy like a bull, demanding he move.

Mei's laughing on the other end, and I can't help but join her.

"I mean, who does that? I practically barked at him!" I groan, rubbing my temples. The more I tell this story, the more I feel a little embarrassed.

"All that, and he still decided to flirt with you?" Mei teases, and I can hear her grinning.

"Yeah, somehow. I have no idea why he'd flirt with a walking red flag," I say, shaking my head. "Maybe that's just how he deals with complete psychos."

I enter my apartment as Mei demands to know every detail about how this Thorne guy looks.

I try to keep the conversation as innocent as possible. He's a stranger. I owe him that much, right? But dang, was he hot.

As I wrap up the convo, I'm already pulling on my pajamas and flopping on my bed.

Mei reassures me that the guy has probably already completely forgotten about the interaction, but I still cringe at my boldness.

With a yawn, I tell her, "That was today's problem. I'm going to bed. Love you."

We say our goodbyes, and I end the call.

The exhaustion of the day washes over me.

2

CHAPTER TWO

The fluorescent lights hum above me, I blink against the brightness, but it's relentless, piercing through my closed eyelids. A shadow moves across the light, blocking out its searing intensity. For a moment, I think someone is there to help me, to explain where I am. But the shadow grows darker, consuming the light entirely,

The world shifts beneath me, and I'm falling—plunging into endless darkness with no ground in sight. I claw at the air, desperate for something solid, something to anchor me, but there's nothing. Just black, stretching endlessly in every direction.

My ears fill with urgent voices overlapping. The words are muffled and distorted, as though I'm hearing them through water.

A light flickers to life above me. Then, I see them—shadows moving in the corners of the room. Their faces blurred like smudged ink, but I sense their eyes, cold and searching, fixed on me. The figures grow closer, their hands outstretched as if to grab me, but they never touch me.

"Where am I?" I try to scream. The floor beneath me collapses, and I'm falling once again.

I wake with a gasp, bolting upright in bed. Sweat slicks my hair to my forehead. My chest heaves as I clutch at the sheets.

It was just a nightmare. I'm in my room, safe.

I have to calm down.

That's the thing about dreams—they blur the line between what's real and what's not. One moment, you're tumbling through an endless darkness, your mind and body convinced you're falling to your death. The next, you're in a world so beautiful, so perfect, you'd do anything to stay asleep. Dreams can cradle you in their arms or drop you into the abyss, and the cruelest part? Sometimes, waking up doesn't bring clarity. Sometimes, it leaves you wondering which reality you truly belong to.

Dr. J. Wiese - Psychologist

"I need to increase the dosage of my psych meds," I say as soon as I sit down on my therapist's couch.

Dr. Wiese nods. "Why don't we start with you telling me what's been going on? Then we can discuss your medication options."

I sigh, "Yeah, okay." I fidget with the pom-poms on the throw pillow. "Work has been adding a lot of pressure, as I told you last week. But the stress has just been piling up. It's starting to affect my entire life, so I think it's time for a med adjustment."

"I'm not objecting to changing your medications," she assures me. "But I want to fully understand what you're experiencing so we can get you on the best treatment plan. What changes have you noticed the most?" She asks, pulling her notebook onto her lap.

"Well, I've noticed I am running out of patience extremely fast. I feel like I am always on the cusp of a mental breakdown." I admit. "Yesterday,

I was so stressed about my workload that a stranger sitting in my usual seat at the coffee shop almost caused me to have a full meltdown."

"It sounds like you are burnt out. Your nervous system is stuck in fight or flight mode," she suggests. "With your medical history, I'm sure you are aware of your added need to take care of yourself. Have you been getting enough sleep?"

I trace the pattern on the pillow, too ashamed to make eye contact with her. "I try-" I hesitate. "I have a lot of nightmares and restless nights. I know I should try to do better, but this job means everything to me. If the boss needs an article at two in the morning, I am going to make it happen. No matter the consequences."

"I know I don't need to remind you of what happened last time you pushed yourself too hard," Dr. Wiese pauses and flips through the brochures in the top drawer of her desk. "Before we reach emergency level," she says, handing me two flyers, "it's important you start taking care of yourself. The first pamphlet has some meditation and mindfulness activities to practice throughout the day. The other–" Her demeanor is more serious, "is an inpatient option for psychiatric care."

I roll my eyes in disbelief. "A grippy sock vacation? That's your suggestion?" I scoff.

"Inpatient care isn't anyone's first choice," she concedes. "But it was very successful in treating your anxiety in the past. I don't think we need such drastic actions right now, but I want to have all of your options on the table in case we need them later on."

As much as I don't like Dr. Wiese's idea, I know deep down that she's right. In-hospital care has been a lifesaver for me in the past. But I know I can handle it on my own this time. I don't need nursing staff hovering over my every move. Would work even give me time off for that? It's not like psych wards are known for their excellent Wi-Fi and WFH options. It's not even a possibility right now. I have too much on my plate that I am not willing to throw away.

"I appreciate the concern, Dr. Wiese. Truly," I offer as sincerely as currently possible. "I will read over the mindfulness techniques and put them into practice. In the meantime though, can we please just up my dosage? I just need something to help me get through the added stress right now, and then I'll be happy to discuss more long-term options."

Dr. Wiese nods again. "Alright," she says as she looks through my file. "Currently, you're taking 50MG, let's go ahead and bump you up to 75. I'd also like to increase your appointments to once a week until we start to see improvement in your mental state."

"I can do that," I say as I glance at my watch. "I know we only have a few more minutes, but I wanted to ask—" I hesitate, suddenly realizing that my question may actually land me in a mandatory psych hold.

"Yes?" She inquires.

I take a deep breath in search of bravery. "Do you think nightmares are just our mind playing tricks on us, or could they be trying to warn us that something bad is going to happen—something we can't see yet?"

3

CHAPTER THREE

I sit on my bed and go over my new mindfulness activities. Why does taking care of yourself have to look and feel so stupid? Still, it worked. I am calm and ready for a good night's sleep.

Then, of course, just as I'm about to drift off, I hear the chime of my laptop. More work emails. I sigh, staring at the ceiling, debating if I'll just *pretend I didn't receive* it until morning.

I groan, pulling my laptop onto the bed, knowing I can't afford to slack off. Not now, not when this job is the key to unlocking my dream of becoming a big-time journalist. *This is my stepping stone.* If I don't hustle, someone else will.

As the screen flickers to life, lighting up my dark bedroom, I open the urgent email and immediately feel its weight.

The paper needs an emergency piece tonight. A twelve-year-old girl was killed by a drunk driver on her way home from school.

My chest tightens as I read the details, feeling the grief of her family in my heart.

They want a PSA-style article, collecting stats on drunk driving in New York, the injuries, the deaths, and the grim reality of it all. There is no time to waste. There never is with the news.

I dive right into research, pulling up statistics and cross-referencing data. There has been a significant increase in accidents involving drunk drivers in recent years. This is so important I cannot make any errors. Even though I am beyond tired, I can't stop now.

I grab my phone and place my usual 12 AM order of two energy drinks, a bag of sour gummy worms, and a family-size Salt & Vinegar chips. The order is placed, and I dive right back in.

I'm completely absorbed when the doorbell rings.

I stretch, feeling the stiffness in my back, and quickly throw my hair up into a messy bun. Straightening my pajamas, I make my way to the door.

When I open it, a pimple-faced teenager is standing there, holding my bag. I swear I see a spotlight and hear angels cheering like he's holding the Holy Grail.

I slip him $5, flashing him a grateful smile. "You're an actual lifesaver," I say.

He nods and hops back on his bike.

Bag in hand, I shuffle back to my room.

I crack open the first energy drink, take a swig, and get back to the grind. I find myself tearing into my snacks like I haven't eaten in days. The night is far from over, but at least I have what I need to power through.

4

Chapter Four

The shrill sound of my alarm startles me awake, and I bolt upright, my heart racing. My immediate panic turns to relief as I check my computer. Thankfully, I'd finished and sent the article before crashing hard.

I glance around, only to find my bed covered in chip crumbs and stains of sour powder.

Ugh.

I chug the last bit of my leftover energy drink and grab my phone. It's Saturday, which means breakfast with Violet.

I scramble out of bed, desperate for a shower.

I take my time, letting hot water rush over my aching body.

Once I'm mildly relaxed, I turn off the water, leave the bathroom, and walk into my closet. I forgo anything fancy and pull on sweatpants and a baggy t-shirt, my wet hair hastily piled into a bun.

I throw on my favorite Vans and make a dash for the door. I'm running late and barely functioning, but there's no way I'm canceling on my sister.

I slide into the booth across from Violet, immediately apologetic. **"I'm exhausted. Sorry if my signing is sloppy."**

"**Your signing is always perfect. Don't worry about it,**" she grins up at me. "**Why are you so tired?**"

"**I've had so much work. I had to work late last night to meet deadlines,**" I gesture.

"**You're taking on too much work. Your mental health never does well when you're this tired.**"

"**I'm fine. Work is important. I can handle it.**"

I can tell immediately she doesn't believe me. Thankfully, she doesn't fight me on this.

Our food arrives at the perfect time, and I am absolutely ravenous. We both dig in and then it hits me. I wave to get Violet's attention.

"**Yesterday, I met this hot guy at the coffee shop, Thorne Something. He was sitting in my seat, so I told him, 'Move it or lose it, buddy.' He took the hint and went his merry way.**"

"**Oh, T-H-O-R-N-E? 258,**" she fingers spells his name with a dramatic flare. "**What happened?**"

"**He was such a flirt! He was so full of crap I could actually see it coming out of his ears. Said he'll come back to see me sometime, which for the life of me, I do not understand. I did not flirt back even the slightest, *au contraire*. I was like a bull in a china shop.**"

"**It couldn't have been that bad.**"

"**Oh, it was! He was all, 'What's a beautiful girl like you eating alone for?' and I ever so politely told him to get away from me. It wasn't my greatest moment as far as manners go, but in my defense, I had a lot of work to get finished. Flirting with a stranger was not on my bingo card yesterday.**"

"**Seriously? I thought if I had taught you anything in this life it would be that when a nice, hot guy flirts with you, you definitely flirt back. What is wrong with you?**" She laughs at me now.

"**Shut up! It's not funny. I possibly met the cutest guy on the planet, and I practically told him to run away and never look** back." I drop my head into my hands and feel the regret sink in. **"I am so embarrassed by how I acted. He said he'll see me around, but I think I might have blown it. Big time."**

"I wouldn't worry about it. Maybe he'll come back, and you'll get a second chance. It could make for a fun story in the future. The two of you will get married and laugh about the first time you met. The flirt and the jerk. You can decide who is who."

"I guess I learned how to be a jerk from my beautiful big sister," I tease, sticking my tongue out at her.

I, of course, fill Violet in on Thorne's appearance, and we giggle over my explanation of his striking green eyes. I recount his effortless charm and his completely comfortable ability to flirt with a total stranger.

I also update her on Dolly Purrton. I mention that I'm still hoping to adopt her once she's spayed and ready for a new home.

I show Violet the photo of the Brooklyn deli and explain how the newspaper is trying to draw attention to its legacy in hopes it won't be closed forever.

Violet shares some exciting news of her own. Her art has been selected for an elite art show next month, and she asks if I can help her pick which pieces to highlight. I add it to my calendar because, with everything else on my plate, unfortunately, I know I'll forget.

I am shocked to learn Violet has also been commissioned to create a premier piece for a new reality TV show. The show plans to feature art from local *underprivileged minority* artists.

We roll our eyes at the thought of her hearing status being the only reason she is considered, but who's to look a gift horse in the mouth?

Violet is proud to be a Deaf artist, and she deserves every good thing that comes her way. Her work will be showcased on weekly television. Her name will be in the credits of every episode, which could mean a huge career boost. I could not be more thrilled for her. I will always be her biggest fan.

We laugh for a few hours, taking advantage of the bottomless mimosas.

Violet and I talk about everything important and some things that are not. These weekly breakfasts with my sister are the only thing that keeps me sane sometimes. She grounds me in ways that nothing else ever has. Being the protective big sister that she is, she again reminds me to not take on too much.

"Don't worry, I'll be fine," I assure her. I know she doesn't believe me, especially when she offers to run my errands so I can get some sleep.

I quickly brush off her suggestion. She is just trying to help, but I can't bring myself to admit I might need it.

My weekends are never long enough to accomplish everything I need to get done. I live my life by routine and patterns, which is what is familiar to me. My most popular pattern? Pushing people away when they reach out.

I prefer to shoulder my burdens alone rather than acknowledge I cannot handle everything on my own.

It was easier when Violet and I still shared an apartment, but I understood when she decided to move into the loft above her art studio. Letting her know I'm overwhelmed feels like admitting failure, and I'm not ready to do that.

Violet snatches up the bill before I can even object. I promise I'll get her back next time, both of us knowing that's probably never going to happen.

My sister pays, and we leave.

Outside the restaurant, we share a long, warm hug before heading off in different directions to our respective apartments.

I walk on, feeling gratitude and utter exhaustion. Maybe, just maybe, I should squeeze in a quick nap before tackling the laundry.

Arriving home, I collapse into bed. I stare at the ceiling, my ever-growing to-do list swirling in my mind. The pressure is weighing heavily on me. Even my personal chores feel like a ticking time bomb. One mistake away from a disaster.

I hear my phone play Mei's signature text tone.

Mei: *Wanna grab dinner and a movie tonight? I texted Violet already. She and her boo (yuck) are in. Let me know, and I'll buy our seats together.*

I stare at the text. *I want to go, really.*

Rose: *I'll call you later.*

Deep down, I know I'm not going.

"You're taking on too much work. Your mental health never does well when you're this tired." My sister's words run through my brain.

I am fully aware that my mental health is a delicate balance. It has been ever since I was a teenager, and I had to spend two weeks in the psych ward because I allowed myself to become *too preoccupied* with state finals.

My whole life has been the same story. My sanity is tethered tightly to my success. The result is always the same: If I don't exceed expectations, I launch into a full downward spiral. If I slip up even once, my whole world turns into a black hole that can collapse in on me at any time.

Work email pings. Another rush assignment. Of course, I accept. It's a journalist-eats-journalist world out there. I don't have a choice but to stay ahead. My work comes first - always.

I push aside my fear of failure. *No time for meltdowns.*

5

Chapter Five

For the first time in recent history, I am caught up at work. The newspaper took on an intern from NYU, and thankfully, he helped take on some of my workload. Part of me is relieved; the other part is endlessly worried that he might overshadow me and get my big breaks. It's a man's world, and your girl is trying to hustle it.

With my newly available time, I've taken the opportunity to catch up on some self-care. I got a haircut, the girls and I got our nails done, and I even used the facial gift certificate that I won through work almost a year ago.

Now that I'm home, the only thing I feel I really need is a twelve-hour nap. I don't even take the time to change.

I walk into my bedroom, dropping my pants in the doorway. Before crawling into bed, I unclasp my bra and slide it out the armhole of my shirt.

I lay starfish on the bed under the cool breeze of my fan. I have attained perfect napping conditions.

My blinks become slower and slower as the familiar beige bedroom walls slowly fade out of focus.

When I open my eyes, I am no longer in the safety of my bedroom. There is a strange, muted light filtering into the room. The walls are painted a soft sage green.

Under normal circumstances, I might list the color as one of my favorites, but this room feels sterile. The air is heavy and damp with the scent of strong disinfectants mixed with something earthy.

Confused, I glance around. Plants. They're scattered around in mismatched pots, their green leaves trying their hardest to soften the look of the place.

The faint smell of medicinal alcohol lingers just beneath the surface. This doesn't feel like a hospital, but it sure smells like one.

Despite the room being warm, a chill runs through my spine.

I close my eyes, hoping to return to my bedroom, but I can tell it's a useless endeavor.

I can still hear the hum of the overhead light and the rhythmic ticking of a nearby clock. There's a creak from the floorboards, almost like footsteps. I throw my eyes open, the room coming into focus. I panic that I may not be alone here. The footsteps seem to be getting closer, but when I glance around, I see no one.

A sense of unease twists in my stomach as I try to shift my body, only to realize that I can't.

Panic flares in my chest, sharp and electric. My eyes dart around the room wildly, trying to take in everything, but I'm unable to move my head. It's then that I notice the beeping. A steady, rhythmic sound echoes through the room.

I shift my eyes as far down as I can and catch a glimpse of wires and tubes. Now, I can feel the IV needle taped to my arm. I'm in a hospital bed. I am connected to machines. I can feel the slick coolness of the pillow beneath my head, but I can't turn to see more. I'm trapped, unable to do anything but look straight ahead. I am helpless.

Panic chokes me from the inside out. The machine to my right beeps louder and faster now. It's echoing the heartbeat that thuds wildly in my chest.

The footsteps reach my ears, subtle at first, but they quickly turn into hurried, urgent steps, coming straight for me. Before I even see him, I hear him.

"You need to calm down, Junie," the man urges, his voice soft and firm. "Try to slow your breathing."

Junie? Who is Junie? I want to scream that I'm not Junie. My name is Rose! My throat is frozen solid, and no sound escapes.

The man steps into view. The first thing I see is just a torso. He's wearing gray sweatpants and pulling on a blue varsity sweatshirt like he's just rolled out of bed. I notice his wild, unruly salt and peppered beard. His silver hair is a mess, sticking up in every direction. Absurdly, the first thought that crosses my mind is whether I know him. *Have I seen him before?*

My brain scrambles, rushing to make sense of everything.

His eyes lock on mine as he moves closer. There's an edge of desperation in him now. "Junie, please! I need you to calm down. Everything is fine, I promise."

Fine? Nothing about this is fine.

The beeping, the machines, the fact I can't move. I can't even scream for help. I don't know this man, and it's perplexing me why he's talking to me like I should trust him.

The panic surges again, bile rising in my throat. I try hard to swallow it down, but I can't. There's something lodged in the way. *Oh God.*

My mouth is dry, I can feel plastic pressing against the back of my throat. I can't swallow on my own.

The realization hits me, I'm not even breathing on my own. The machines are doing it for me.

None of this makes sense. The panic twists around me like a vice. I feel myself spiraling deeper.

"Why are you doing this to me? I don't want to keep you drugged, you know that. You have to know that," he says, defeated.

Doing this to you? You're the one threatening to drug me. My thoughts race so fast that I don't notice the large needle he's holding until it's too late.

He inserts the needle into my IV port and injects a clear liquid. The world rapidly goes black. I swear I hear the man apologize before the room completely disappears from my vision.

My eyes shoot open, and the familiar, safe, beige walls surround me like a warm hug. I am drenched in sweat, and my heart is still racing like I've been running for miles.

I'm here. In my bed. Safe.

The dream... It was just a dream.

I sit up, rubbing my eyes. I physically shake out my limbs, hoping to rid myself of the eerie feeling that clings to me.

"It's nothing," I mutter, hoping that if I put it out into the universe, I will believe it. "Just a weird dream, that's all."

I run my fingers through my hair, pushing away the images - the hospital bed, the man, the machines. It doesn't mean anything. Violet was right: I've been working too hard. That's all it was. Stress can make you have nightmares, right? It's just my mind being overworked and overactive.

I head into the bathroom and splash ice-cold water onto my face. "Back to reality," I whisper to my reflection.

I force a small smile on my face despite the knot in my stomach. I've got a full day ahead. I can't afford to get caught up in nonsense.

It was just a dream.

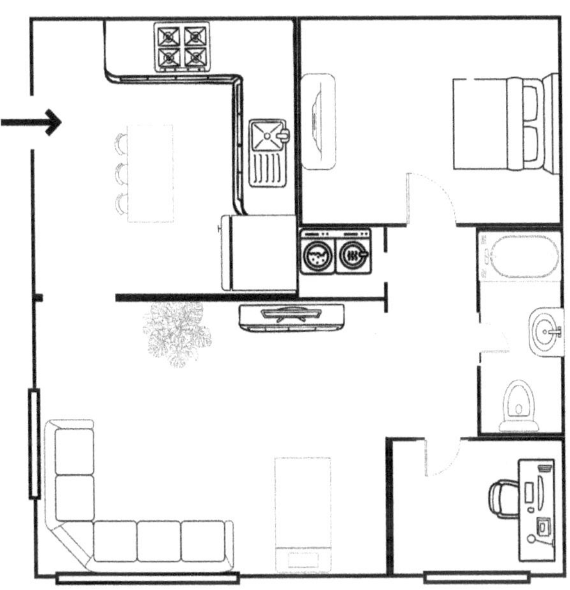

THE ROOM

6

CHAPTER SIX

It's been a week since I first experienced "The Room." It has a name now because for reasons unknown, I have been trapped there every time I fall asleep. My solution? Sleep as little as possible.

I stand in front of the mirror, rubbing my temples, trying to push away the throbbing that has been my constant companion this week. I swear the pounding behind my eyes burrows straight through my brain. Between the sleepless nights and the nonstop pressure at work, it's no wonder I live with a constant headache. "Just stress," I mutter.

I grab my faded blue jeans and tug them on, and I finish the outfit with my favorite Silly Goose hoodie. It's not my standard work attire, but I do not have the energy to give even a minimal level of care for how I look today.

I throw back some pain pills and head for the door. For the first time since I started this job, I'm running late, and it's stressing me more than I'd like to admit.

It takes me fifteen minutes of brisk walking and lugging my laptop bag to arrive at the coffee shop.

When I enter, Sam immediately jokes, "I was about to call the cops and request a search party if you hadn't shown up in the next ten minutes."

He smiles, but I can tell he is halfway serious.

Sam tells me he needs to remake my drink since the one he prepped on time is now cold.

I stop him before he starts. "Can you just make me an XL Shaken Espresso? With like six shots of espresso? Is that a thing?" I say, feeling the total weight of my coffee-inept embarrassment. I'll be the first to admit I'm not a coffee drinker, but today it's a must.

Sam fakes a heart attack, clutching his chest. "Six shots? Who are you, and what have you done with Rose?" Sam laughs, wide-eyed in mock horror.

He's right, though. I've never ordered anything even close to that strong.

"I've got a killer headache," I explain, pointing to the sunglasses still on my face. "I need the caffeine."

I agree to allow him to make me his choice, marketing it to me as a miracle cure. He also rattles off the pastries of the day, but I shake my head and opt for pancakes and eggs instead. There's something about a hearty breakfast that feels oddly comforting right now.

"Pancakes? I don't even know who you are anymore," he teases, pretending to be scandalized.

I roll my eyes and tell him to charge it to my work account, and I slump into my booth.

I stare at my laptop and internally scream. *Why today?* I finally land an assignment for a front-page feature, and I don't even want to do it—a high-pressure investigative piece that I can feel is draining me just by thinking about it.

It's the kind of project that usually fuels me. That's my bread and butter. But today, I am not a happy-go-lucky Rose. My energy is tapped out, and the normal excitement I feel for this type of assignment is missing. I have a mountain of research to tackle, on top of making phone calls, juggling leads, and proving to myself that I can handle all of this.

Sam looks like an actual saint when he appears with my food and coffee.

I take a huge sip of liquid gold, the caffeine hitting me like a small jolt of relief. I try to comfort myself with the warmth of my meal as I eat between tasks.

Just as I'm getting into a rhythm, my phone rings. It's my boss pushing me for more and demanding quicker results.

Internally, I want to tell him to shove off. But instead, I assure him that I'm working on all possible leads as we speak. "Nothing to worry about. I'm on it."

He offers to send an intern to assist, but a painful stab runs through me when he states that my work hasn't been of the usual quality lately.

I dismiss the idea immediately, asserting my independence. I don't need help; I can handle this.

Deep down, I fear he's right. But my obsessive nature kicks in. I'm too focused on proving I can manage this, and I won't allow anything to disrupt my determination. If I can just get through this story, everything will be fine.

After what feels like days, I slam my laptop closed. Work is finished, and I am miserable.

I put my phone and laptop in sleep mode, I won't be handling any more calls today.

I step outside the cafe and flag down a taxi. I give the driver my address and start to drift off in the back seat.

When my eyes flutter shut, I am transported back to The Room. I jolt awake realizing that I cannot fall asleep until I'm back in the safety of home.

The taxi drops me off, and I enter my apartment. I leave my bag at the entrance and make a beeline for my bedroom. I crawl directly into bed, pulling the covers up over my head. For the first time, I do not care what The Room has in store for me. I just need sleep.

Hello, hospital bed, I think as I awaken in my nightmare.

7

CHAPTER SEVEN

I'm blinded by the light streaming through the windows. I look at the clock and do the mental math. I slept for thirteen hours. I don't feel great, but I get up and dress for the day anyway.

Somehow, it's already Saturday again, and canceling on Violet would be more suspicious than just showing up not feeling well.

I don't remember talking to her at all this week, which is unusual, but I've been... distracted. I wouldn't have even remembered our breakfast date was today, except my phone reminded me three times already this morning. I guess I've been setting more calendar reminders because my days are starting to blur together.

Everything in me screams to cancel, but Violet would know that something is wrong immediately if I bail, and I don't need her trying to do a psych evaluation on me. Besides, she is calm. Being with her can do me some serious good.

I straighten my hair in an attempt to look more put together than I feel. I throw on some blush and mascara just to feel less like a sleepless goblin. I toss some headache meds into my fanny pack and throw on my sunglasses.

Every inch of light bleeding into the room feels like daggers stabbing into my skull. I take a deep breath, slip on my shoes, and head out the door.

I approach our table and can already see purple and red hair peeking from the top of the booth.

"What's up, guys?" I try to act casual, but I feel like I've been set up.

With an overwhelming amount of sass, Violet signs, **"Do you care to explain what's been going on with you?"**

She's leaning forward with a serious look. It almost makes me want to laugh, but I can tell this isn't the time to make a joke.

I glance between Violet and Mei, feeling my defense walls rising.

"What do you mean?" I reply.

"You haven't talked to us all week. That never happens. We are worried about you," Mei interjects.

I see the concern on her face, and yet I feel like I can't make eye contact with her.

"I don't know, I've just been busy with work. You know how it is." I shrug.

I can't explain why I am hiding my feelings from them. They have never treated me like I'm crazy. But that's just it, isn't it? I think I'm losing my mind, and I don't want anyone to know. Not even the people closest to me.

I manage to convince them that I am fine, even if what I tell them isn't the whole truth. I tell them how I took the weekend off work to do some self-TLC. They don't need to know that it was mandated by my boss.

The rest of breakfast goes by smoothly but undeniably awkward. They're still watching me closely, even when the conversation moves on to easier topics.

We finish breakfast, and after we say our goodbyes, I head to the store to pick up essentials I'll need to get me through the weekend.

My boss told me to take the weekend off and re-evaluate my priorities. I admit I may have taken on more assignments from the lead journalists than I could handle, hoping they would "put in a good word" for me. I just want to prove myself.

This is my dream, and I'm willing to work myself to the bone to attain it. I took on over fifteen assignments this past week, and I gave my best. I really did. However, my performance review returned my results as sloppy and unorganized. Hence the mandated "vacation."

I wander the grocery aisles, tossing random things into the cart. I just need easy, microwaveable comfort foods. I'm not leaving my apartment until Monday, and I don't want any plans that require lifting a finger.

As I look through the glass doors of the freezer section, peering at the frozen dinner selections, I realize the boxes are fuzzy. No, just the words are fuzzy. My eyes are blurry, and I can't seem to focus.

A wave of dizziness hits me, like I'm about to black out, and for a moment, I swear I can smell the strong and now familiar scent of antiseptic.

I stumble to the bathroom and splash cold water on my face, trying to shake the feeling of losing grip on reality.

When I finally look up into the mirror, my heart drops. It's not my reflection staring back at me - it's The Room. The walls, the bed, the machines.

I blink hard, trying to clear the vision, but it won't go away.

"I need to get home. Now."

I leave the store, purchasing what I've already thrown in the cart. I will just have to make it work.

I stumble back to my apartment and lock the door securely behind me once inside. I put the groceries in the fridge, whether they need it or not.

I shuffle into the living room and collapse on the couch, flicking the TV on for some background noise. Thankfully, I find a rerun of Forensic

Files that I've seen a million times. Nothing like a good ol' comfort show to keep me from my thoughts.

My body feels like it's on the verge of a breakdown, and there's nothing I can do to stop it. I can feel the tears coming, slow at first, then all at once, pouring down my cheeks. I bury my face in the pillow and cry myself to sleep, exhaustion finally taking over.

8

Chapter Eight

I already know where I am before I even open my eyes. It's becoming routine, but some things do change. At first, I noticed the small things. The blanket covering my body is different from last time; there's a window open somewhere that I can't see, but I can feel and smell the fresh air.

One change bothers me every time, and I am unable to ignore it: my clothes are different.

I can't move my body, but I can see enough to know the clothes I'm dressed in are never the same twice. I try not to think about it because, somehow, that raises questions I am not ready to ask.

Before I can dwell on it too long, the door creaks open. The man steps in again, his smile eerily polite, too measured, like something he's rehearsed in front of a mirror. His grin doesn't reach his vibrant green ... empty eyes.

He doesn't say a word; just walks over and pulls back the blanket.

A chill rushes over my skin; my body wants to recoil from his touch, but I can't move.

He exposes my legs, pale and unfamiliar, thin like brittle branches.

I want to scream at him, 'Why are you touching me?' But the words stay lodged like cement in my throat.

My heart thuds as he grips my ankle, his fingers cold and clinical. I notice he's wearing a wedding band, but when I glance down at my hand, I'm not.

He moves my leg, bending it in ways that make my muscles ache. I feel like a doll that he's just pulled out of storage. His hands are, sure, methodical like he's done this a thousand times before—to me.

A sharp pressure crawls up my spine. *Who is this man? How can he be so comfortable manipulating my body?*

I don't know him, yet there's something so unnervingly routine about the way he moves and massages my limbs.

My body feels too thin, too frail. I could be looking at someone else's body entirely. *Is this really me?*

He still calls me Junie. Not once has he slipped, not even accidentally. Not one time has he called me Rose. Does he even know who I am? Do I?

A question gnaws at the back of my mind, dark and unsettling: What if I'm not me anymore? What if this has never been me?

I can't contemplate that question for too long because my brain is overwhelmed by the pain. Each pull and twist sends sharp pain rippling through my legs, so intense at times that it borders on unbearable.

I want to scream, to cry out, but nothing comes. Just silence, my thoughts forever trapped in my throat. My body betrays me, locked in its prison.

The man finishes with the stretches, wiping his hands as if he's completed some ordinary task. But then, he reaches for a bottle of lotion.

His hands touch my skin again, this time rubbing the cool cream into my calves, working it in slow, deliberate circles. This moment feels... intimate. Too intimate. Like he's taking care of something fragile, something that he owns.

My mind recoils, but another part of me wonders: why doesn't this feel wrong? I can't help but accept the touch as if it's familiar, like he's been doing this for days, weeks, maybe even months.

A shiver runs through me as my thoughts begin to twist. *Why does this feel normal? Shouldn't I be horrified? Is this what dreams do? Make the strange feel ordinary*? Or... my stomach tightens at the thought. Has he cared for me so long that I feel some sort of gratitude for him?

I'm hit by a wave of nausea as I push the thoughts away, but stubbornly, they linger.

His hands move down to my feet, rubbing them with the same eerie precision.

My mind floats away, lost in the sickening confusion of whether this is care or control. Then I feel it, the soft fabric sliding over my toes. He's putting socks on me.

I stare at my feet, frozen. My mind stumbles over itself, trying to explain it away. Could it be a coincidence? No, it can't be. They're my socks. My favorite Cookie Monster socks. How could they be here unless... unless reality is starting to bleed between the cracks?

That thought should make my skin crawl, but it doesn't. Oddly enough, it's comforting in a twisted sort of way. If my socks can find their way here and can cross the line between whatever this place is and my world, then maybe I can, too. Maybe, just maybe, there's a way out.

My attention is brought back to the man as he makes a booming clap that terrifies me.

"Psst, stop it!" he yells, disciplinary and sharp.

I hadn't registered the sounds of cat claws on fabric before this moment, but now the sound is undeniable.

"You know better than that." He is tired.

There's a cat here.

"That darn cat," he mutters as he injects something into what I assume is a feeding tube and pats me on the thigh. "There, now you're taken care of," he says. "Can't say I never did anything nice for you."

I think that is a joke, but it's so hard to tell with his cold demeanor.

He sits on the couch to my left, almost completely out of my line of sight, but I hear him as he clicks on the TV. It's the Food Network, some kind of grocery store cooking challenge I vaguely recognize. I've never cared about these types of shows, but as the contestants start their player introductions, I find myself oddly engrossed. It's distracting, at least, and I let myself get pulled into the competition.

The man makes a comment about one chef's terrible ingredient choices, and my body lets out a shriek that I think is supposed to be a laugh. At least, that's what I am hoping for.

My suspicions are confirmed when the man says, "Thank you, thank you, I'll be here all week, and I am full of comedic gold."

It's so weird, but his commentary adds to the show. I find myself agreeing with all his remarks, which is probably the strangest thing about all of this. I'm not even fighting it.

Somehow, this bizarre scene feels... normal. The longer I lie here, the more I realize that I don't mind it. I'm almost... enjoying it? There is no pressure, no responsibilities weighing on my shoulders. No endless list of tasks or chores to complete, no forced conversations to navigate, awkwardly filling the silence with meaningless small talk. Here, I can just be. I can finally rest.

I close my eyes for a moment, savoring the strange relief. *Maybe this isn't so bad.*

But something inside me shifts—SNAP OUT OF IT! *What are you thinking?*

My eyes snap open, my heart pounding. *You're not safe here!*

The creeping fog that had settled over my mind clears, peeling back to reveal the raw reality beneath it. *You're not resting, you're trapped.*

I try to sit up, but my body remains unresponsive, heavy as stone. The helplessness surges back, a wave of panic crashing against the edges of my calm.

This isn't rest. This is a cage.

My thoughts race, colliding with each other as I struggle to make sense of it all. When did I start feeling like this place is a sanctuary?

A shiver runs down my spine. *No. No. This isn't right.*

The man, the way he touches me, the strange familiarity, the way he calls me Junie, it's all wrong. And I let myself relax into it, let myself be lulled by the ease of it all, like a frog in a pot of water slowly coming to a boil.

I squeeze my eyes shut, forcing myself to focus, to remember. *You're trapped. Don't forget that. Don't let yourself forget that.*

The eerie sense of calm begins to slither back like poison in my veins. *Rest*, it whispers.

But I know now. I know that voice isn't my own. *Fight it*, I tell myself. *Stay awake. Stay alert. You are not safe.*

I've been here too long. Far too long. I know it, even if I can't prove it.

The past week has been filled with dreams that only lasted a few hours, max. But now? Now I sit here, watching cooking shows, episode after episode, while an entire day passes. The light climbing in through the windows when I first arrived has now gone dark. How did that happen?

"You are a research journalist. This is not like you. You need to question everything," I say to myself.

I go back to the beginning and try to remember everything I have experienced up to this point, but it feels too detailed for a dream. Could my mind be creating all this, down to the precise pattern on the socks and the random choice of TV programs? Or, more terrifyingly, what if this place keeps going even when I'm not here? What if it's a world of its own, continuing while I'm back in my real life, unaware of how much time passes here?

I am terrified by that thought. I try to focus back on the TV, but it doesn't help. I'm no longer relaxing. I can't.

There's something wrong about this place. It feels too real and too lived in. I have been here longer than I think. Maybe... longer than I even remember.

9

CHAPTER NINE

I wake up in my own bed, confusion lingering in my mind about how I got here.

The sharp pain immediately hits me, cutting through the fog of sleep like a knife. "Welcome back, old friend," I say to my headache.

I'm home now. I'm lying here, letting the tension roll off my shoulders, when a thought suddenly occurs to me. The difference between reality and The Room. It's the migraines.

In the waking world, my headaches are constant and unbearable. But in the dream... they're dulled, barely there. The more time I spend there, the less pain I feel.

I stand and shuffle into the kitchen, my legs still stiff from... whatever that was. The dream? I don't know anymore.

I grab a frozen dinner from the freezer, barely glancing at the label before popping it into the microwave. Salisbury steak, mashed potatoes, corn, and a sad excuse for a brownie. The kind of meal that tastes like cardboard but feels like a hug when I'm too tired to care.

I stare at the microwave's countdown, the numbers ticking away in their relentless rhythm. Three minutes.

That's when I feel it creeping up the back of my mind like a shadow. I'm craving it. The relief of the dream world.

My stomach tightens, and I press a hand against the counter to steady myself. *What is happening to me?*

I close my eyes, my thoughts swirling. The dream world, The Room. As terrifying and strange as it is... there's no pain there. No aching joints, no heavy limbs. No constant barrage of stress and worry gnawing at the edges of my mind about work and unpaid bills. No deadlines, no responsibilities. Just silence. Stillness. And... him.

My chest tightens as my mind flashes to the man. The one who stretches my legs and calls me Junie, the one who rubs lotion into my skin with unsettling precision. He asks for nothing in return and just tends to me like some silent caretaker. And as twisted as it is, part of me wants to go back.

No. No. That's not right. That's not normal. What is happening to me?

The microwave beeps, startling me out of my thoughts. I blink at the flashing numbers before opening the door, the steam wafting up from the tray like a cheap imitation of comfort.

I poke at the food with my fork, feeling a knot form in my stomach. Why do I want to go back? I should be terrified of that place. Terrified of that man. And I am, but my brain? It's like Stockholm syndrome for a nightmare.

I let out a bitter laugh as I prod the rubbery steak. Great. Just what I needed. My subconscious is falling in love with my own personal hell.

I lean against the kitchen counter as I take that first steaming bite. I glance down at my legs, my real legs. The difference is clear. My legs feel heavier, curvier, and not nearly as frail. It's strange feeling the weight of my own body like this, almost foreign after how light I've felt in the dream world.

Maybe I just need more sleep, I tell myself.

I toss the plastic tray into the recycling bin and drop my fork into the growing pile of dishes in the sink. Grabbing a cold Dr. Pepper from the fridge, I head to my room.

On the way there, I open my phone and scroll through social media, letting my mind go completely numb.

I'm taking a refreshing sip of my drink when I spot a picture of Violet and Cam from their date tonight. I smirk and type the obligatory sibling comment, "Ew Gross. Stop swapping cooties, you two."

Almost immediately, my FaceTime lights up, showing Violet's face. I ignore the call as I flop onto my bed, knowing she probably just wants to tell me about her date.

I shoot her a quick text.

> Rose: *Exhausted, Going 2 bed early. TTYT ILY.*

After a few minutes, my eyelids feel like they're weighed down by bricks. I toss my phone onto the nightstand and sink back into my pillows. I can feel the lure of sleep pulling me down fast.

10

CHAPTER TEN

When I come to, everything is dark. I can't see anything; it's just pitch black all around me. My heart skips a beat as I try to move, but I can't. I'm face down on the bed, unsure of what's happening.

I feel something, someone, moving my body. There's pressure on my limbs, a pull at my clothes. I hear breathing hard and heavy. He's grunting softly as he moves me, his hands firm but methodical.

Panic shoots through me. *What is he doing? Am I being hurt?*

I squeeze my eyes shut, trying everything I can to wake up and get out of this place. I don't want to be here, not like this. *Please let me go back. Just let me wake up.*

But nothing happens, I'm still trapped in this body that refuses to listen.

I can feel my clothes being pulled off, my skin suddenly exposed to the cold air. A sickening dread rises in my throat, but I can't do anything. I can't scream. I can't fight. I'm stuck, helpless, afraid, while he does whatever he wants with me.

Minutes pass. Long, agonizing minutes where all I feel is the absence of my clothing and numbness running through my entire body.

After some time, I feel my clothes being slid back onto my body.

Suddenly, I am flipped over onto my back, and I see him. He's standing over me, sweaty, his chest rising and falling heavily as if he's just run a marathon.

My eyes dart around the room. I am terrified, but nothing is different. The room looks the same as always, calm and normal. The things I see are at complete odds with the panic roiling inside of me.

He leans over, brushing the hair from my face. "Don't worry," he says, his eyes still blank.

I can't decipher his expression.

He continues, "I'm not upset with you."

Not upset? Why should you be upset? my mind screams. *I'm the one who should be upset!*

But then I see it: the pile of dirty laundry in the corner, the stained sheets bunched up at the foot of the bed.

Embarrassment washes over me. *Oh God.*

I realize what happened. I must've had some kind of accident while I was out, and he was just... cleaning me up. Changing my clothes, making sure I wasn't lying in my own mess.

I'm still completely unsettled by the entire situation, but it's starting to shift in my mind. The way he touches me, the way he cares for me—it's clinical, almost detached. He isn't hurting me. He is taking care of me.

But then, a cold realization settles in my gut. Not me. Junie.

There's a distance between who I am and this woman he seems to know. Junie. Whoever she is, she isn't me. She can't be. I don't know her. I don't feel like her. I can't even begin to comprehend why, let alone how I am dragged back to her consciousness every night. But I have a sinking feeling it won't stop until I figure that out. *Find the connections, Rose.*

I begin to channel my inner journalist, rewatching every Charlie - Junie interaction in my mind. Some scenes feel tender, like he cherishes her. Others feel violent and frustrated. I can't get a true read on their relationship. *Focus on what you know, draw conclusions from the facts.*

If I'm right about the ring on his hand, then he's married. From where I'm stuck, I haven't seen any other evidence of that. If I'm wrong about his marital status, though, could that be why he takes such care in everything he does? Or is this all part of some sick fantasy? Keeping her weak, making sure she's completely dependent on him, unable to advocate for herself so that he can swoop in as the selfless savior, the knight in shining armor tending to her every need?

I've watched enough true crime to know there are all kinds of sickos out there. I remember one docuseries that delved into the psychology of a man who kidnapped a college student after hitting her with his car. He had convinced her that she had amnesia from an accident and that they had been married for years. He had been stalking her for so long that he knew enough to make her comfortable, so she didn't figure it out until years later. Is something similar happening here?

The questions coil like a rattlesnake deep in my gut as I process it all to make any sense of this warped reality. I can feel its poison getting ready to strike at any moment.

This man's kindness feels hollow, robotic, and emotionless. There's something about the way he watches me, always a few steps away, that sends a shiver down my spine.

I don't trust him. Not by a long shot.

Every interaction with him leaves me feeling off-kilter. There are no real answers, no explanations, just vague gestures and that ever-present gaze. He never speaks to me, not really. But even if he did, how could I respond with this broken body of mine? My mouth won't form words; my limbs refuse to obey.

And then there's the IV. The steady drip of medication pumping something into my veins. I don't know what it is, and that uncertainty gnaws at the edges of my mind. How can I be sure it's not him keeping Junie like this? What if he's the one keeping her paralyzed, and the drugs are somehow bringing me back night after night? Is this mirage just a tortured woman's cry for help? Could I be here to save Junie in some way? I try to swallow, but my throat is tight and dry.

The thought unfurls like a dark shadow in the back of my mind. Maybe this is his fantasy. Keeping a girl bedridden, helpless, completely dependent on him for everything. Her entire life, my entire life, revolves around him. He gets to play the hero, the one who nurtures, protects, and cares for me. He's the one pulling the strings...

Real life is not a fantastical world of good versus evil, heroes conquering villains. But if I've learned anything from my true crime addiction, it's this:

Monsters are real. And they hide in plain sight.

The knot in my chest tightens, the fear winding tighter and tighter. I can't escape the feeling that something is deeply and terribly wrong. And the worst part? I have no way of knowing for sure. Not until I can figure out how to leave this place for good.

He moves around the room quietly. Trying not to disturb me. His steps are measured and calculated. There's something about the way he navigates the space that feels too deliberate, too purposeful, as if this is his everyday routine.

My heart picks up its pace as I stare at him. The textures of the sheets beneath me, the faint hum of medical equipment, the electrical buzz of the overhead lights—it's all so real. I can smell the sterile air tinged with a hint of something floral, like someone's tried to mask the clinical atmosphere with fake freshness. It's real. It has to be.

I can feel it all, the cool air slipping across my exposed arms and the weight of the bedding pressing down on me. The way the man moves, the rustling of his clothes, the soft scuff of his shoes against the floor. It's all so vivid.

And him...

He's not a figment of my imagination. There's something too familiar about him. I can't put my finger on it, but it's there, just out of reach. The way he stands, his silhouette against the low light, it's too solid. Too present.

I've never seen him before, but I know him in that strange, gut-wrenching way you feel when you see someone from your past you can't quite place. He's real. More real than a dream should allow.

What is this place? It feels so wrong and yet, in some twisted way, so right. Everything about it is tangible. And more than anything, the absence of pain is intoxicating. It's like I've traded the ability to have my autonomy for this pain-free refuge as if this room was designed to shelter me from all the stress and chaos that's been weighing me down for so long.

It's a mental vacation from reality.

My mind drifts back to my life outside of this place. The deadlines piling up at work, the constant pressure to deliver, the gnawing ache in my brain that never let up. I shouldn't be surprised that I've been having nightmares. My mind has been cracking under the weight of all that stress, searching for an escape. And maybe, just maybe, this room is that escape. A place where I don't have to be Rose, the woman who is constantly suffocated by the pressure of everything. Here, I don't have to juggle responsibilities or keep up appearances. There are no emails to send, no articles to finish, no crushing sense of failure creeping up on me. No stress.

But I know, deep down, it's not that simple. Because to stay here, to exist in this strange refuge, I've had to trade my body. It's not mine anymore, is it?

I can't move. I can't speak. I'm completely at the mercy of this man, whoever he is. And I don't know if that's something I'm willing to accept.

But why does it feel like I am?

I close my eyes, the weight of everything settling over me like a shroud. I shouldn't want to stay here. I should be fighting to leave. Yet, there's a part of me that's drawn to it. The peace, the quiet, the lack of pain. The freedom from everything that makes real life feel so heavy.

But the cost...

I'm chasing my thoughts in circles when I notice something I swear wasn't there before.

Right at the edge of my vision, a glimmer catches my eye. It's metallic and glints in the light, but what is it? If I could just convince my neck to move a little, I might be able to get a better look.

But I can't.

I can only see that it's small and attached somehow to the hospital bed.

I wrestle with my thoughts, willing every muscle in my body to co-operate. Is it something for the IV? Some type of machine? A chain? It looks like some type of restraint system.

My imagination races, conjuring dark scenarios that make my skin crawl. I try to dismiss the nagging fear creeping in. My mind is just trying to fill in the gaps of my fractured reality. But no matter how I try to shake it off, my brain won't relent: What if I'm being kept here?

I close my eyes to steady the frantic rhythm of my heart. I'm being ridiculous.

I tell myself I'll wake up soon, go back to my real life, and all of this will fade away like any other dream. But deep down, I know. This isn't fading.

Panic surges through me, hot and wild. My heart races, pounding against my ribcage like a caged animal desperate to escape. I can feel it thrumming in my neck, pulsing in my head, drowning out all rational thought. I'm trapped, my instincts scream.

The walls of this room close in around me, and nausea churns in my stomach, making me feel as though I'm going to throw up. Why would he need restraints? *You don't have to restrain a person that can't move.*

Maybe Junie could move before... before whatever he did to her. Perhaps she fought her hardest to get away from him, and he had to restrain her until he decided on the drug concoction he'd been injecting her with.

The thought rattles around in my mind, echoing louder with each beat of my heart. My breaths come in short gasps, shallow and frantic, and I fight against the rising tide of fear. What if Junie is being held captive here? The question twists my insides, planting seeds of dread.

I can't. I won't let this be my reality.

But the metallic glimmer from earlier haunts me, and my thoughts spiral deeper into darkness. What if this is real? What if I'm trapped here forever, always afraid to close my eyes?

I wrestle with my growing sense of dread, desperate for any thread of hope, a scrap of clarity in the chaos swirling around me. But all I feel is the cold, hard grip of fear wrap around my throat, tightening with every passing second.

Then, the man's phone rings, breaking the silence. My heart skips a beat as I watch him reach for it.

He answers in a way that feels familiar and foreign. "Go for Charlie."

There's a tone of happiness, a warmth that I've never heard directed toward me. It cuts through the fog of confusion, unsettling me further.

I want to scream out to whoever is on the other end of that call to beg for help, but it's trapped, locked away like the rest of me.

"Honestly, I've been struggling," the man says, the happiness completely stripped from him. "It doesn't even feel like she's trying. She fights me every step of the way. I don't know how much longer I can do this. Some days, I don't even want to deal with this anymore."

Is he talking about me? *Of course, I'm fighting you. I don't want to be drugged up and paralyzed anymore.*

I can hear a woman's voice on the other end for several minutes, but I can't figure out what she's saying.

Then the man speaks again, sounding more frustrated now. "And dump her like garbage? She's my problem. I have to figure something else out."

Just then, I make eye contact with him.

"Hey, let me put you on hold. I gotta take care of something, then I'll be right back."

As he speaks, I notice a flicker of something in his eyes, a tension, a weighty consideration. I can see the thoughts churning beneath the surface.

He lets out a deep sigh, almost resigned, and it sends chills skittering down my spine. His body language betrays him; his shoulders tense, and the way he holds the phone tightly suggests a decision is being made, one that could seal my fate.

I struggle to piece it together as the weight of his words hangs heavy in the air. *Figure something out? Dump me?*

The implications gnaw at me, and I'm filled with a desperate need to escape.

"I'm sorry, Junie," he says, pulling out a needle-tipped syringe from his pocket. "But I can't deal with this right now."

I try to move my arm out of his reach, but my body lays still, helpless and trapped.

The syringe glints in the dim light as he plunges it into my IV port.

The world begins to blur, the edges of my vision fading to black.

Everything is slipping away, but my thoughts are sharp, repeating over and over again.

Charlie. He said his name was Charlie.

11

Chapter Eleven

Dr. J. Wiese - Psychologist

I sit in the waiting room, staring at the muted floral wallpaper. My name is next on the clipboard, but I'm not ready to face Dr. Wiese—not today. Not after last night. Not after learning *his* name. Charlie. It should mean a step forward, knowing more about him, but instead, it feels like he's taken another dangerous step closer to me.

The nightmares are worse now. Louder. More vivid. More real. I don't want to tell Dr. Wiese that the increased dosage isn't working. I don't want to admit that despite all the pills and exercises, I'm still trapped in a spiral of falling, suffocating, running—but never waking up. She'll just look at me with that kind smile, the one that feels equal parts comforting and pitying, and tell me we need to "reassess." I don't want reassessment. I want freedom.

"Rose Piper," a nurse announces, and she leads me back to the room.

The doctor's office is cold, unnervingly so — the chill sinks into my bones, making everything feel off. My hands are clammy, and I have a death grip on the chair's armrests, as if letting go would send me spiraling into another universe.

Across from me, the therapist sits quietly, her gaze patient, waiting for me to speak.

"Sorry, did you ask me something? I'm just a little distracted."

I don't know why I'm making excuses, but I am what I am.

"I just asked how things have been going for you." Her tone is warm but neutral.

"I don't know where to start," I admit, my voice sounding smaller than I'd like. "Everything feels wrong, like I'm not even in control of my own life anymore."

Dr. Wiese nods slowly.

The clock on the wall ticks in time with my pulse, but I can't tell if the sound is coming from the room or from inside my head.

"Why don't you start by telling me what's been stressing you the most?"

I sit there under the weight of her gaze. All I can feel is the looming pressure of something dark and haunting. I let out a sigh, leaning back in the chair as I run my fingers through my hair.

"Honestly, I've been having these dreams. Well, they're not exactly dreams. They're more like... experiences." I pause, trying to find the right words. Saying this out loud feels dangerous, like once they're out, I'll never get them back again.

"I dream about a room. It's always the same room. I can't move. I can't speak. There's a man..." My breath catches in my throat. "Charlie, I think. He calls me 'Junie.' And he - he's taking care of me, I think, but it also feels like I'm trapped there. It feels like I wake up in someone else's body, paralyzed in a hospital bed, in an apartment I've never been to in the waking world."

She raises her eyebrows, her interest clearly piqued. "These dreams, do they happen often?"

"Every night, every time I close my eyes for too long," I say, barely above a whisper. "And it's like time slips away from me when I wake up. I'm losing hours. Days. Weeks, even."

She's quiet for a moment, then says, "Rose, sometimes when we experience trauma, our brain tries to protect us by creating barriers — shields — to keep us from facing the full weight of it all at once. What you're describing — headaches, time lapses, confusion — can sometimes be signs that your brain is trying to process something it hasn't fully dealt with yet."

I blink, trying to process her words. "Trauma?"

"Yes, it could be recent or from long ago. Sometimes, our minds find ways to connect the past and present, especially when there are unresolved feelings involved."

"Honestly, I can't think of anything that could be causing this," I say. "The only thing stressing me is work."

"That may be the only thing you are mentally aware of," Dr. Wiese says. "But our subconscious and our nervous system holds onto things much longer than we may realize."

"I don't feel traumatized," I say, my irritation growing.

Dr. Wiese sets her notebook on the desk and leans toward me. "That may be," she hesitates, "but I definitely think it's something we should explore. Before your appointment next week, try to think about your family, your childhood, anything that may have caused you anxiety or stress, even if it was long ago. Make a list and we will talk more about it then, alright?"

I half-heartedly agree to do my "homework," even though I don't think this will actually provide any real answers. Doesn't matter right now. I have to get to work. Life waits for no one.

12

Chapter Twelve

I'm standing in line at the coffee shop, holding Dolly, who found me before I even made it to my seat. She purrs as I scratch behind her ears, blurring out the hum of espresso machines and background chatter.

I have another long work day ahead. My mind is already flipping through the list of tasks waiting for me. Deadlines. Edits. Emails. I've been ignoring it all over the weekend. I would rather spend my day figuring out who Charlie is and if he's even a real person, but I know I don't have enough information at this point to find any real answers.

The bell over the door jingles. I glance up, only for a second, but long enough to catch a familiar figure walking in. Thorne.

Of course, it has to be him.

I quickly look back at the menu, pretending I hadn't noticed him walk in.

Sam runs me through the pastry specials of the day, but I am only half listening.

"I'll take whatever she's having," a voice interrupts from behind, as smooth and confident as the first time I heard it.

I turn to face Thorne, who stands with his hands in his pockets and that same easy smile playing on his lips.

I catch Sam raising an eyebrow as he glances between us.

Not missing a beat, Sam says, "Alright, two Apple Chai Lattes it is."

"Never tried it," Thorne says as he's handing over his card. "Maybe this will be my new favorite."

I hesitate, completely unprepared for this sudden intrusion into my morning routine. "You don't have to—"

"Don't worry about it." His smile widens with every word. "I insist."

I don't know how to respond. There is something disarming about his confidence. He seems to slide into my life as if he belongs there.

I can't protest because Thorne has already paid.

I feel a wave of guilt. I didn't outright reject his gesture. Something inside me wants his kindness.

"Thanks, but you really didn't have to," I say with a grateful nod.

I make my way to my booth and set up my laptop with a sigh. Maybe I should tackle the mountains of unread emails before diving into the mess of research assignments.

"Mind if I join you?" Thorne stands there, holding our drinks.

The look on his face feels like he is daring me to refuse.

I pause, weighing my options. *Just say no. You need to focus. You don't have time for this.*

But instead of saying my thoughts out loud, I find myself nodding.

"So you bought my drink just to bribe me for the best seat in the house, huh?" I aim for casual, but it sounds too playful and borderline flirtatious. *What am I doing?*

He slides across from me as if it is the most natural thing in the world. Thorne places my latte in front of me and settles in like he belongs here. Belongs across from me.

Thorne takes a sip of his drink. When he sets it down, I can't help but notice he is now sporting a frothy milk mustache. I smirk at him shyly, feeling butterflies flutter in my gut.

"You have excellent taste," he says with a wink.

I am immediately blushing. How can he know what I am thinking? "Uhhh, what do you mean?"

I am starting to believe it's possible to die of embarrassment. But he just lifts his mug slightly into the air.

The drink. He meant the drink.

I shake my head, trying to push the shame out of my head. "Oh, I'm glad you like it. I drink the same drink every morning, Monday through Friday. I strangely believe I can't accomplish my work without it."

He looks at me as if I just told him the most interesting fact in the world. "I think this latte might just be my lucky charm too."

I can feel myself blushing deeper as I shyly push my bangs behind my ear. I cannot explain why I am acting this way. This is not typical Rose Piper behavior.

Thorne continues to sip his drink. We are both sitting in comfortable silence.

I blast through my emails, occasionally glancing up at him, sometimes catching him smiling back at me. Other times, he's just typing away on his phone.

"So," he says, leaning back slightly. "How have you been since our little meet-cute? I think that's what they call it in the movies."

I give him a quick smile, but my eyes stay fixated on my screen. "I've been working nonstop," I reply.

I'm typing an unnecessarily long reply to an email simply because I need something to focus on. I don't want this conversation to wander too far.

"You really are a workaholic, huh?" He chuckles softly. "No wonder you live in a coffee shop. You need a constant stream of caffeine."

He lifts his mug again as if toasting the exact beverage that keeps me functioning.

I let out a small laugh. "Yeah, something like that."

"You know, they say all work and no play isn't good for anyone," he says teasingly.

"I play." My tone sounds more defensive than I mean it to.

He raises an eyebrow. "Ok, I'm listening. What does the ever-so-serious Rose do to relax?"

Ever so serious? I am internally annoyed, knowing that's how he views me. "If you must know," I say, pushing my laptop to the side. "I have a weekly breakfast date with my sister, Violet, that involves bottomless mimosas. My best friend, Mei, and her family own the greatest local Chinese restaurant that I have hung out in every Friday night for as long as I can remember. And sometimes, if I'm feeling really crazy," I emphasize. "I go to the movies."

He throws his hands in the air, a dramatic show of defeat. "I was so unbelievably wrong about you," he teases. "You are a real party animal."

I can't help it. I smile at him. Just a little.

He is so charming in such an effortless, annoying way. Surprisingly, I do not mind his company.

After some time, Thorne asks about my sister. "Is there a story behind the flower names?"

"Actually, yes."

I explain that Violet was born in February and how my mother, Joy, loved the fact that violets were February's official flower.

"Then, when Violet was born deaf, mom found out that violets symbolize faith and inspiration, and she felt that those words would be the adjectives to describe my sister's entire life."

I continue, "Then fast forward two years, Mom was pregnant again, with me. This time her best friend is pregnant at the same time. My mom was already thinking along the lines of June's flowers so her options were rose or some variation of honeysuckle. When mom's friend gave birth to a beautiful baby girl only two hours later, my mom decided Rose was the only option since they are a symbol of love and friendship, and I was destined to be best friends with the girl who now shares my birthday."

"So, did your new best friend get to join the flower club too?" he says jokingly, but he somehow guessed correctly.

"How'd you know?" I joke in response. "Mrs. Wong loved the idea of flower names, so she decided on Mei. It means plum blossom in Chinese. The three of us have been best friends our entire lives."

I open my phone and show him a picture of us all together. "I don't know what I would do without them."

"Wow, you guys are committed to the bit."He chuckles, pointing to our hair colors. "I guess I don't need to ask who is who."

"Ha Ha. Very funny," I retort.

I seem to completely forget about work as I tell him more about the two most important women in my life.

"So," he says curiously. "If your sister is deaf, does that mean you know sign language?"

I shake out my hands with a flare of showmanship and sign, "Does this answer your question?"

I have to admit that he looks kind of cute when he's stumped.

"You have to teach me," he says, leaning forward.

I spend way too long teaching him some basic greeting signs. I also teach him about sign names, showing him mine (r-flowers), Violet's (v-flowers), and Mei's (m-bloom).

"So when do I get my sign name?" he asks, genuinely interested.

"You would want one?" I am weirdly surprised. I recognize immediately that I have activated his flirt switch.

"Well, if I'm ever going to meet your family, I think I'll need to know how to communicate," he says with a wink. "I think the first step would be getting a name, right?"

"Well, that makes you wrong about two things," I say defiantly. "Firstly, I'm not sure why the coffee shop stranger would need to meet my family. Secondly, you have to get to know the Deaf Community. If you fully immerse yourself, you'll receive a sign name. The deaf have to get to know you first. A sign name says something about you. They aren't given out lightly. The first step would be to learn how to communicate with them."

"Got it," he says matter of factly. "So when do we start lessons?"

I don't know how to describe the feelings welling inside me. I've never had someone so interested in being able to communicate with my sister. I can tell by his expression that he's serious. He wants to learn my sister's heart language, our language.

I shake myself out of the trance that thought has me in. "I will teach you some more signs under one condition. You must promise to take it seriously and try not to butcher it. ASL is important to me and my family. It's accessible communication, not just a ploy to learn swear words in another language."

He puts one hand to his chest and the other raised in the air. "Scout's honor."

"Ok then," I say with a smile. "I'll be happy to teach you."

I'm overwhelmed by emotions as memories take hold of me, and tears fill my eyes.

"Hey," he says softly, putting his hand on mine. "I promise I'll take it seriously."

For some reason, I don't pull my hand away. "It's not that. I just..." I trail off.

"What is it then?" His face is full of worry. "Did I say something wrong?"

I chuckle softly as I wipe my tears on my sleeve. "Quite the opposite, actually."

Despite my usual walls of defense, I let him see into the darkest corners of my heart. I explain how my mom died when Violet and I were still young, and after that, we were primarily around Dad's side of the family, who unfortunately couldn't be bothered to learn sign language to communicate with their family member.

"I remember so many family dinners where Violet looked between the faces of all our relatives as they laughed and joked around the table. I tried to interpret as much as I could for her, but there's only so much a little kid can do. At night, I would hold her while she cried. From that point on, I decided that I would never allow her to feel that alone again. And I think I've kept that promise."

"Wow," he says slowly. "I can't imagine how difficult that must've been for the two of you."

"Yeah," I continue. "It was hard sometimes, but mostly it brought us closer. Violet and I have been inseparable our entire lives. Once we moved out on our own, we only kept people who could communicate with Vi in our lives. Throughout my life, I've had a lot of first dates, but if the guy isn't willing to put in the work to communicate with my sister, they don't get a second date. Needless to say, I don't have many second dates. No one seems to understand why it's so important to me."

I look down, suddenly feeling embarrassed that I may have shared too much. "Until you."

"I think having a second date with you would be worth every sacrifice a man could make," he says quietly.

"You'd be the first."

"Oh my, Rose. Are you asking me out on a date?" He's joking, but his tone is eager.

I push his arm in an attempt to be flirtatious. "That wouldn't be very ladylike of me, now would it?" I tease. "Besides, I don't know your life story yet."

He shrugs. "It's not poetic like yours. Maybe I can tell you over dinner sometime."

I feel the heat immediately rush to my face. "I might just have to take you up on that offer."

He leans toward me, "I'll hold you to that. No takebacks."

I chuckle, shaking my head as I turn back to my laptop. I can't help but feel a growing attachment. Thorne's laughter is infectious, and despite my best efforts, I find myself smiling more often than I ever intended.

"If you're going to make me wait till some future possible dinner to tell me about your family," I poke fun. "Can you at least tell me something interesting about yourself?"

He takes a long sip of his drink, then leans forward as if to tell me a troubling secret. "I have a ridiculous habit of talking to my plants." He is whispering so seriously as if this is top-secret information. "I swear, they are the only ones I can trust. Sometimes, I tell them all my problems and then apologize for dumping all my issues on them."

I look up from my laptop, faking concern. "I wish you would've warned me from the start that you're a crazy person."

Thorne grins, clearly enjoying this turn in the conversation. "Well, it's not like they talk back. But they also don't judge me. Maybe you should give it a try."

"I'm not judging," I protest. "Everyone has their quirks."

"It's honestly a nice way to unwind after a hard day," he says, glaring down into his mug.

As if realizing he took the conversation down a serious path, he adds, "Plus, I stick to a strict routine with my plants. I have to sing while I water them, or else I feel that they will end up dead. I know, it sounds pretty silly."

I grin at him, finding the idea oddly endearing. "Silly, yes. But also a little bit sweet."

For a moment, I feel a strange sense of connection. Here is Thorne, sharing something personal, almost vulnerable, and for some reason, it feels completely natural. There's a comfort in his presence, a familiarity that's strangely freeing.

I push that feeling aside, reminding myself of the ever-growing mountain of work waiting for me. *No more distractions, no matter how charming Thorne is.*

I can't lose sight of what's important.

"Well, I suppose if talking to plants helps you unwind, then keep at it. I, on the other hand, have a mountain of deadlines staring me in the face." I sound ruder than I intend, but my resolve is to stay focused on work.

I see Thorne's smile fade. "I get it. Work comes first." He sounds like a little kid who just lost his favorite action figure. "If you ever want to take a break or just want to chat, I'm always just a text away."

He jots his number on a napkin and pushes it toward me.

I nod, grateful for his offer but also resolute. "Thanks. I'll let you know." I slide the napkin into my laptop bag. "For now, though, I need to get back to work."

Despite knowing I am doing the right thing, seeing Thorne's discouragement is like a stab through my heart.

"I'll let you get back to saving the world, workaholic." He tries to crack a joke, but he sounds so serious. "Don't be a stranger, okay?"

I watch him go, feeling relief and disappointment. I bury myself in my work, no longer having to face a man of undeniable charm.

Even as I tackle task after task, my mind keeps wandering back to our conversations. I find myself replaying his comments, his smiles, and the way he seemed genuinely interested in the little details of my life.

The clock ticks away, and the workload lightens with it.

After a few more hours, I turn in all my assignments before their deadline. I take a deep breath, letting the relief sink deep into my bones.

I glance out the window with a pang of longing to see Thorne walking down the street. I can't help but wonder when I'll see him again.

As I pack up my things to head home, I come across the napkin with Thorne's number on it. I add him to my contacts list but will not text him. At least not now.

I hit save and flip over to my messaging app. I hesitate, open the chat labeled "The Daisy Chain," and type a message.

The Daisy Chain

Rose (4:53 PM): U won't believe the day I had.

Mei (4:55 PM): ????

Rose (4:55PM): 4 hour coffee "date" w/ Thorne. 'Member tall, dark hair, & green eyes?

Violet (4:55 PM): DETAILS. ASAP.

Rose (4:56 PM): IDK. He bought my latte & we sat talking all day. We both flirted, I think.

Violet (4:57 PM): AND???

Rose (4:58 PM): wdym AND?

Rose (5:00 PM): I smiled like a dork. Idk girls… There's something about him. The way he talks, the way he teases me. I can't stop thinking about him.

Mei (5:01 PM): Sounds like true love to me.

Violet (5:01 PM): VEE-VEE! Thorne & Rose sittin' in a tree K-I-S-S-I-N-G!

Rose (5:02 PM): SHUT UP! Nothing happened. Idk if anything WILL happen. I'm focusing on my career, remember?

Mei (5:03 PM): Who says you can't have your dream job and your dream man?

Rose (5:04PM): He DID ask for my number… & sort of asked me out on a date. So we will see.

Violet (5:04 PM): Y DIDN'T U LEAD W/ THAT??

Rose (5:06 PM): Idk, not important.

Violet (5:07 PM): NOT IMPORTANT? My baby sister is getting married!!

Rose (5:09 PM): OMG, hold your horses, missy. He only asked me out for a date because he wanted free ASL lessons. It's not a whirlwind romance.

Violet (5:10 PM): He wants to learn ASL?? I love him already.

Mei (5:12 PM): Sounds like a keeper to me, Rose. I know how important having someone who can communicate with Vi is to you. I think it's at least worth a go.

Rose (5:26 PM): Legit can't tell you guys nothing. Drama Queens.

Violet (5:27 PM): Took u long enuff 2 respond.

Mei (5:28 PM): It's because she knows we are right. She was totally delaying to gain extra time to think of a comeback. She still didn't come up with anything clever.

Rose (5:31 PM): NOT TRUE! I was walking home and didn't want to have my face plastered to my phone. TRAFFIC SAFETY.

Violet (5:31 PM): RIIIIIIGHT.

Mei 5:32 PM): You may not get it yet, but we sure as heck know it.

Rose (5:33 PM): & what's that exactly?

Mei (5:33 PM): Every Rose has its "Thorne."

Violet (5:33 PM): <3

13

CHAPTER THIRTEEN

Every rose has its thorn, I think as I brush my teeth. "What a cliche," I mutter.

I'm going through the motions of my nightly routine, but my brain is only fluttering to one thought.

Thorne.

I think back to our effortless conversation. I picture his imperfect but gorgeous smile in my mind. I roll my eyes at the memory, cringing at the fact it makes me smile even now. He slipped past my defenses, and as much as I hate to admit it, it feels... nice.

I slip into bed, the cool sheets brushing softly against my skin. "*Hey, Google, turn off bedroom lights.*"

My room is swallowed by darkness.

I'm lost in Thorne's laughter. A part of me is hoping I'll see him again tonight, but this time, in my dreams. No hospital bed. No creepy feelings. Just... him.

I close my eyes, focusing on his face. If I think about him long enough, I'll have no choice but to dream of something good. "Just... let me have this," I plead with my brain.

When I open my eyes, I'm surrounded by something that resembles static, but I can feel something in the dark. Not something, someone, just ahead of me. It's a man standing directly in front of me. I can't see his face, and his back is toward me. But I know that stance, the way his shoulders rest, relaxed yet confident. My heart skips.

Thorne. It has to be him.

The tension I didn't even know I carry begins to melt away, leaving only relief in its absence. This is what I wanted.

I try to reach out and touch him, let him know that I'm here. But something is off.

The air turns colder, and the room is quiet and still. He starts to turn toward me, his face coming into focus. The dark hair in my mind's eye changes rapidly to white.

My blood runs cold. Not Thorne. Charlie.

The room around me snaps sharply into clarity. The bed, the IV, the green walls, the orange couch, the TV, everything. How could I have not seen it before?

The tall, athletic build, the green eyes... they're the same. But that's where the similarities end. Thorne's face holds warmth, humor, and an irresistible spark that draws me to him. Charlie's is devoid of all of that, just a flat, unreadable mask.

Their features echo each other yet stand worlds apart. Thorne's black, wavy hair stands in stark contrast to Charlie's silver locks. Plus, nothing about him compares to Thorne's amazing dimples that shine when he smiles and eyes that radiate with life.

Charlie resembles more of a looming shadow, with a thick, monochrome, Viking-esk beard that looks like smoke. He is always disheveled and gives... Walking Dead character. Nothing like my coffee shop crush. He is completely devoid of Thorne's exuberant and enticing personality.

Still, despite the harsh contrasts, I can't deny the strong similarities between them. They shouldn't be connected in any way. Could it all just be a twisted joke my mind is playing on me? A sick way of coping with my real-life stress? Am I losing it for real?

Charlie's eyes are locked on me now, and something about how he looks at me makes the hair on the back of my neck stand up. He looks disturbed, and his demeanor is completely different from that of his previous dreams.

He takes a step toward me, slow and deliberate. I want to run far away from him, but this body refuses to cooperate. Charlie is inches from my face. It feels like he is peering into the very depths of my soul.

Charlie backs away from me without saying a word. It's only then I notice his eyes. He looks so tired like he's carrying the weight of the world on his shoulders. There's something broken in them, something that makes me feel sympathetic and terrified.

Suddenly, he turns and walks away, leaving me in the suffocating silence.

There's a knock at the door. More than ever, I wish I could scream. "Help! I'm in here! Call 911. Please. Anyone? Help me."

But of course, no sounds escape me.

After a few moments, I hear Charlie again in the distance. His voice is low as if he's talking to someone, but I can't make out the words. Then it grows louder, sharper, like the rumble of a storm about to break. I hold my breath, straining to catch any details, my pulse quickening in sync with his rising anger.

The frustration builds, each word more jagged than the last. My heart skips as he lets out a deep growl of fury.

I still can't understand what he's saying, but the menace is clear. It feels like a dam ready to burst. Then, without warning, there's a guttural grunt, followed by the unmistakable sound of something heavy slamming against metal. My heart jolts at the noise. *What is happening?*

The clatter of metal echoes through the house, followed by the sound of something being dragged across the floor. My imagination conjures up chaotic scenes: objects flying, fists slamming, the sound of a struggle that I can't see, can't understand. The noise is brutal and violent. And then, just as suddenly as it began, it stops.

The silence that follows is suffocating, thick with tension and unanswered questions. I can hear my pulse pounding in my ears, the quiet stretching out as if the entire house is holding its breath.

Every second drags, a stillness so unnerving that it feels like I'm waiting for something to snap. And then it does.

Charlie storms into the room, his steps heavy, purposeful, the sheer force of his presence sucking the air out of the space. His face is twisted with fury, his eyes blazing with a kind of intensity I've never seen before.

My stomach flips when I see him up close. His shirt is untucked, his hair a wild mess, and his once-white t-shirt is now smeared with red. Is that...blood? My thoughts screech to a halt. *It is blood. Oh my God, it's blood.*

The sight sends my mind spiraling. *Whose blood?*

The question claws at my insides, panic swelling in my chest as I watch him stride across the room, tightly gripping a towel in his right hand, knuckles white from the strain. A singular blood drop from his palm falls to the floor, a stark reminder of the violence that just unfolded beyond these walls.

Charlie's eyes meet mine, locking me in place with a cold, piercing stare. I try to look away, to pull my gaze from the crimson streaks on his shirt, but I can't.

His voice is low, like a growl, when he finally speaks. "It's nothing. Just an accident."

I feel a chill race down my spine as he stalks past me toward the bathroom, just at the edge of my vision. His movements are stiff and deliberate. Charlie slams the door shut behind him with a force that rattles the walls, the sound reverberating through my chest. I stare at the closed door, frozen, my mind racing. I can hear running water, but beyond that, I'm surrounded by silence.

What accident? Whose blood is that?

The seconds drag on, each one heavier than the last, until finally, the door creaks open again.

Charlie steps out, his hand now wrapped in pristine white bandages. The bloodied towel is gone as if it was never there, but the image is burned into my mind. Something is very, very wrong.

His eyes flicker to me, cold and unreadable, and I feel the weight of that look pressing down on me like an unseen hand crushing my windpipe.

He doesn't offer any explanation. He doesn't tell me what happened or why his shirt is stained with blood. He just vanishes into the kitchen, his footsteps heavy as they fade from the room.

I can hear him moving things around, muttering, too low for me to understand. The silence that follows is excruciating. I'm left alone with my spiraling thoughts, panic simmering just beneath the surface.

Is someone else still here? My mind races, trying to make sense of the noise, the blood, the rage.

Is Junie in danger now? Am I in danger? The questions burn through my skull, my imagination running wild with dark possibilities.

Footsteps make my heart stutter. He's back, but something's different now. He's shirtless, and his movements are calm and deliberate as if nothing out of the ordinary has happened. I watch him wide-eyed, my body tensing. Charlie doesn't sit down. He just stands there, looking at me with that same icy detachment.

"I'm sorry you had to hear that," he says, his voice disturbingly measured.

The fury that burned in him minutes ago is gone, replaced by an eerie calm. His lips twitch into a ghost of a smile. "I'll be back in a little while.

I have to take out the trash, and then I'll pick up some dinner. I'll be back soon."

Before I can process his words, he leans, brushing my hair back with a tenderness that sends a shiver down my spine.

Charlie presses a soft kiss to my forehead, lingering just a moment too long, and for a heartbeat, I feel trapped beneath the weight of his presence. The sweetness of the gesture feels wrong, like something tainted.

He goes toward the bathroom again, this time turning left to go down the hallway. He reappears a few moments later in a black button-up shirt. *There must be a bedroom down that hallway.* I attempt to create a mental layout.

He's rolling up his sleeves to three-fourths and then grabs his wallet, phone, and keys off the TV stand. If he hadn't been covered in someone's blood just moments earlier, I can confidently assume most women would describe him as a "silver fox."

He gives me a mock salute, and then, just like that, he's gone.

The silence rushes back in, suffocating me as the door closes behind him. My pulse races, my skin cold with dread. What just happened?

I glance around the room, taking everything in with fresh eyes. I am trying to find anything that can help me make some sort of sense of the chaos that just unfolded. But nothing comes. I am truly alone in this place. Completely and utterly helpless.

My fear feels raw, but the longer I am here alone, the more the adrenaline rush starts to ebb away. Now feeling a sense of determination, I glance around the room once more. I force myself to pay attention to the finer details. My view hasn't changed. My body is still unwilling to move, even in this desperate situation. Despite seeing this room every night, I look closer with fresh eyes. It doesn't take long to notice characteristics that I hadn't registered until now.

The curtains on the window are slightly frayed at the edges, the light switch plate is askew, and there are scuff marks under the table from the chair being repeatedly slid in and out. I hadn't paid attention to any of these details before, but now... they stand out. This place is more real than I ever thought.

But it can't be real. Can it?

I look again. The furniture, the decorations, the wear pattern in the carpet - all of it looks too lived in, too detailed. I can see the texture of the wooden TV stand and the soft, worn edges of the couch cushions. What if this isn't just a dream? What if it's something else, something I can't understand?

I don't know how much more I can take. I am convinced now that I have lost my grip on reality, and I don't know how long it'll be before I lose my mind completely. I don't have time to dwell on these thoughts as I'm interrupted by the sound of keys in the lock. He's back.

I can hear his footsteps come closer, each step echoing as it hits the hardwood floor. He sounds relaxed now. Still, I feel acid climb my throat. I don't want him to come in here. I don't want to face him.

He took out the trash that was undeniably full of bloody clothing and who knows what else. I'm not ready to be in the room with the psychopath who can just pretend like a slasher movie wasn't just reenacted in their kitchen.

For the first time, it feels like I'm truly present in this place. My eyes flutter, and I realize something strange: it doesn't just feel like an automatic reflex anymore. This time, I feel in control. I'm not just blinking—I'm choosing to blink. My heart skips as I focus harder. One blink, two... I made it happen. I can control this.

It feels like one of those lucid dreams, where one suddenly realizes they're dreaming and starts to have a sense of control over the storyline. Unfortunately, the only thing I can seem to control in this nightmare is my eyelids.

I try to make sense of this newfound power over such a tiny movement. Why hadn't I noticed it before? I've been able to look around this room, but it is like my body does it on its own, like I am watching from a distance. Every movement I make feels automatic and dreamlike, as if I am not fully in control. But this—this is different. This is me.

If I can control my blinking, what else can I control? Can I wake myself up? Am I even asleep?

I grapple with the realization that I've never experienced anything like this in my dreams before. This room, this life, none of it feels like a dream anymore. It feels like a trap. I have to get out.

I squeeze my eyes shut, forcing myself to wake up, to shake myself out of this nightmare.

But nothing changes. I'm still here.

My eyes are wide when Charlie enters the room. Upon seeing my expression, his eyes soften, the tension in his face loosening as he steps closer.

"Junie..." His voice is gentle, almost apologetic. "I didn't mean to scare you."

I concentrate, blinking with every ounce of will I have left.

I'm in here. Please, see me. My mind screams the words, hoping, begging for him to understand. But my body remains frustratingly still.

He steps closer, his brow furrowed as he examines my face.

"Your blinking is getting stronger. Can you understand me?" He holds onto an unfamiliar curiosity and fragile hope.

For a moment, something flickers in his expression. Recognition, perhaps. Does he see me? Does he realize I'm not this "Junie" he keeps talking about? I blink frantically, trying to drive the point home. *It's me. Not Junie. Please.*

His gaze sharpens, and for a fleeting second, I can almost see it: the gears turning in his mind, the pieces of the puzzle coming together.

Charlie's lips part like he's about to speak, to acknowledge what's happening. My hope for escape is rising dangerously.

But then it slips away. I can see it so clearly. The hesitation in his eyes. His brows knit together, and his whole face tightens as he backs away. It's like he's pulling the curtains closed on his revelation, retreating from the truth, convincing himself that any sign of life was just a figment of his imagination. The flicker of hope inside me snuffs out.

His voice hardens, distant now. "You're still in there, aren't you, Junie?"

There's a tremor in his words, one he tries to hide beneath his calm demeanor. He wants to believe that everything is still the same, that he hasn't lost his version of Junie yet. The cracks in his facade are small but unmistakable. The way his hand lingers at his side, the way his gaze falters ever so slightly before looking away.

"You have to be."

Why? I scream silently. *Why can't you see that I'm not her*?

But he's already made up his mind, retreating into the safety of denial. Whatever glimmer of recognition he had, whatever hint that he might've seen me, is gone now, buried beneath layers of grief, guilt, or fear, too thick for even reality to penetrate.

Charlie shakes his head, more to himself than to me. "I know you're with me. I can feel it," he mutters as if reassuring himself more than anyone else.

Then he turns away, leaving me trapped, unseen, unheard.

The room falls silent once more, and I'm left with the suffocating weight of knowing that he was close, so close, to seeing me. But in the end, he couldn't. Or wouldn't.

He sets a bag on the table, and the familiar smell hits me before I even see it: fresh dim sum, steamed buns, and dumplings. For a split second, I am almost comforted by the scent that brings Mei to the front of my mind.

The logo. The food doesn't just smell familiar. It is familiar. It's actually from Mei's restaurant. It's from my life, my home.

My mind stumbles, trying to process what I'm seeing. How is this even possible? Mei's place is real. It's part of my life, outside of this nightmare, not part of this room. How could Charlie have gotten this? Mei's restaurant shouldn't even exist here.

I stare at the bag. This isn't a coincidence. It can't be. My world is seeping into this prison. I have no idea what any of this means, but it feels like the walls are closing in on me. The boundaries between dreams and reality are becoming increasingly thin. I am bombarded with questions that I don't have any answers for.

Charlie moves around the room, talking to himself, but his words do not even register.

I can't tear my eyes away from the bag, the logo, the undeniable proof that my life, my real life, is intertwined with this nightmare. I don't know what's happening or how it's all connected, but I am more determined than ever to figure it out.

14

Chapter Fourteen

I bolt upright, gasping for air as if I had been drowning. I glance at my clock—6:00 AM.

Every inch of me trembles. I can still feel Charlie looming over me—the intensity of his eyes, the anger, all the blood.

I press my palm firmly against my chest, begging my heartbeat to slow down. It was just a dream.

I throw off the blankets and scramble for my laptop. My fingers tremble as I flip it open. The dim light illuminates the darkness, casting shadows around my room.

I open a webpage while trying to recall every single detail. Charlie, the restaurant, anything.

I create a new document called *"Operation Charlie."* My fingers fly across the keyboard, typing in a flurry of desperation.

Charlie NYC

Nothing useful. Too many Charlies in New York.

Charlie, Junie (Surname?) New York City

Still nothing. I stare at the endless list of random Charles and Charlies.

Charlie, NYC, Apartment sage green walls

Even though I know it's hopeless, I wait for something to pop up. Something that could explain everything that has been happening to me.

I'm missing something.

I stare at the screen for a moment. What would I do if this was for the newspaper?

That thought gives me a spark of inspiration.

Charlie and Junie wedding records NYC - Search.

Charlie Junie Marriage License NYC - Search.

No results found.

Something pushes me to keep searching.

Junie, Missing Woman NYC - Search.

Junie / Juny / Juney / Jooney + Missing Woman + NYC - Search.

Junie paralyzed woman - Search.

Junie + Disabled Woman + Kidnapped - Search.

I bite my lip, anxiously waiting for each result. Nothing. It's like they don't even exist, and I feel the weight of that realization settle into my bones. I'm chasing smoke. The more I start to get a grasp, the further it slips away.

"Come on, come on," I whisper, my eyes darting over pages of useless information.

Every search is completely fruitless. I am not nearly as afraid of my dreams now as I am of absolutely losing my sanity.

THE DIM SUM BAG.

A light bulb turns on in my brain. There's no way food from Mei's restaurant could have been a coincidence.

I look at the clock: half past seven. "She should be up already," I convince myself.

I grab my phone and press Mei's contact with shaky fingers. "Come on, pick up."

"You've reached Mei. I can't come to the phone right now. Leave me a message and I'll get back to you as soon as possible. Thanks!"

BEEP.

"Mei, it's Rose. I need to talk to you about something super important. Please call me back as soon as you can."

I end the call, frustration bubbling inside me. My mind races with all of these unanswered questions, each more disturbing than the last.

I can't just sit around waiting. If I don't do something soon, I'm going to lose it. I need answers, and I need them now.

But first—clothes.

I rush to the corner of my room, where a mountain of laundry has taken on a life of its own. I dive in, grabbing the first shirt I find, and give it a cautious sniff.

Nope. That's not going to work.

I toss it aside and dig deeper. A pair of jeans? Also questionable.

I sniff again, this time quickly regretting it as I recoil. Definitely not.

I spot a hoodie buried halfway down the pile and yank it out. After one sniff, I nod. Passable. That'll do.

I toss it on, still reminding myself I need to do laundry soon. That will be tomorrow's number one mission. But right now? That's not my priority.

I manage to find some halfway-clean jeans that don't smell like gym socks, and after a quick mental pep talk about not looking like a complete disaster, I'm out the door, heading toward the restaurant. Everything else will have to wait.

The streets are quiet this early. My mind, however, is not. My pace quickens as every step closer to Mei is one step toward unraveling the mess of fears and doubts that I've been calling life as of late.

Whatever is happening, I need to confront it head-on. Mei is my only true lead at this point, and I am holding onto the hope that I will find some semblance of clarity after all this.

I push through the back door of the restaurant, the spare key cold in my hand. I've used it dozens of times during busy periods when Mei needed an extra hand, but tonight, it feels different—like I'm sneaking into an evidence locker.

The dim, empty dining room is unusually still, but my heart pounds in my ears.

I don't have time to process the guilt of breaking into the Wong's restaurant. I am on a mission.

I make a beeline for the computer, my fingers shaking as I log into the system. The screen hums to life, casting a blue glow around me.

I scroll through the list of orders from last night, my pulse racing as I try to remember exactly what I saw in The Room. Dim sum. Steamed buns. Dumplings. I scan for anything that matches.

Three orders pop up that seem close enough.

My heart stutters as I check the timestamps, each one aligning with the moments I imagined—or rather, remembered—from last night. But it still doesn't make sense.

I push my chair back and head toward the security monitor.

I click through the footage from the times of each order pickup, my eyes glued to the screen. The first one: an older woman, hunched over with a cane, slowly walks in and out, clutching her takeout bag. Definitely not Charlie.

I fast-forward to the next. A man in his twenties, looking more like a student, rushing in and out between classes wearing earbuds and barely glancing at the cashier. No match.

My breath catches as I click on the final one.

The footage rolls and the seconds tick by agonizingly slow. My stomach twists in knots.

I hit pause when the last customer steps into the frame. My heart leaps into my throat. It's a tall man of similar build, but obviously not Charlie. It's another stranger, some random guy in a business suit. He had grabbed his order and walked out. *Charlie wasn't here.*

I lean back, staring at the blank screen, the silence of the room crashing in on me. No matches. Another dead end.

How could this be?

The room spins around me as I sit frozen, trying to comprehend what I've just seen—or rather, what I haven't seen. Charlie wasn't here. But I saw the food. I know I saw it.

I curl into the chair, pulling my knees to my chest. My breaths come in short, shallow bursts. Tears prick my eyes. *What is happening? Am I losing my mind?*

He is real. He has to be real. The blood. The fight. His voice. The panic inside me builds into an uncontrollable sob as I bury my face in my hands.

I try to steady myself, forcing deep breaths through the sobs. But all I can hear is the echo of my own thoughts, louder than the empty restaurant. How could something that felt so vivid, so terrifying, be nothing but a figment of my imagination?

I wipe my eyes, staring blankly at the empty screen in front of me, the reality—or nightmare—setting in deeper. Nothing makes sense. Nothing.

My phone buzzes, and I shake my head, tears rolling down my cheeks as I read an incoming text from my boss.

Stacey (8:10 AM): Zoom meeting in twenty minutes. Cameras on. Don't be late.

15

CHAPTER FIFTEEN

I storm into the coffee shop with only minutes to spare.

"You're late," Sam says teasingly. "What's your excuse this time, missy?"

"I'll tell you later," I blurt as I hurry past him. "Just give me my usual. No pastry. I think I'm gonna be sick."

I get to my booth and fumble with my laptop, finally logging into the Zoom meeting. I connect my earbuds to my laptop just as Sam brings my latte.

"You doing ok?" he asks.

"Cameras on everybody," a voice from the meeting calls.

I look up at Sam as I put in my earbuds and smile. "In meeting, chat later," I tell him, pointing to the screen.

He rolls his eyes, just a little gesture to remind me that he won't forget to ask again.

The meeting is exactly as I fear: a monotonous parade of corporate buzzwords and obligatory team-building jargon. My boss drones on endlessly about the need to "do better" and "exceed expectations."

I try to focus. I really do. But I have way too much on my mind right now to care about this company "being like a family."

I catch occasional snippets of what's being discussed, but my thoughts drift right back to the dream.

I complete the tasks required of me and half listen as my boss praises the team's efforts and outlines this quarter's goals.

Finally, the meeting finishes, and I close my laptop with a sigh of relief.

I take a sip of my tea, allowing the brief silence to roll over me. I lean back against the booth, closing my eyes.

"Rough day?"

My eyes shoot open to see Thorne sitting across from me. His voice is laced with genuine empathy.

"You have no idea." I chuckle in response.

"Well, why don't you tell me all about it?" His tone is soft.

I scramble to come up with an answer that doesn't make me sound like a psychopath. I stare at him for a moment; the uncanny resemblance to Charlie haunts me, yet Thorne's calm demeanor offers me a strange sense of grounding. Still, I can feel the anxiety growing inside me.

Desperation is clawing up my throat, and without thinking, I blurt, "Can I see your right hand?"

Thorne raises an eyebrow, a playful smirk spreading across his face. "You're not some weird palm reader, right? Because I have no interest in learning how or when I'm going to die."

I chuckle nervously. "No, I don't believe in that stuff. Just give me your hand."

Clearly curious and amused, he places his hands on the table. I grab his right hand, my fingers trembling as I turn it over. I'm inspecting his hand closely from every angle. There are no cuts, no bandages — nothing that resembles the injury from my dream. His hand is perfectly intact.

"If you wanted to hold my hand, all you had to do was ask," he jokes with a flirtatious wink.

I melt with relief. There is no way this gorgeous man in front of me is Charlie, and now I have irrefutable proof. An injury so severe could never heal overnight.

"Very funny," I say, trying to match his playful attitude. "Say, you don't, by chance, have an older brother?"

He clutches his chest in mock pain. "Already wanting to replace me, huh?"

I roll my eyes, letting out a small laugh. "It's not that... I just saw a man last night who looked a lot like you. Thought maybe you were related."

Thorne shakes his head. "Must've found my doppelganger. No brothers, only one sister, and she lives in Louisiana. Even if she was here, I don't think she'd get mistaken for a man. She is the prettier of us two."

I mumble, "I doubt that."

I can feel myself blushing, and I'm immediately embarrassed.

As we continue to chat, his genuine nature eases my frazzled nerves. His stories give me a much-needed distraction, and I feel the spark between us growing.

As the workday wore on, the weight of my fears lift. Maybe it is just a nightmare.

Thorne's laughter and the ease of our conversations create a sense of safety that I haven't felt in quite a while. He talks about his passions, his love for cooking, the challenges of running a restaurant, and his dreams for the future. He paints a picture of his life, filling the silent spaces with warmth and humor.

I need this. He is the greatest distraction.

Hours pass quickly. As I wrap up my workday, Thorne turns to me with a grin.

"Care to join me after hours at my restaurant? We can cook together. Just you and me, no interruptions."

I blink, taken aback by the unexpected invitation. The offer is surprising and intriguing. "You wouldn't get in trouble?" I ask, contemplating a date that sounds straight from a movie.

"I own the place—my house. My rules," he says with a big, cheesy grin.

"Well, then, I'd love to. That actually sounds amazing." I'm excited and nervous. "I could use the distraction."

His smile widens, and his energy is infectious. "Great, Sunday at nine? I'll text you the address."

"Yeah," I smile back at him. "Nine works for me."

My heart races again, this time out of curiosity about what might happen next.

My phone lights up with the address.

"Got it," I say.

"Awesome," he says, packing up his things.

I'm almost tempted to ask him to stay.

"Dinner rush starts in an hour; I better check that my kitchen is staffed and ready."

I look down at my hands, trying to hide my disappointment. "Right, of course. The dinner rush waits for no man."

I try to laugh it off, but it comes off as awkward.

He places a hand on my shoulder, looking down at me. "I'll see you Sunday, nine sharp."

With a final, deep breath, I watch him walk away. I gather my things and head home.

I walk through my front door straight to my couch and sink into it, the weight of the day pressing heavily on my chest.

The confusion from my nightmare still haunts me like a ghost I can't shake. Everything feels out of focus and unreal, as if my life has blurred into two distinct worlds — one dark, filled with unanswered questions, and another that shimmers with possibility.

But the more I think about Thorne and our upcoming date, the lighter the air around me feels. My real life with him feels like a plot from a Nicholas Sparks movie that I never want to end. If Thorne is just part of some weird dream, maybe, just maybe, I don't want to wake up. For the first time in a long time, I can't wait for tomorrow.

6

Chapter Sixteen

My body feels rigid and heavy. The beeping and hum of the machines fill the air before I even open my eyes. The tightening knot in my chest is begging me not to look. I don't have a choice.

I glance around —- more machines, sleek and sterile, line the walls around my bed. The once sparse room feels more cluttered now, blurring the lines between hospital and apartment.

Charlie comes into my line of vision, balancing a tray full of medications. He's calm, his expression unreadable as he methodically prepares each vial. I can feel the strain on my eyeballs as I work hard to make out the labels, but the writing is a blur. Whatever he's giving me, I can't tell what it is.

"More meds to help you out," Charlie says as he administers the first dose.

He inserts the syringe with practiced ease. "Just want to make sure you're comfortable. You need to keep your strength up."

Strength. Internally, I scoff at his choice of words. He's not helping me gain strength. I am being kept weak, restrained under the guise of care. Each dose of medicine feels like just another chain binding me here.

"This will all be over soon," he says with a half-hearted smile. "You just have to trust me, alright?"

Trust him? Each word out of his mouth sounds like a hollow echo, meant to soothe me but only amplifying the nervous thoughts in my brain. How can I trust someone who keeps me like a prisoner locked in a cage of his own making?

Blink, I command myself, willing my eyelids to cooperate.

Maybe if he knows that I understand, something will change.

Blink, blink.

Each movement is a struggle; my eyelids feel weighed down, but I need to communicate something, anything, to Charlie.

Finally, he looks in my direction. I'm searching for a flicker of recognition crossing his face. He turns back to the tray of medications, oblivious to the significance of my efforts.

My heart sinks. *Did he not understand?*

This isn't just random blinking. I'm trying, fighting with everything I have to break through this suffocating fog he has cast over me. *I'm here. Please notice me.*

As he begins putting the medications away, each passing moment intensifies the chasm between us. Charlie busies himself with the equipment. He's never going to acknowledge me.

The sudden burst of sound from the TV snaps me out of my fading thoughts. I can tell that Charlie is sitting on the couch beside me now. I glance toward the screen and immediately recognize the familiar local news station logo.

A woman's voice fills the room, both serious and urgent. "We're following a breaking story this morning. A woman's body has been discovered in Main Street Park. Authorities have yet to release the victim's identity, but sources tell us the investigation is being treated as a homicide..."

My pulse quickens. *Main Street Park?*

I know exactly where that is. I've been there many times before. Just when I convince myself that this is all just a figment of my imagination, something from reality drags me deeper into this nightmare.

Charlie breaks into my thoughts, sounding almost conversational. "That park, it's right outside."

I can hear him move to the window, just out of sight.

"I can see the lights of the police cars from here," he murmurs unbothered.

His words bounce off the walls of my brain: The park right outside. The police lights. A dead woman.

Memories from the last time I was here with Charlie surge to the front of my mind. The blood, his red-stained shirt, his trembling hands. The vague, distant sounds of a struggle. No, a fight. His haunted expression when he assured me, *"It's nothing. Just an accident."*

An accident. Was that a lie? I can feel my mind spiraling, connecting the dots with terrifying clarity. Had Charlie killed someone? Was this woman's blood on his clothes? Maybe he took out more than just the trash.

The machines around me beep incessantly, an out-of-body warning that my anxiety is escalating to dangerous levels. I have arrived at the only possible conclusion: Charlie may be far more dangerous than I ever thought. Even more horrifying, I am completely at his mercy.

The piercing sounds of alarms fill the room. My heart is beating out of my chest, the relentless beeping a perfect mirror of my terror. Every instinct screams at me that I am in grave danger.

Charlie comes into view, his face tight with frustration. "Seriously, Junie?" he mutters.

His presence feels cold and annoyed as he grabs another syringe from the medicine tray. "How many times do I have to tell you? You need to stay calm," he snaps.

He jams the needle into my arm. "You're making this so much harder than it needs to be."

The cold liquid runs through my veins, and the effects come on fast. He's mad at me. I can't keep up with his violent mood swings. It's terrifying.

As the drug takes its hold on me, the world around me warps. My body relaxes against my will, the fight draining from my muscles even when my mind screams to stay alert. *Just stay awake a little longer.*

The medication is too strong. I am consumed by the sound of his heavy, exasperated sigh. The weight of his impatience fills the room as though my very existence is an inconvenience to him.

And then everything goes black.

17

CHAPTER SEVENTEEN

I blink, disoriented, and stand in the library entryway. *How did I get here?* I don't remember walking here.

The library is only a couple blocks from my apartment, but not being able to recall how I got somewhere makes me look at the distance completely different.

I look down at my hands, which tremble slightly, and see I'm holding a flyer. It's advertising a coding class at the library. *Coding? What the—? Why would I care about that?*

A strange unease seeps into my mind, but I shake it off. *Focus. There are bigger things at play right now—the woman in the park.*

My feet feel heavy as I walk deeper into the library like I'm wading through wet mud. The quiet atmosphere amplifies the sound of my breathing.

I drop my bag by an old, forgotten computer tucked into a dark corner and move the mouse to wake it; the screen flickers as it boots up.

As I pull up the local news website, my fingers tap against the keyboard, mechanical and cold.

For over an hour, I scroll through article after article, hunting for anything that would match what I'd seen on the TV last night. But there's nothing. No reports of a body. No incident at Main Street park. No active crime scenes.

My chest tightens, and I want to scream, to throw the keyboard across the room.

Am I losing my mind?

I feel nauseous. I think of Mei and Violet. They're right. My stress is driving me insane. What if I'm imagining it all? Could everything I've experienced be a twisted fabrication of my mind?

I push myself back from the computer desk. This is getting me nowhere.

I look out the window at the passing cars. If I can't find the answers here, maybe I can find them out there.

I leave the library and take a taxi to Main Street Park.

The cabbie drops me off, and as I step into the park, the afternoon sun filters through the trees, casting shadows on the walking paths. From a glance, it feels like any other day: joggers stretching after a run, a couple walking their dog, and kids playing on the swings.

I walk the entire park perimeter, scanning for any trace of a crime scene. But there is nothing here. No tape, no officers, not even a scrap of evidence to suggest something so gruesome had taken place here within the last twenty-four hours. The more I search, the more I am convinced of my own insanity.

My eyes dart between the nearby high rises. I've memorized every detail of Charlie's apartment. From this vantage point, I hoped I could match something to what I had seen in The Room with one of these faceless structures. But none of it fit.

Every building looks wrong; there are no recognizable curtains and no sage green walls peeking through the window. All the details I started to believe were real are now slipping through my fingers.

I stand frozen in the middle of the park, my mind spinning with a confusion I can't shake. Everything around me feels painfully familiar and unsettlingly wrong like I've wandered into a half-remembered dream.

My hands shake as I pull my jacket tighter around me, though I'm not sure if it's the cold or the unease that's making me shiver. I came here searching for answers, desperate for concrete proof that what's been happening is real. But all I've found are more questions. Doubts I can't even begin to unravel.

The heavy air presses down on me. The trees sway, their branches whispering secrets I can't hear.

A flicker of movement catches my eye, but when I turn to look, there's nothing. No matter how hard I try to ground myself, the lines between my reality and... something else keep blurring. I don't know what's real anymore.

I'm paralyzed by fear in the middle of an NYC park. And that's not even the most terrifying part. My worlds are merging in ways I can't explain, bleeding into each other until I don't know what's a memory, a dream, or something worse. I can't trust my mind.

I close my eyes, trying to calm the storm inside me. Reality feels slippery and fragile as if it could shatter at any moment, and I'm falling into whatever lies beneath.

18

Chapter Eighteen

I invited Violet over to watch movies because I couldn't handle the thought of being alone. Not tonight.

She tells me about her new side hustle. She's taken on some art students and has opened up her art studio for other artists to use. I nod along, grateful for the distraction.

I let Violet pick the movie while I head to the kitchen to make a bucket of popcorn. I pop the bag into the microwave and head toward the pantry. Since we were kids, Violet and I have always dumped our boxed candy into our popcorn to make our own movie trail mix.

Surveying my options, I decide on Reese's Pieces, Sour Gummy Worms, and Milk Duds as our cavity fuel of choice.

Once I no longer hear the faint sound of corn kernels popping, I pull the steaming bag from the microwave and dump it, and all the candy, into my largest bowl and toss it all together.

I head back to the living room and hand the bowl to Violet. She shrieks excitedly, clapping while doing a happy dance as she pops the first bite into her mouth.

I watch her, trying to lock this moment into my permanent memory, and a sadness rushes over me that I can't explain.

She smacks my thigh, and I shake my head, looking at her confused.

"What about this?" she signs, gesturing to the screen with the remote still in hand.

She's chosen *Alice in Wonderland*, and we both know it's only because her "hear me out" crush is Johnny Depp as the Mad Hatter. He's on my list, too, though I'll never admit it.

I agree and pull the fluffy blanket off the back of the couch for us. Even though my couch is large, we sit in the middle together.

I lay my head on her shoulder as the movie plays. It's nice just being here with my sister.

My eyes start to flutter closed. Darn the movie-time drowsiness.

As my eyes get heavier, I am struck with the strangest feeling of *Deja Vu*.

Violet nudges me awake. The credits roll in the background.

"Typical Rose," she signs. **"You have never seen a whole movie all the way through."**

She's teasing, but she might be right. I've never been known to stay awake, even at the cinema.

I sit up, and an unexpected wave of dizziness crashes over me, sending the room spinning. My vision blurs, and I blink hard, struggling to steady myself.

The air around me feels different, heavy like it's pressing down on my chest. When I finally focus, there's blood. So much blood.

Violet sits in front of me, her face a mask of horror. Crimson streaks drip down her forehead from a deep gash across her skull, soaking into her shirt. My stomach lurches, and a cold sweat breaks across my skin.

I can't breathe. I can't think. I let out a shaky gasp and reach out, my hand trembling as it brushes her arm. "V-Violet?" My squeak, barely above a whisper, my throat tight with terror.

She blinks at me, confusion clouding her eyes. Her face... it's normal. No blood, no wound. Just Violet—whole, unharmed, staring at me with wide, concerned eyes. The nightmare shatters like glass, leaving me breathless in its wake.

"What's wrong?" she asks, her face full of concern. **"You look like you've seen a ghost."**

My chest heaves as I fight to control my breathing, my mind still reeling. I force myself to swallow the bile rising in my throat and push down the images still burning behind my eyes. **"Nothing... it's nothing,"** I manage to sign somewhat clearly. **"I—I just... zoned out for a second."**

Her eyes narrow, suspicion flickering across her face, but I pull her into a hug before she can ask more.

I hold on too long, my grip tight, as if the warmth of her body is the only thing keeping me here.

Violet's concern visibly manifests in her shoulders. But I can't explain. Not like this, not now. Whatever is happening, I'll handle it. I have to.

I pull away, giving her a weak smile that I hope masks the fear still twisting in my gut.

"Rose, talk to me," Violet urges gently, searching my face for answers. **"This isn't like you. You're scaring me."**

I force a laugh, the sound hollow. **"I'm fine,"** I lie. **"Just tired, that's all."**

She watches me, her eyes full of worry, but eventually, she nods. **"Alright,"** she gestures in defeat. **"But you know I'm here, right? For whatever's going on."**

I nod. Could I even explain what I just saw? It felt so real. Maybe I'm starting to hallucinate. Whatever it was, Violet doesn't know about it, and I'm going to keep it that way.

Violet decides to crash on my couch tonight. She feels "too lazy" to walk home. Typically, I am thrilled by the thought of a sister sleepover, but I can't shake the image of Violet's bloodied face. It lingers in the back of my mind, and deep down, I know this isn't over.

Not by a long shot.

19

CHAPTER NINETEEN

I stare at my reflection in the mirror, smoothing down my dress and applying the final touches of my makeup. I spent the whole day consumed by questions, but tonight isn't for answers. Tonight is for Thorne.

The drive takes twenty-two minutes, and whens I arrive at Thorne's restaurant, I flip down the visor to double check I don't have any lipstick on my teeth and re-fluff my curls. I take a deep breath, get out of the car, and head for the front door.

The place is stunning. Polished wood floors, low amber lighting, and sleek modern decor that screams elegance without being pretentious.

"Come on," Thorne greets me with a warm smile. "I'll give you the grand tour."

I follow him through the dining room, and Thorne explains the intricate layout, his deep voice guiding me through every detail.

Eventually, we settle into a quiet corner of the kitchen, and he pours glasses of wine.

As we sip the most divine red I've ever had the privilege to taste, our conversation flows effortlessly. He tells me about his early days in the city, working his way up through various kitchens, the struggle of balancing passion, and the reality of owning a fine dining establishment.

As the evening goes on, I laugh more than I expect to. I'm surprised that I am drawn into Thorne's world of culinary stories.

The kitchen buzzes with warmth and energy as he sets up the ingredients for dinner.

"Think you can handle chopping these veggies?" Thorne teases, handing me a knife.

I smirk, deliberately fumbling with the blade. "I can try, but I'm no pro like you."

He raises an eyebrow, clearly seeing through my act. Without missing a beat, he comes up behind me, his arms brushing against mine. Gently, he takes hold of my hands and guides my movements.

"Like this," he whispers, his breath warm against my ear. "In culinary school, they call this 'the motion of the ocean.'"

Our hands rock together, slicing the vegetables with determined precision. The intimacy of this moment sends a jolt of electricity running through me, a spark that I haven't felt in forever.

I glance up at him, our eyes meeting for just a moment. *Keep it cool*, I remind myself.

My heart races a little faster as I return my attention to the vegetables. Even after he steps away, my skin is warm from where his arms have brushed mine.

Thorne teases about my poor knife skills, but it's clear that our banter holds a deeper undercurrent now.

I'm internally repeating his mantra, "motion of the ocean," as I glide the chef's knife through the action.

Suddenly, I feel him close behind me and he puts a spoon in front of my face.

"What is it?" I ask.

"Just try it," he urges. "Tell me what you think it is."

As soon as the spoon touches my tongue, I am madly in love. It's sour and sweet, and my tastebuds are dancing.

"Well." He grins. "What do you think?"

I put my hand in front of my mouth. "I think that's the best thing I've ever tasted. What is it?"

He shakes his head in a teasing manner and backs away. "Not telling ."He puts his finger to his lips. "You have to guess."

I am almost embarrassed to guess. Something inside me wants to impress him with my grand (non-existent) culinary knowledge. "It's fruity." My words sound like a question. "It's sweet and sour."

He looks at me like that's not a satisfying enough answer.

"Is it tropical?" I ask.

Thorne shrugs back at me.

Think, Rose, think.

A lightbulb goes off and I do a little jump. "Oh! Oh!" I exclaim. "Is it passionfruit?"

He nods, giving me a smile that really highlights his dimples. "I knew you would get it."

Using a bench scraper, he scoops all of my cut veggies into a sizzling skillet. "I didn't know it was possible."

Thorne looks at the stovetop as the kitchen fills with the most intoxicating aroma.

"And what's that?" I ask snarkily, preparing myself for another punchline about my horrible knife skills.

"That I could love cooking any more." He slides his hand onto mine. "But having you as my sous chef has proved me wrong. I could cook with you by my side forever."

The oven timer dings, saving me from an awkward moment.

Thorne isn't just goofing off and flirting anymore. He is really enjoying my company.

I must admit that I am enjoying his even more. I don't even know how to respond, and thankfully, he doesn't act like he even needs a response.

Thorne flutters around the kitchen, prepping food, tasting this, adding salt there, and occasionally sending me a heart-melting smile.

In no time, he's plating all of the delicious dishes. "Garnish, garnish, garnish," he mumbles as he looks around the island.

"Aha!" he says as he triumphantly holds a blood orange in the air. "Watch this." With practiced precision, he slices off the top and bottom, exposing the crimson flesh.

His knife glides smoothly along the curve of the fruit, peeling away the pith and bitter white rind in fluid strokes. Each motion is deliberate and clean. "Learning how to supreme an orange was a pivotal moment in my career. I had seen chefs on TV do it growing up, and I felt like once you could master supreming, you were at Master Chef level."

Turning the orange in his hand, he carefully slides the blade between the thin membranes, freeing perfect segments of glistening red flesh. Juice drips onto the cutting board, staining it with its rich, dark hue.

My intrusive thoughts imagine him slicing straight through the orange and right into the palm of his hand. I shudder. I can't push it away, instead I blurt out, "I can't look! You're gonna cut right through your hand!"

He laughs but, in a comforting way, says, "I'll be careful, I promise. Honestly, I have done this so many times, I could probably do it with my eyes closed."

Thorne arranges the delicate wedges on the plate with precision, each slice a bright jewel ready to be savored.

The plates are finished, and we sit down to a candle-lit dinner. The food is exquisite — fresh, flavorful, and full of the love that Thorne had poured into every dish. Paired with the rich red wine, the ambiance wraps around me warm and soothing.

As we eat, our conversation flows easily again. His smile and his laugh all make me feel something I haven't allowed myself to feel in a very long time: hope. A glimpse of happiness even.

For a moment, I realize I haven't thought about Charlie or The Room for hours. The fears and doubts that have haunted me feel… distant, almost like they belong to someone else. Here, with Thorne, I feel a very welcomed peace.

Hours later, the last of the wine is gone, and our dinner plates are completely empty. I stand to help clean up the mess we've made. Thorne just shakes his head at me, waving me off with a soft smile.

"I've got it," he says gently. "You should head home and get some rest. I'll walk you to your car."

We leave the messy kitchen, and Thorne escorts me out.

As he opens my car door, he steps closer, his hand lingering on my arm before leaning and pressing a gentle kiss on my cheek. The warmth of his lips on my skin leaves me momentarily stunned, a soft blush heating my face as I smile up at him.

"Goodnight, Rose," he mutters, soft and full of meaning.

"Goodnight, Thorne," I whisper in return. "Thank you for a lovely evening."

As I drive home, I feel lighter than I have in days. I lower my windows and let the cool night air hit my face. I can't stop smiling. The warmth of his kiss still lingers on my cheek. It's been such a long time since I've allowed myself to just enjoy the moment.

I arrive home, and the memory of Charlie and The Room that await me when I close my eyes comes crashing back. I shake my head, pushing the thoughts away.

For the rest of the night, I am going to allow myself to just breathe. Whatever darkness waits on the other side of my dreams... I will deal with it when it comes.

20

Chapter Twenty

I'm back in The Room. *This is just a dream*, I remind myself. *Nothing more.*

No matter how real it feels. No matter how convincing the details are, none of it can touch me. There's no evidence of The Room in my waking life. There's no Charlie, no active crime scenes, no murdered woman. I've scoured every corner, every thread of logic. Nothing.

It's a dream, Rose. And dreams can't hurt you.

The Room is the same as always. Sage green walls, the vague hum of machinery, the strange orange sofa, the TV stand. And, of course, Charlie.

I glance around, waiting for something new to happen, but there doesn't seem to be much going on today. Perhaps now that I've come to accept what this room is or isn't, my brain no longer wants to invent new ideas to torture me. It's as if I've been caught in a pause like time no longer exists here.

If I have a choice, I'd rather be mentally reliving my evening with Thorne right now. When I'm with him, I feel like I belong, like his presence alone can tether me to something good. Instead, I'm stuck here in this suffocating box of a room where nothing is truly alive.

I'm tired of this place. I am tired of waiting for some shift. For some grand revelation that never comes.

In the real world, my days blend together in a blur of deadlines and meetings. I am always running, always chasing the next big story. But here in this room? It's like the world just... stops. Every visit to this dreamscape has stretched longer and longer. Every second smears into the next until I can't tell how long I've been here.

I stare blankly ahead at the television set, willing it to turn on so I have something to distract me from this boredom.

I wonder where Charlie is. Maybe he's also ceased to exist since my grand understanding of this place. None of it is real.

Minutes, maybe even hours pass. I close my eyes and will myself to wake up—enough of this. I'm done. I don't want to waste another minute here.

I'll wake up any second now—any second.

When my eyes snap open, I'm not where I expect to be. It takes a moment for my brain to catch up to what I'm seeing. I'm in my bed, the sheets tangled around me, the faint light of morning creeping through the blinds. I should feel relief, so why do I feel... off?

The throbbing in my head has returned with a violent appearance. The base of my skull aches, sharp and insistent. I squeeze my eyes shut, willing it to pass, but the pain lingers and intensifies. And then -

I can't move.

My body feels cemented to the bed, heavy and unresponsive. I try to shift, to lift an arm, a leg, anything — but nothing happens. The Room's paralysis has bled into my real life. *Move. Just move.*

And then, as suddenly as it comes, the feeling slips away. My body jerks back to life. I sit upright, staring at the blank wall in front of me. For a moment, just a moment, I swear The Room had followed me here.

I shake my head, swallowing hard. It's just my mind playing tricks on me.

I grab my phone and do a quick internet search. Sleep paralysis, that's all it is.

It's a common condition that can be frightening but not dangerous.

I read the search results aloud. "Can lead to intense fear and apprehension in the patient as they lie awake without the ability to use any part of their body."

Happens to people all the time. Maybe that's what I've been experiencing this whole time.

Sleep paralysis, nothing more, nothing less.

21

CHAPTER TWENTY-ONE

I stare at the sign hanging over Mei's family restaurant. The soft glow of the neon dragon wraps around the frame, lighting the night. I've been here a thousand times before. I could probably get here with my eyes closed. So why do I feel so uneasy?

I can't remember how I got here.

I shake my head, trying to force the hazy feeling from my mind. I look down. My feet are solid on the ground.

The familiar scent of ginger and garlic wafts from the kitchen, but my brain scrambles to fill in the gaps. Did I drive? Take a taxi? Did I walk here?

"Rose!" Mei's voice calls from inside, breaking me from my thoughts.

I force a smile, pulling open the door. The usual buzz of the dinner rush surrounds me, but I feel strangely disconnected, like I'm floating just above this moment, watching myself from a distance.

Low blood sugar. It has to be. Have I eaten anything today? I can't seem to remember.

Violet waves me over to our usual table, and I thread my way through the crowded dining room.

Mei is already seated, her red hair pulled into a loose bun. She's folding napkins and greeting customers as they pass.

I slide into my seat, trying to ground myself in their presence. This is good.

"You look out of it. Everything okay?" Violet asks.

I hate that she's always been able to read me so well. I force a laugh, rubbing my temples. **"Just a long day. I forgot to eat. Low blood sugar, that's all,"** I sign back.

Mei raises an eyebrow, clearly unconvinced, but doesn't push. Instead, she signals for her mom to bring over our usual orders. She doesn't need to ask me what I want. We've been doing this every Friday for years, like clockwork.

But as I sit there, listening to the chatter of the restaurant, I can't ignore that something feels wrong. The disorientation hasn't passed. The more I try to push it away, the more it clings to me like a shadow.

I glance at Violet and Mei. Their faces are lit up by the restaurant's soft glow. They're talking, laughing, filling the space with the kind of easy comfort resulting from years of friendship. But I can't focus on what they're saying.

A stranger watching me might assume I don't even know ASL with how unresponsive I am to their conversation. My thoughts are tangled. I feel as if I'm not really here, like I'm somehow watching a memory from the outside.

Violet pauses mid-sign, her eyes narrowing. **"Rose. Earth to Rose."**

She is trying to make light of the situation by pretending to be a NASA communicator, but her concern is real.

I blink, trying to snap back to the present.

My face must scream confusion because Mei grabs my hand. "YOU'RE ZONING OUT. YOU'VE BARELY SAID A WORD SINCE YOU GOT HERE."

I brush it off to tell them I'm fine, but the words get stuck. I can't keep pretending. I've been holding everything in for too long, and I know they can see right through my act. They always have.

With a deep breath, I lower my gaze to the table, tracing the pattern on the Formica tabletop with my finger.

"I... I think I'm losing my mind."

My words hang in the air, heavy and raw between us. There's a strange relief in finally saying it out loud.

I can't even look them in the eye, but everything starts to spill out. The dreams. The Room. The way it feels so real. So tangible. Even though every molecule of common sense knows it's impossible.

I tell them about all of the things I have researched to find proof of The Room in the real world, but my searches always turn up empty.

A lump forms in my throat, and I feel tears prickling the corners of my eyes, but I blink them away, determined to hold myself together. I don't want to become the girl who falls apart. Not in front of my sisters. Not here.

After I've laid my soul bare, I know I have to look at them and deal with the concern on their faces. But when I look up, I'm alone.

Where did they go? They were right here.

My vision fades, and I can hear my heartbeat over everything else in the restaurant.

"This isn't funny!" I yell into the crowded dining room.

I feel a panic attack coming on. *Where did they go?*

I look down the aisle of booths and can't see Violet or Mei anywhere. "Playing a joke on the crazy one. Very funny. Ha-ha, ladies. You can come out now," I say dryly.

But Mei doesn't answer me. No one does.

I head for the kitchen, the dizziness getting worse as I stand.

The gold dragon wallpaper swirls in my vision, slowly transforming. I blink hard, trying not to lose consciousness.

I reach out to grab the metal counter hoping to stabilize myself, but when my hand reaches the level of the counter there's nothing there. I look down and see... a cat?

My hand is resting upon lush white fur, and it's purring. I blink again, shaking my head.

When I open my eyes, my hand has a white-knuckled grip on the prep counter. What is happening?

"Mei! Violet!" I yell.

I glance at the kitchen, but what I see isn't right... I see The Room: the green walls, the TV, the orange couch.

No, no, no, no. I close my eyes. *Wake up, wake up.*

When I open my eyes, I'm back in the restaurant.

I slide down to the floor and pull my legs to my chest. The sobs are uncontrollable. Just as I start to contemplate another grippy sock vacation, I hear Mei's laugh. I get back on my feet and look around. Mei and Violet sit at our table. Laughing like nothing happened.

I'm furious as I storm toward the table, arms crossed, ready to give them a piece of my mind. Was this just a joke to them?. They've never done anything like this in the past. How could they just walk away as I'm pouring my heart out?

Before I can say anything, though, Mei looks up at me. **"You made it!"** she signs.

"PAH!" Violet agrees.

"I've been here for a while," I say, confused.

"Did you sit at the wrong table?" Mei asks.

Both erupt into laughter.

"Sit! Sit! Sit!" Violet exclaims. **"I have something I am dying to tell you both!"**

Still dazed, I slide back into my seat. Violet turns away from Mei and me. She digs in her purse for something. She enthusiastically turns back toward us, holding her left hand in front of our faces. **"I'M EN-GAGED!"**

Mei and I barrage her instantly, **"WHAT?" "WHEN?" "CAM?" "HOW?" "DETAILS, NOW."**

Violet laughs softly and tells us how Cam proposed last night over dinner, painting a vivid picture of the scene.

The confusion of tonight's events blur my memory.

"But you and Cam haven't been together that long... it's only been—"

"It's been a year," Violet signs, seeming disappointed. **"More than a year, actually."**

A cold pit forms in my stomach, the shock of her words cutting right through me. *Over a year.*

I thought it had been... months, maybe. But a year? How could I have missed so much?

"Are you sure? It doesn't feel like it's been that long."

Violet nods. **"Yeah, I'm sure. Time's been moving faster than you think, sis."** She slaps her hand down on the table. **"Besides, Cam told me he asked for your permission because he knows I care more about your opinion than Dad's."**

She pokes me in the forehead. **"So why are you acting like you had no idea he was going to ask?"**

"He did?" I can tell by Violet's face that she's growing concerned. **"Right, yeah, of course he did. He's always been good at understanding the importance of The Daisy Chain."**

I try to smile and be happy for her, and I am—-truly—-but there's a nagging fear overpowering my joy. Time is slipping away, and I am missing things I should be holding onto. I'm losing pieces of my life, and I don't know how to stop it.

Violet's face is true-biz glowing as she continues to share details about the proposal. Her excitement is contagious even though I'm still reeling from everything.

She pulls out her phone, scrolling through ideas and plans for the wedding she has already saved. A spring wedding, small, intimate, but beautiful.

Violet tells Mei about their plans for Cam to move in with her above the art studio after the wedding so that she can keep her business running efficiently. I can't pay attention to the details of the move because I'm distracted. I only have about eight months to stop losing my mind.

I watch them, feeling like I'm standing just outside a window, looking in. I'm so happy for my sister, unbelievably happy. But a year. How could I have not known that she'd been with Cam for over a year? She's planning a life I can barely keep up with.

I push my thoughts aside, determined not to let them overshadow her moment. This is what she deserves - happiness, love, everything.

"Oh, and another thing." She excitedly tells us of their decision to have the entire ceremony in ASL.

They will have interpreters for the hearing guests, but she and Cam want their wedding to be fully accessible.

My heart swells a little at that. The thought of a deafie wedding makes me smile.

"That's a beautiful idea. I love that," I say, and I mean it.

Violet's smile deepens as if she has been waiting for my approval. Then I notice her hesitation.

She continues, **"Cam's...not going to wear his hearing aids during the wedding. He just wants to experience our day in our language, our way."**

I let that thought sink in. Cam is hard of hearing and usually relies on his hearing aids in busy or important situations. But opting to go without them for the wedding shows he wants to fully immerse himself into Violet's world. I can feel how much that means to her, to both of them. He really is a great guy.

"That is true-biz perfect!" Mei exclaims.

Violet nods, her eyes shining with emotion.

I glance at Mei, who gives me a knowing smile. We've both been there through every heartbreak, every high and low of Violet's relationships. And now, watching her prepare for this next chapter with someone who truly sees her, who understands her... it feels right like everything's falling into place.

We spend the next hour discussing dresses, venues, and flower arrangements. All of this is so important to Violet, and it reminds me how much I love her. I push down all of my fears and focus only on her joy. I have to be present for her now, I have to be the sister she needs.

A spring wedding will come sooner than I think.

$$22$$

CHAPTER TWENTY-TWO

I sip a latte with my laptop open in front of me, the words on the screen blending together like a foreign language I'm struggling to decipher.

It's strange, miraculous even, that I've managed to keep up with my work. I've turned in articles, met deadlines, and kept up with the basic flow. But if someone asks me to recount what I've actually written or what meetings I've attended recently, I won't be able to say.

I rub my temples, willing the headache to ease, but the dull throb only seems to worsen. I can't even remember when the headache started this time. A few days ago? Weeks? Time feels tangled, and I can't shake the fog that's been hanging over me.

A light bell rings in the distance as the cafe door swings open, and I hear someone approach my table.

"Well, well, well... if it isn't my favorite ghost."

I glance up to see Thorne standing there with a grin. His hair is tousled, and he's wearing a leather jacket that he has no right to look that good in.

I catch myself staring as his words settle in. "Ghost?" I repeat, confused.

He arches a brow, crossing his arms with playful accusation. "Yeah, it's been two weeks, Rose. You haven't called, haven't texted... I was starting to think you just used me for restaurant access and then decided to ghost me once you got what you wanted."

"What?" My brain is unable to process what he just said.

"Don't tell me," he begs dramatically. "My food scared you off, didn't it? It couldn't have been that bad, right?"

I can tell he's joking, but my mind is reeling. *Two weeks*? There's no way two weeks could've passed.

I shake my head slightly, trying to make sense of it. "No… no way it's been that long. I… I swear, it feels like our dinner was just a few days ago."

Thorne laughs, but it's gentle, not mocking. He slides in across from me and leans toward me. "Well, either time is flying, or you have been avoiding me."

I try to laugh it off, but I can't. More time slips. *You're losing it, Rose.* "I'm sorry, I didn't mean to disappear."

His grin softens, and he reaches across the table, closing my laptop screen. I can't explain it, but with the click of the lid, all my anxiety about the time slips fades.

"Make it up to me then." He winks.

"Oh, yeah?" I raise an eyebrow, falling into the easy rhythm we find ourselves in since we met. "How do you suggest I do that, Mr. Thorne?"

"You can start by letting me take you on another date," he says, dropping just enough to make my stomach flutter. "Preferably sometime in the next two weeks so I don't have to search for you again."

I chuckle, looking down into my drink. "I think I can manage that."

I lift my gaze to see his eyes twinkle with amusement, but his expression grows more serious as he watches me. "You okay, though? You seem… distracted."

I hesitate, glancing out the window, begging the tears in my eyes to dissipate. "I've just been dealing with these headaches," I admit. "They've been throwing me off. I can't seem to focus on anything. Half the time, I don't even know how I get from point A to point B."

I turn to face him.

He frowns, his eyes screaming with worry. "How long have they been going on?"

I shrug, feeling the frustration bubbling inside me. "I don't even know. It feels like time is slipping through my fingers. I'm losing track of entire days. I have another appointment with my therapist, I guess I'll be getting an official 'off my rocker' diagnosis soon enough."

Thorne nods, and a sympathetic look smears his face. "It's good to ask for help when you need it. If you need someone to take you, I'm free. Seriously, Rose... I'd be happy to drive you."

I smile, touched by his offer, but shake my head. "Thank you, but I'll be fine. It's just a consultation, nothing too serious. I appreciate it, though. Really."

"I care about you," he says softly. "A lot."

There's a weight to his words that makes me pause.

He reaches across the table again, resting his hand on mine. "Just let me know what the doctor says, okay?"

"I will," I promise, squeezing his hand just a little. "But hey, I have some good news."

"Oh?"

"Violet's getting married," I say, smiling at the thought. "She just got engaged, and I've already been designated the maid of honor. I wanted to ask if you'd be interested in being my plus one?"

Thorne's eyes widen in surprise, but there's a hint of a smile tugging at his lips. "Your plus one? At your sister's wedding?"

I nod, feeling the butterflies in my stomach again. "Yeah. I'll be busy most of the time with my maid of honor duties, but I'd love for you to be there. With me."

For a moment, I wonder if it's too much, too soon. But then he gives me that playful, easy grin I've come to love.

"I'd be honored. Besides, I've been keeping up with my *Lingvano* courses like you suggested. I think I'll be able to impress your sister with my new ASL skills."

A genuine laugh bubbles up. "She'll love that. And so will Cam. They're having the whole ceremony in sign language."

Thorne leans back, looking impressed. "That's amazing. I'll be ready."

As the conversation shifts to wedding plans, something soft brushes against my ankle. I glance down and see Dolly, now fully healed from her surgery. She looks up at me with those big, soulful eyes, and I can't help but smile.

"Well, look who's back," I say, pulling her into my lap. "She just got spayed, but she's all healed up now. I've been wanting to adopt her since the day she was born. But I think it's best if I wait until I am feeling better."

Thorne watches me with a silent contemplation. "You really love her, don't you?"

"I do," I admit, feeling a pang of longing. "Sam's holding onto her for now. He promised he won't let anyone else have her. I just want to be sure I'm in the right mental place before I take her home, you know?"

He nods thoughtfully. "Makes sense. You deserve to feel your best before adding any new responsibilities."

"Yeah," I murmur, giving Dolly one last scratch before she scampers off.

Thorne is right. I want to be better. Better for myself and everyone around me.

As we finish our drinks and prepare to leave, Thorne lingers by my side, looking down at me with a quiet intensity. "Promise you'll call me after your appointment?"

"I promise," I say, standing on tiptoe to press a kiss to his cheek.

His skin is warm, and I whisper, "Thanks for caring. And... for not giving up on me."

He smiles, soft and sincere. "I'm not going anywhere, Rose."

As I watch him walk away, that same fluttering returns, stronger this time. Maybe everything isn't as tangled as it seems. Maybe, just maybe, things are starting to fall into place.

23

CHAPTER TWENTY-THREE

DR. J. WIESE - PSYCHOLOGIST

Dr. Wiese sits across from me, her hands folded neatly in her lap. "Have you thought more about what we discussed last time?" she asks, tilting her head just slightly. "About the possibility of trauma or PTSD being connected to your nightmares?"

I nod, fidgeting with the hole in the knee of my jeans. "Yeah, I've thought about it," I say. "But honestly, I can't think of anything. I mean, my childhood wasn't great, sure. My family was kind of a mess, but—" I shrug, trying to downplay it. "None of that really bothers me now."

Dr. Wiese doesn't look convinced, and her silence speaks louder than her words. Finally, she leans forward slightly, her tone gentle but firm. "Sometimes, the things we think we've moved on from have a way of lingering under the surface," she says. "They don't always announce themselves until we're ready—or forced—to confront them. Let's dig into that a little more today."

I want to argue, to tell her there's no point, that whatever ghosts she thinks are haunting me are ancient history. Instead, I just nod in agreement.

"Great," she says with a click of her pen. "So you said your family situation was a mess. Can you tell me more about that?"

I shrug. "Not a lot to tell," I admit. "Nothing worth mentioning anyway. Just the typical dead mom and absent father situation. Hundreds of people have identical childhoods, but they aren't being tortured with nightmares."

She sets her notebook to the side and lets out a sympathetic sigh. "True, in my career, I've had a lot of people with similar childhoods sit in that chair. None of us react exactly the same to the experiences we go through. However, nightmares are more common than you might realize. Tell me more about your family."

She pulls her notebook back onto her lap and patiently waits for me to respond. I haven't thought about my parents in a long time. It's easier to just pretend that my family consists only of Violet and Mei.

My throat tightens as memories I've buried resurface. I really don't want to revisit the past. "My mom died when I was four. My dad isn't really in the picture anymore. We had a falling out. Long story short, my sister and I don't really talk to him anymore. And I guess that leaves my sister, Violet. She's my entire world. Many times, she was my only reason for breathing."

Dr. Wiese taps her pen on her chin. "I see. Sounds like you have a complicated family history. It makes sense that your sister would be so important to you. What did you mean by that last sentence?"

"Nothing, really," I say as I tap the rubber toes of my Converse together. "It's just... when my mom died, things got really hard at home."

I take a deep breath, trying to find the courage to dig up long-buried memories. "My dad never learned to use sign language fluently for Violet. I guess he felt like he had more important things to do than practice fingerspelling. But when Mom died, it was like the light in our house had disappeared."

I pause for a moment, trying to conjure an image of my mother in my mind. It's only now that I realize I have forgotten what my own mother looked and sounded like. It's been so long since I've seen her that the memories are just blurred faces— the details unclear.

I don't want to allow myself to get caught up in the emotions. I clear my throat and continue.

"Dad turned to drinking and yelled more than he spoke. Violet couldn't hear it, but she still tried her best to protect me from his anger. She took a lot of hits. Sometimes, I think it was a blessing that she couldn't hear his words... It would've broke me if she knew the things he called her."

I squeeze my eyes shut, trying to force away the sudden flashbacks of broken glass and swearing being thrown around my brain. When I look back up at Dr. Wiese, I see that she is offering me a tissue. I hadn't even realized I started crying. I take a tissue, pat the tears away, and apologize. I wasn't expecting to get so emotional.

"It's quite alright," Dr. Wiese assures me. "I'm sorry to hear about that. Loss affects each person so differently. Essentially, you lost both parental figures when your mom passed. I can imagine that must've been hard for you."

"It was, I suppose. But Violet and I got used to our new life pretty quickly. Dad went back to work immediately after the funeral and expected Vi and I to take care of all the chores and tasks that Mom used to do."

"By the age of eight, Violet was the best budgeter and couponer on the block. She even filed Dad's taxes for him and got, quote: 'the largest refund I've ever seen.' At least that's what he said." I chuckle.

"I would take care of cleaning and making sure that our bedding got changed once a week. I remember this one time Violet made spaghetti. It was pretty early on after Mom died. Anyways, she brought out a plate to Dad, where he was watching TV. He takes one bite, and the plate goes flying, smashing against the wall."

I imitate the action of throwing an invisible dinner plate across the room.

"He was so angry his face looked like a tomato and spit was flying from his mouth. Obviously, Vi couldn't understand him so I was trying to interpret for her as fast as I could. I guess the recipe called for half a cup of sugar in the sauce, but she had accidentally used salt. He thought she was trying to poison him. I was laughing so hard, but I think I was the only one who thought it was funny."

I always looked back at that memory as a humorous event. But now I sit here in silence, realizing how incredibly *not funny* the entire situation was. Violet didn't deserve that. She was just trying to help out.

Dr. Wiese breaks through my silent contemplation, "So you and Violet had to grow up pretty fast then, huh?"

I have never thought about my childhood this way. I twist my hands together anxiously. "Yeah, I guess we did. Violet really took on Mom's role, which, looking back, might've not been the best for a little kid."

"I'm sure that was never the life your mother had hoped for you both. There are often unrealized 'side-effects,' if you will, for children who are parentified too young — forced to be an adult."

She glances at her watch and closes her notebook. "We have made really great progress today," she says cheerfully. "Next time, I'd like to delve more into you and Violet. What do you say?"

I let out a sigh of relief. "Violet is easy to talk about. She's the glue that holds me together."

"Great," she says, standing from her chain. "I look forward to hearing all about her."

On the way home, I pull out my phone and send a quick text to The Daisy Chain.

Rose: *Just saw my therapist. Will fill you in later.*

I hit send before my anxiety kicks in. It feels like a relief to let them know I'm taking steps forward, even if I still feel lost.

Next, I call Thorne.

He picks up on the first ring. "Rose? How did it go?"

"Hey," I say. "The appointment was...good. She has more she wants to talk about next week. So we'll see."

"You sound exhausted," he says gently. "How are you holding up?"

Thorne's genuine concern forces the sobs to come out before I can stop them. I take a few deep breaths.

"I'm sorry. It's just... the therapist... she brought up some things I hadn't thought about in a very long time. Things I didn't even remember," "Violet and I weren't allowed to be children..." I trail off.

"You don't always have to be the strong one, Rose. And you definitely don't have to carry all of this alone."

His words make something inside me crack, but this time it's different. I feel lighter. I can't help but feel a deep sense of gratitude. Thorne's here for me, not just in a physical sense, but really here, willing to shoulder things I've kept buried for so long.

"Thank you," I say.

He's quiet for a moment, then says, "Do you need anything? Want me to come over?"

I shake my head even though he can't see me through the phone. "No, I'm okay. Just needed someone to talk to."

"I'm always here. Remember that."

"Thanks, Thorne. I'll talk to you soon, okay?"

"Take care of yourself, Rose."

I end the call when I approach my apartment.

I park and head inside, dropping my laptop and coat by the door, and drag my feet to my bed.

The headache intensifies as I lay down. Hopefully, getting some sleep will give me some kind of reprieve.

24

CHAPTER TWENTY-FOUR

It's quiet here tonight. No Charlie. Just silence. Uneventful, as far as The Room goes, but somehow, that makes it worse. There's nothing to distract me from my own thoughts.

I stare at the cracks in the ceiling, and my mind drifts to my therapy session earlier today. Dr. Wiese's words keep echoing: *Sometimes, the things we think we've moved on from have a way of lingering under the surface.*

I didn't think anything from my childhood mattered now. But with nothing but time to kill and a whole lot of silence, more memories start creeping in.

I think about the countless hours I spent trying to get my father's attention. The way he would brush me off with a distracted nod or tell me to "go play" while he stayed glued to the TV. Every time he promised to come to my school play or my soccer game, I'd hold my breath, praying this time would be different. But it never was.

It wasn't all bad, I remind myself. But even the good memories feel different now. Back then, I thought working harder and being better was the only way to stand out. To be noticed. To be worthy. That same work ethic has carried me through my adult life—through school, through my career. All of my hard work has been for what? To prove I deserve to take up space? That I matter to anyone or anything?

The realization stings in a way I wasn't prepared for. Maybe the ghosts aren't as dead. Maybe I've been carrying them with me this whole time, disguised as ambition, disguised as success.

The hum of the overhead light seems louder now, an unwelcome reminder of where I am. I acknowledge that my life has been far from perfect, now I just wish this nightmare would let me out of it's grasp.

25

CHAPTER TWENTY-FIVE

I can't explain the comfort I feel from being in Sam's *Mews & Brews* today. The hiss of the espresso machine, the low murmur of voices, and the occasional clink of mugs on saucers fill the space. I don't think I could handle any more silence. I take a deep breath, willing myself to settle into the day.

My latte is warm between my hands, the intricate leaf pattern in the foam already fading away. The blueberry scone is perfectly baked and delicious, as always. But today, none of it is enough to rid myself of the strange ache in my chest.

I should be focused on work. My laptop is open, the day's assignments neatly organized, and the cursor blinks in an empty document where the first article is waiting to be written. But the words won't come.

Instead, there's a persistent sadness, raw and unrelenting, and I can't ignore it any longer. It's strange, really. I haven't felt this way in years—like something inside me is broken, calling out for help I don't know how to give.

I tear off a piece of the scone and chew slowly, trying to anchor myself in the simple act of eating. But even that feels hollow today, like going through the motions of someone else's life.

My recent therapy session comes back to mind. Dredging up the past. The memories I thought I'd left behind. Is that why I feel like this now? Like my inner child is clawing at the edges of my mind, begging me to pay attention?

I glance out the window, watching people pass by on the sidewalk. My reflection stares back at me in the glass, and for a moment, I don't recognize myself. There's a hollowness in my eyes that I've refused to acknowledge for far too long.

I've been holding back depression, burying it beneath work and routines, convincing myself that if I just keep going, I'll outrun it. But today, it's finally caught up to me.

Before I can overthink it, I grab my phone and open my messages. My fingers hesitate for only a second before I start typing:

Hi, Dr. Wiese. Can I come in later today? I think I need help.

I hit send and set the phone down, a small wave of relief washing over me. Admitting it feels like the first real thing I've done all morning. I pick up my latte again, sipping slowly, and stare at the blinking cursor on my screen. For now, I'll sit here in this booth and try to tackle my workload. It's not much, but it's a start.

26

CHAPTER TWENTY-SIX

DR. J. WIESE - PSYCHOLOGIST

I t feels like the walls are closing in. I sit across from Dr. Wiese, clutching a tissue like a lifeline, my eyes already sting with tears. "Thank you for fitting me in on such short notice," I say quietly.

Dr. Wiese offers me a kind smile, her hands folded in her lap. "Of course, Rose. I'm glad you reached out. You've been through so much, and I want to help in any way I can. But I'll admit...I'm worried about you."

Her words break something loose inside me. The dam bursts, and tears spill freely as I bury my face in my hands. All the pressure I've been holding back, all the pain I've been pretending doesn't exist, comes crashing down in waves.

"I—I don't know how to do this anymore," I manage between gasps, the tissue crumpled in my hand. "I thought I was okay, that I could handle it, but...I'm not. I'm not okay."

Dr. Wiese leans forward slightly, her voice gentle but firm. "Rose, it's okay to feel this way. It's a sign that we're touching on something important. These emotions, as overwhelming as they feel, mean we're making progress. You don't have to face this alone."

I nod, wiping my face, though the tears keep coming. "I don't even know what I'm feeling anymore. It's like everything is just...too much. The nightmares, the memories, and everything we talked about last time. I don't know how to keep going when it all feels so heavy."

She hands me a fresh tissue. "Would you like to talk about Violet today? Or is there something else that's weighing on you more?"

I stare at the floor, my vision blurred, and I shake my head. "I just want it to stop," I whisper. "The Room, the nightmares, all of it. I don't want to face any of this anymore. I can't."

She's silent for a moment, and when I look up, her eyes are full of sympathy but also resolve. "Rose, I know it feels impossible right now, but avoiding it will only make it harder. These dreams, these feelings—they're telling us something important. We can figure it out together. You don't have to do it all at once, but you do have to let yourself feel it."

I don't want to face it. I don't want to face *any* of it. But the way Dr. Wiese looks at me, steady and patient, makes me wonder if she's right. "If you say so," I say, defeated.

"I promise this will get easier. It hurts now, but it's going to be worth it in the end." She sounds so confident that I decide to trust her judgment.

She readies her notebook and pen, "So, if you don't object," she says cautiously, "I'd like to pick up where we left off last time."

I nod.

"We established that you and your sister had to grow up faster than most children. Did that have any effect on you as a teenager?" she asks.

"I guess." I shrug. "I remember when we were teenagers, Violet started acting out pretty badly. She had this friend, Scott Something. Anyway, she would sneak out sometimes to see him. Dad would disappear into his work for weeks at a time, and he 'wasn't gonna take care of a bastard baby' if she got pregnant. After that, he sent her away to an all-girls Deaf School. I always felt bad for her getting shipped off. I knew her and Scott weren't having sex. I don't think they were even interested in each other like that. She just wanted a safe place to relax and get some sleep."

"How did things go at home with Violet being out of the house? That must've put a lot of responsibility on you."

"It did. Suddenly, I had all of my chores and Violet's. Dad's anger turned to the only outlet. Me. I was never as strong as Violet. I had so many responsibilities at home, and I had mounting pressure from school to ace my SATs and take the career aptitude test to determine my best future."

It seems silly to be so stressed out about SATs now, but it dawns on me that I still have the same attitude toward my work. I always put myself in the same situations, even when they aren't good for me.

"I remember being so tired, beyond tired. I couldn't keep up with everything. I told my best friend Mei that I wanted to die. That I couldn't keep doing it anymore. Looking back now, I don't think I really would have done it, but I was exhausted. I had a lot on my plate. It just felt easier, ya know? Mei's mom, Mrs. Wong, drove me to the emergency room as soon as she found out. I was so mad at Mei for tattling. But who knows? Maybe she saved my life."

Dr. Wiese nods, "Sounds like your support system was not in your home anymore. It's good that you found solace with your friend's family. Is this when you were admitted to inpatient care?"

"Unfortunately, and thankfully, yes. Initially, I was put on a forty-eight-hour psych hold. Not my proudest moment. I quickly realized that my life inside the psych ward was easier than being at home. The doctors gave me time to rest, time by myself, and they encouraged my hobbies. Most importantly, I wasn't expected to take care of anyone else but me."

Even now, the thought of having a break from expectations sounds divine. Not that another psych ward stay is on my To-Do list right now.

I continue, "When I was nearing the end of my forty-eight hours, I had another status evaluation. The thought of going home to the screaming, to the fights, to the endless list of chores, everything - it caused me to completely break down. I think maybe I was just being dramatic, but the doctor didn't think so."

I explain how the forty-eight hours turned into a week, then into two. "In the second week, I was allowed visitors. Mrs. Wong and Mei came first. Mei was crying and apologizing immensely for 'putting me in here.' Of course, I told them both how nice it had been to have a break. I thanked them for caring about me so much."

"On the other side, Dad never came to visit, but Violet did. Mei told her I was in the hospital, and she took three different buses over six hours to come see me. I've never held on to someone so tight."

I feel sick that my biological father couldn't be bothered to visit his suicidal daughter in the hospital. I shouldn't have to get on my knees and beg to be loved... *Right*?

Dr. Wiese interrupts my thoughts, "That all makes sense. Sometimes, our brain just needs a break from trauma to recenter ourselves. It's possible that your dreams may be directly linked to your experience during your hospital stay. Perhaps your brain has learned to associate comfort with a clinical setting. We will return to that later. Tell me, what happened after you were discharged?"

It takes a moment for that possibility to sink into my brain. *Yes, let's come back to that later,* I think. "Violet had visited a lawyer while I was in the hospital and had filed for emancipation. Thirty days later, she picked me up from Dad's house. Apparently, Dad didn't even try to contest her emancipation. When Violet told him that she wanted me to live with her, he agreed that would be for the best. He said my mental health was 'too hard' to deal with. Everything had been arranged behind my back. That's how a sixteen-year-old and a fourteen-year-old came to live in a tiny apartment off the back of a bakery. We didn't have a lot of money, but it was the first place that actually felt like a home since mom died."

Dr. Wiese tries to hide the shock on her face, but it's undeniable. "That's a lot for a fourteen-year-old to go through. Do you think these lack of options you were given as a child may be impacting your dreams?"

"What do you mean?" I'm genuinely confused, I can't see the connections.

"The dreams make you feel like you've lost all sense of control, right?" she asks.

I scoff. "It's not just a sense. I literally can't control anything. Not my body, not the TV, nothing. If Charlie doesn't do it for me, I just sit and stare at a blank wall."

Dr. Wiese writes vigorously for a brief time. Then, as if connecting the dots, she states,"It'd be reasonable to assume, then, that these thoughts may be spurred on by the unresolved trauma of not having a say in your own life growing up, wouldn't you say?"

"I don't know. It feels more real than that." I admit.

"I'm sure that being admitted to a hospital without your consent probably felt very real to you, too. Your dad giving you up. Your sister deciding that you would live with her without so much as asking your opinion. I'm sure all of that felt very real."

I don't know why exactly, but tears start to roll down my cheeks again. I've never thought about those aspects of my childhood like this before.

"I guess," I whimper.

"So if the trauma felt very real, wouldn't it make sense that the solution your brain has concocted would also feel very real?"

"How do I make it stop?" I practically beg.

"Well, when you were facing these situations, what made you feel better?"

"Violet. It's always been Violet."

Dr. Wiese jots down a few more notes. "Ok, that's a good start. Describe what it was like growing up with a deaf sister. Sure, she was your comfort, but it couldn't have always been easy."

My voice cracks as tears blur my vision. "It was hard sometimes, but it was always worth it. Most of the time I was the one who communicated for her. When she cried, when she needed something - I was the one who had to figure it out. When we were little, we'd make up hand signs, gestures, and expressions - anything to understand each other."

My fingers twitch as though I am trying to sign even now. "Then, when Violet started school, she finally learned the real way to communicate. Proper sign language, and suddenly, she was the one teaching me. We had spent so many years isolated, trapped in a home where no one listened to her silent screams. I still don't understand how Dad didn't even try to communicate with her. With either of us, really."

I exhale, feeling the weight of those years sink in. "Sometimes, I think he was relieved when she learned ASL at school like it gave him an excuse to stop pretending to care. He checked out completely. But I never could. I was the only one left to make sure she didn't feel alone in that house. We didn't deserve to grow up like that."

Dr. Wiese's expression softens. "No, you didn't. You were responsible for each other in ways a child shouldn't have been. That kind of pressure can stay with you. What happens to us in our developmental years affects how we communicate and how we handle emotions, even as an adult."

I bite my lip. "But why now? What does that have to do with the dreams? The headaches? Why do I feel so disconnected from my life?"

"It's possible that your brain is revisiting your childhood traumas in your dreams. The inability to speak in the dream may be a manifestation of how powerless you felt as a child when it came to communication. You mentioned that you and Violet had to create your own language. Maybe your subconscious needs you to find a way to communicate again."

I nod, not truly understanding what she's telling me. "So... what do I do?"

Dr. Wiese taps her fingers on her notepad. "I think it would help if you found a way to communicate in the dream world. If speaking isn't possible, maybe there's another method."

I sigh in frustration. "There is no other method. I can't move, I can't speak, I definitely can't lift my arms and sign. The only thing I seem to have control over is my eyelids. If I use every drop of energy I can muster, I can control my blinking."

Dr. Wiese leans toward me, "If you can control your blinking, perhaps you can send a message that way. Perhaps now that you're more self-aware, you'll find you have more control. Before you go to sleep tonight," she recommends as she hands me a flyer. "Try reading up on Eye-Guided Communication. There are many technological advancements that have allowed disabled people to regain their ability to communicate. Perhaps if you research that before bed, you'll be able to bring what you've found into the dream world."

Suddenly, I'm struck with the faintest flicker of hope. "Yeah, I could do that. I hadn't thought about that."

"Could be worth trying. The dreams might be your mind's way of asking you to break through a communication barrier that you couldn't as a child. Perhaps once you find a way to communicate, the dreams will stop. And it may be worthwhile to explore your options of trauma-focused treatments to help you process everything."

Dr. Wiese looks at the clock. "I'm afraid our time is up for today."

I swallow hard, standing up to leave. "Thank you again for fitting me in today." As I walk out of her office, the weight of her suggestions settles in. I have a lot of work to do.

27

Chapter Twenty-Seven

I sit on the bed, looking into every lead for Eye-Guided Communication. There are many good options for eye-tracking communication devices.

They have a learning curve, but if I can get one of these machines to appear in the room, maybe I can at least get a simple message across.

I look through pages of Reddit members talking about the "Blink Once for Yes, Twice for No" method, but that requires someone else with more communication abilities to assist me. I immediately disregard that idea. I don't think Charlie is willing to help me out in this endeavor.

I chuckle at that idea. What else?

I stumble across an article about using Morse Code as a way for mute people to communicate.

> Dots: One second
>
> Dashes: Three seconds
>
> Spaces between dots and dashes: One second
>
> Spaces between characters: Three seconds
>
> Spaces between words: Seven seconds

I don't have the time or desire to learn Morse Code tonight, but that may be an option for the future. No equipment or willing participants are required.

I feel the drowsiness pulling me under. I repeat my goals in my mind. Eye Tracking Communication.

Blink-To-Live.

EyeGaze.

Tobii.

If I keep it in the forefront of my mind, maybe I can trick my brain into giving me this.

$$28$$

CHAPTER TWENTY-EIGHT

I'm back. The familiar scent of soil and greenery surrounds me, but tonight something's different. The tension in the room is suffocating, and I hear Charlie pacing the room.

"I didn't ask for this!" Charlie yells sharp and bitter. He reeks of frustration. "I'm not going to kill her. But sometimes... sometimes, I don't know, man. Sometimes, I wish she'd just... die." He falters. There's a long pause before he continues, "I am not lucky."

Who is he talking to? My heart races as he continues, his words piercing through me even though I am only able to hear his side of the conversation.

"I don't have a wife. All I have is a breathing corpse." He lets out a shaky breath. "No... I can't do that to her."

I feel sick. *What is he talking about?*

"I don't know how much more I can take," he mutters. "Money is running out. If I have to go back to work, what am I going to do? I can't just leave her here. It's not safe."

There's a brief silence before he continues, "The drugs keep her pretty quiet, but if I get caught... I'll end up in jail, man. All it takes is one person finding out about her, and I'm screwed."

He suddenly turns, making eye contact with me, and my heart nearly stops. Charlie looks ragged — exhausted, unhinged.

"Oh my God," he stammers, dropping his phone. He clammers to pick it back up. "I gotta go. I'll call you back later."

He rushes toward me, his face twisted with guilt. "I'm so sorry, Junie. I thought you were still asleep. I didn't mean for you to hear any of that."

Charlie's hands tremble as he brushes hair from my face, placing frantic kisses along my cheeks and neck.

His hand cups my face, his thumb brushing across my cheek. Charlie's touch is gentle, but there's a hunger in his eyes. I can feel him fighting it, whatever this is. But I can also tell he's losing the battle.

"God, Junie, I need you." He breathes, and suddenly, his lips are against my skin again.

Charlie's hand slides to the back of my neck, pulling my limp body closer to him. His eyes are filled with longing, breath hot against my skin, and I feel the need radiating off him, pulling me into his orbit.

Charlie's mouth is barely an inch from mine now, and I sense the tension within him. How much he wants this, wants me.

"I know I shouldn't, I shouldn't... but I can't stop."

His lips hover just over mine, and my heart races, trapped between fear and something else, something I can't even name.

Charlie's eyes burn right through me, filled with a silent rage. His hand slides down my arm, gripping me tighter than I think he even realizes. He kisses me on the lips forcefully.

His hands move aggressively over my arms, and I want to push him away. I want to scream. He's so lost in the moment, his lust consuming him. But just as fast as the passion rises, I feel it subside.

Charlie pulls back suddenly, breathing hard, his forehead pressed against mine as if he's trying to ground himself.

His chest heaves with emotion, the desire still coursing through him, but I can see the war playing out in his eyes.

"I can't. I can't do this." His voice shakes. "Not like this."

His hands drop from my body, and I can still feel a dull ache from where they were.

Charlie runs his hands through his hair, looking like he's trying to hold on to the last thread of control he has left. "You have no idea what I'm going through," he admits. "But I can't…"

His hand shakes as he brushes a strand of hair from my face. Charlie's tenderness now contrasts sharply with the aggressive behavior just moments before.

He paces as if he needs to put space between us to stop himself.

"What were you thinking?" he mumbles. "You deserve better than this."

I can see the desperation in him — warring between selfishness and guilt. He's barely holding himself back.

Charlie's eyes keep drifting back to me, lingering on my lips and my body, as if he wants to run right back to me.

I stare back at him, internally begging him to walk away.

"I don't know how much longer I can keep pretending… that this is enough."

Stepping closer, his hand trembles as it reaches out, stopping just before touching me. He steps away, clearly defeated.

Charlie slumps as he picks up his watering can, trying to busy himself with his plants. I can see his struggles and how badly he's hurting.

He mumbles now, his frustration clear. "Lucky? How could he call this lucky?" He sounds sharp, almost angry.

He? Who was the man on the other side of the call? What could he have said to Charlie that made him act this way towards me?

Despite my confusion, despite everything that's happened, I almost feel sorry for him. Even though he was ready to hurt me — or at least thought about it — I can see his pain. He's unraveling, and I don't know how to stop it or if I should even try.

I try to make sense of what just happened. I can't shake the feeling of danger that now hangs over me like a storm cloud. I don't feel safe around him, especially not now. The way he looked at me, the way his hands trembled as if he was holding back something darker.

I don't know if his self-control will last forever, and the uncertainty of that terrifies me. I'm trying hard to find some clarity amid this chaos. How can he say that he needs me yet speak of me like I'm a burden? He said he wants me to die.

My mind is a tangled mess of fear and confusion, and I can't trust my instincts anymore.

I think about the conversation. Why would he go to jail if someone found out about "her?" If someone finds out about me? About Junie? Or does someone know about the woman in the park?

29

Chapter Twenty-Nine

I wake up. My heart pounds, and my head feels like it's splitting open.

The dream lingers, every word from Charlie's mouth echoing in my skull.

I sit up, gasping for breath, my mind racing. Dr. Wiese is right. I need to break this. I need to communicate. Morse code. It might be my only way out.

I grab my phone and do a quick search for "Learn Morse Code." I'm going to learn to speak, even if I have to do it with my eyes. I learned ASL for my sister, and I'm sure as heck going to learn Morse Code to save myself.

I approach the table, my heart sinking with every step. This isn't how I imagined introducing Thorne to my sisters. *Wait, did I invite him? When did we all decide on tonight?*

I can't remember planning it, and now here he is, casually signing with my family as if they've known each other for years.

The shock tightens as I watch Thorne's hands moving with ease as he talks sports with Cam. His ASL is good, like really good. It hits me hard.

Violet throws her head back, laughing, and Mei looks equally impressed. Everyone seems so comfortable with each other, except for me.

Thorne catches my eye and stands to make room for me at the table. "Hey babe," he says cooly as I slide into the booth.

Babe?

His arm drapes over my shoulder the second he sits beside me. It's so smooth, so natural, like he's done it a hundred times before. But something feels off about this whole scenario.

Everyone pauses mid-conversation to greet me.

Mei smiles, Violet wiggles her eyebrows, playfully looking between Thorne and me, and even Cam gives me a nod.

The food is already on the table. I pop a dumpling into my mouth, trying to gather myself while tuning into the conversations around me.

Violet animatedly signs about wedding details, something about the invitations, while Cam and Thorne are deep into a discussion about fantasy football picks. I suppress a smile. Neither of them cares about football; I know that for a fact. They're in it for the camaraderie, for the "bro-hood," as Cam would call it.

"We should go to Gallegher's next week instead," Cam suggests.

All heads snap toward him, and Violet immediately scrunches her face in disgust.

"I did not just see you fingerspell G-A-L-L-E-G-H-E-R-S!" she signs dramatically, her face an exaggerated grimace.

Cam throws his hands up in defense. **"It's a sports bar! Tons of TVs, and the WiFi is incredible. Thorne and I can keep track of the game and our fantasy league stats."**

Violet and Mei fake gag in unison, signing the different variations for vomiting like they're in some silent movie.

The whole table erupts in laughter, but I'm too distracted to join in.

My eyes dart to Thorne, and I realize I hadn't even caught what Cam had signed earlier.

"What did Cam just call you?" I whisper to Thorne, confused.

He turns to me with an easy smile. "Violet gave me a sign name last week. I thought I showed you already."

Last week? How could I not remember? "Wait, what day is it?" I ask, trying to act casual, though I feel far from it.

He frowns, a hint of concern crossing his features. "It's Monday. Why?"

"No, I mean the date."

He pulls out his phone. "October twenty-fifth."

October? My chest tightens. I thought it was still September. How could I have lost an entire month? "Oh, right. I knew that," I lie, forcing my face to remain neutral. "I just got mixed up. This headache has been making me feel a little disoriented."

Thorne leans in close to me. This time, he whispers softly, full of concern. "Are you sure you're okay? I can drive you home if you're not feeling up to family dinner tonight."

"No, I'm fine," I say quickly, trying to reassure him — and maybe myself. "Let's just enjoy... 'family dinner.'"

The words feel strange as they leave my mouth. Since when did the five of us start this ritual? Sure, I've always referred to Mei and Violet as my sisters — even if only one of them shares my blood. Cam's practically my brother-in-law now. But when did we all start hanging out together like this?

I glance around the table, and everyone is laughing and chatting, but I feel like I'm on the outside looking in.

The world around me seems to spin faster, pulling me under while I desperately try to stay afloat. Thorne's hand gently rubs my shoulder, and it brings me back to the present, even if only for a moment.

Violet slaps her hand dramatically on the table, startling me.

"What's up with you?" she signs, her eyebrows scrunched in suspicion.

I blink, trying to act normal. **"What?"**

"I asked," she repeats slowly, drawing out the signs for emphasis. **"If we had a small reception at the art studio, would you help me set it up?"**

I nod quickly, forcing a laugh. **"Of course! What kind of maid of honor would I be if I didn't get the parties just right?"**

I hope the joke hides my anxiety.

Everyone smiles and returns to their conversations, but I can't shake the growing dread. I should feel happy. These are the people I love most in the world, my chosen family. But instead, I feel completely alone. I don't remember the last time the five of us all hung out together, and now... it's already October? What have I missed?

Thorne brushes his fingers against my shoulder again, his presence steady beside me. I glance at him and see he's already looking at me, worried. He leans in and presses a soft kiss to the top of my head, almost like a reassurance that he's here and he's not going anywhere. But even his touch feels distant somehow.

I swallow the sadness rising in my throat, pushing it down to deal with it later. I can't let them see how lost I am.

Violet tells a dramatic story about the horrors of finding affordable wedding options, and everyone's caught up in her antics. But all I can think about is how much time I've lost, how disconnected I feel from this moment.

I smile and laugh at the right times, but the pit in my stomach only grows deeper. It's like I'm missing out on my own life, and I don't know what I'm losing.

As the laughter fades and the night winds down, a strange familiarity settles over me. The clinking of the plates, the murmurs - this moment feels like it's happened before. Like I've sat here, in this exact spot, with these exact people, laughing at the same jokes, listening to the same stories. But it's distant and foggy as if I'm watching it from behind a veil. I swear I've done all this before.

I shake the thought away, forcing a smile. Just my mind playing tricks on me again... or at least, that's what I tell myself.

$$30$$

Chapter Thirty

I sit on the edge of my bed, the sounds of the city outside barely reaching my ears. My apartment feels too quiet as if the silence is waiting for something.

The laptop is warm against my legs as I scroll through the email from Dr. Wiese for the hundredth time, trying to convince myself that the strategies listed will work. *Focus on your breathing. Anchor yourself to the present.*

It's all so logical and clear in words, but is it in practice? Panic always comes like a wave, and it is impossible to stop.

My hands tremble as I close the laptop and set it aside. I've done everything I can think of to prepare: practiced the Morse code and read through my grounding techniques, but I'm still not ready. *How do I prepare to face a nightmare that feels more real every time?*

I glance at the clock on my nightstand. It's later than I realized, shadows stretching long and distorted across the walls like dark fingers reaching for me. Time to sleep. Time to face him again. I don't want to go back. Not after last time.

I can still feel Charlie's hands on me when I think about it. His grip, his presence—it lingers in a way that shouldn't be possible. What if he does more next time? What if he already has, and I don't remember? What if I'm not really waking up at all, and this room keeps going, keeping me trapped, even when I think I'm free?

I shudder at the thought, pulling my blanket up around my shoulders as if that can protect me. My heart races, each beat a reminder that there are things I don't understand, things that could be happening when I'm not even aware.

I tuck the blankets tighter around me, another weak attempt at protection, and take a deep breath. Charlie is just a figment of my mind, a symbol of something I'm not facing. Childhood trauma. My dad's anger. I think back to what Dr. Wiese said, but it doesn't make the fear any less real.

I try to remind myself that none of it is real - it's just my brain trying to make sense of the past. I want to believe that. But the way he looked at me, the way his hands lingered... That felt real.

Rolling onto my left side, I pull my knees to my chest, the weight of the blankets no longer enough to keep the fear at bay. My fingers trace the edge of the blanket, the fabric soft and familiar, grounding me in my bedroom, in the real world.

You have to go to sleep.

I dig my nails into the blanket, trying to focus on the sensation. *Focus on what you can see, what you can touch, what you can hear.*

But all I hear is my heartbeat, pounding louder with each passing second.

My eyes dart to the door, half expecting to see him standing there, waiting.

It's just my mind. I repeat it over and over, but the fear doesn't fade.

I reach for my phone, open the notes app, and type out the Morse code I've been practicing:

.-. --- ... . Rose

.... . .-.. .--. Help

... --- ... SOS

.--- ..- ... - / .- / -.. .-. . .- -- Just a dream

I practice blinking the dots and dashes once more. The rhythm of it calms me, a small comfort, though I don't know why. Maybe, just maybe I can break this cycle.

I take a deep breath and close my eyes, summoning the courage to let go, to let the sleep take me.

The Room is waiting.

And so is he.

31

CHAPTER THIRTY-ONE

I open my eyes as the dim, suffocating light of The Room greets me. My breath hitches, and for a split second, I pray it's still my bedroom. But no. I'm here. The sage green walls, now looming and too large, expand around me, closing in as if they know I'm trapped here again.

This place always knows how to pull me back.

Then I hear it.

A child screaming. Piercing, frantic, like their very soul is being ripped apart. The sound stabs the stillness, cutting through the haze of sleep.

Just a dream, I remind myself, gripping that thought like a lifeline.

The panic surges inside me, clawing at my insides. The machines beside me beep louder, faster - syncing with my growing fear. I have to calm down. I can't let him come in here. Not again.

I shut my eyes tight, willing my breath to slow down. *Focus on what you can see, what you can hear, what you can feel,* The mantra echoes in my mind, but the terror still sticks to me.

The child's scream, distant but relentless, makes it impossible. I can't see anyone, but the sound lingers, bouncing off the walls like it's coming from everywhere and nowhere all at once.

I frantically glance around the room, searching for anything to ground me. *Breathe in. Breathe out.* In... out.

The beeping slows just a little. The scream fades as if the child has moved farther away.

The silence creeps back in, filling the void. I'm alone again, for now.

I start blinking in morse code:

.--- ..- ... - / .- / -.. .-. . .- -- – Just a dream

It feels like an anchor in this place where I have no control.

.-. --- ... . Rose

If I keep spelling my name and keep reminding myself who I am, I'll find a way out.

I blink it again, my hope flickering with each movement. There has to be a way I can break this.

Suddenly, the bed dips beside me. I snap my eyes open, expecting to see him - Charlie, with his cold hands and angry eyes - but instead, it's a small child, a boy, sitting on the edge of my bed.

He stares at me.

My heart rate increases as I take him in, dark skin, wild curly hair, and bright green eyes that seem too happy for this place. He looks familiar, but I've never seen him before. I would remember those eyes.

For a moment, we just stare at each other. Then, instinct kicks in. Now's my chance. I have to try.

I start blinking again, quicker now, spelling out my name.

The boy's eyes lock onto mine, and his mouth opens slightly in confusion.

I hear footsteps, heavy and deliberate, approaching. Charlie. He's coming.

I start to blink out HEL... but the boy's eyes widen in terror, and he raises a finger to his lips in a frantic shhh motion. He's scared, too, maybe even more than I am.

Then he does something that sends a shiver down my spine.

He signs, slowly, clearly, **"Help."**

He knows ASL. He's asking me for help. A child, in this nightmare of a place, is asking me for help. But I can't move. I can't scream. I can't do anything.

The boy scrambles off the bed, his small body moving with sudden, desperate urgency. He crawls underneath my bed.

Charlie's voice fills the room like a thunderclap. "Wren, you better not be in here." He says sharply. "You know this room is off limits."

His footsteps are heavy, vibrating through the floor. He's searching for the boy. *Please don't find him. Please, just go away.*

He stomps around the bed, muttering under his breath. Suddenly, there's a soft squeak - a slip of sound from beneath the bed. *No. No, no, no.*

Charlie crouches, his face twisting into a cruel smile. "Got you now."

He reaches under the bed, and the boy lets out a blood-curdling scream. It's a sound that shatters something inside of me. I want to reach for him, to stop this, but I can't. I have never felt so helpless.

Charlie yanks the boy out by his arm, hoisting him like a rag doll and throwing him over his shoulder. The boy kicks and thrashes, trying to break free from his grasp.

"You thought you could get away from me? No one can."

The room spins around me, the walls closing in tighter. Without another word, they vanish from the room, leaving only silence in their wake.

I'm alone again. But I'm not safe. I'm never safe here.

Hours pass, or at least it feels like it. Time moves differently here; it is slower, like each second drags out to a minute. The room has remained quiet, and I'm left with nothing but my thoughts.

The boy's face lingers in my mind—those eyes. I've never seen him before, but there is something unmistakably familiar. Green, piercing, but there is a softness too, a knowing.

Then it hits me. Violet. The boy's eyes are just like Violet's — her exact shade of green. Maybe that's why I felt such an instant connection to him. Maybe this is my mind playing tricks on me again, taking pieces of my life and mixing them up in a nightmare. *It's a projection*, I think. *It has to be.*

My brain scrambles to cope with everything, with the trauma. Why else would I invent a child who not only looks like my sister but knows ASL? Of course, he knew how to sign. It's just my subconscious cataloging worst-case scenarios, throwing things at me to keep me on edge. *God, I'm going crazy.*

But still... Something about the way he looked at me, so terrified.

That scream. It felt real. Too real.

I blink the thought away, but the boy's wide eyes and desperate plea keep flashing in my mind.

Help.

I'm still lost in the memory, when Charlie steps back into the room. His face is flushed, and he's breathing hard like he's been running. But there's something different about him now - he's almost... relaxed. Lighter than I've seen him in a long time. It's unnerving.

"Sorry about earlier," he says, looking directly at me.

He sounds almost conversational, like we're having a normal chat. Like he didn't just drag a screaming child out of here only hours earlier.

Charlie continues, "He knows he's not supposed to come in here. I don't know what got into him."

My stomach knots, and I try to hold his gaze, hoping my eyes can communicate what my mouth can't. What happened to that little boy? What did you do to him?

Charlie's smile widens as if he can understand my thoughts. "Don't worry," he says with a dismissive wave. "I got him good. He's gone now."

My blood runs cold. *Gone?*

What does that even mean? Does he really think I wanted something to happen to an innocent child?

A wave of nausea rolls through me. *Gone.* Like he did me a favor.

My mind races, searching for a logical explanation, but there's nothing—only that awful, sinking feeling.

"I worked up an appetite," he says, oblivious to my terror. "I'm gonna go grab some dinner. Be back in a bit."

He picks up the remote and flips through channels as if everything's perfectly normal. Then he stops. "Oh, your favorite."

He glances back at me with a crooked grin and gives my hand a squeeze before heading for the door.

Forensic Files. Every girl's favorite, right? He just got lucky with that guess.

When I'm sure he's gone, I turn my attention to the TV. Part of me can't help but feel a bitter amusement at the irony.

I get lost in the episode, letting it dull the edges of my anxiety. The details of the murder investigation, the forensic breakdowns, the luminol, all of it fills the silence, giving me something else to focus on. But before I know it, Charlie's back.

He walks in with such a casual ease. "I'm gonna change into my pajamas," he says. "Wanna watch a movie after?"

Charlie looks at me expectantly, like he's waiting for an answer. Is he serious?

He sighs when I don't respond. "Yeah, right," he mutters, his shoulders drooping slightly as if I've disappointed him. As if I had a choice.

Charlie disappears into the other room, and I hear him rummaging around.

A few minutes later, he reappears wearing gray sweatpants and a hoodie, which makes me pause. Silly Goose. I recognize it instantly. It's a joke that Mei and I share. We have the exact same matching sweatshirts. The sight of it soothes me for just a moment, another shard of my real life bleeding into this twisted dream. *This is just a dream.*

Charlie flops down on the couch beside me. He grabs the remote and flips through the options, finally settling on a movie— *The Count of Monte Cristo.*

I hear the crinkle of wrappers as he digs into some fast food, the smell of greasy burgers and fries filling the room. My stomach twists with hunger, the sudden urge for a cheeseburger hitting me hard. It's almost funny how something so mundane could seem so out of reach in a place like this.

I zone in and out of the movie, the images on the screen blending with the swirl of my thoughts.

My eyelids grow heavier, and I fight the pull of sleep, but it's no use. I've always fallen asleep during movies.

Just before I drift off completely, one last thought crosses my mind. *I can't wait to be in my own bed.*

32

CHAPTER THIRTY-TWO

I wake up gasping. The Room. The child. Charlie. But it's not real. It wasn't real.

Just a dream, I remind myself, wiping the sweat from my forehead.

I'm in my own bed. I'm home. I glance at the clock on my bedside table reads, 11:47 AM.

My eyes widen. Almost noon.

I reach for my phone, its screen glowing with multiple missed calls. My boss asked why I hadn't responded to any of the new assignments.

Crap. I shoot back a quick text, calling in "sick." The lie comes easily, and I don't feel guilty.

I close my eyes for a moment, letting the reality of the present sink in. It was just a dream. That's all. But a small part of me nags just enough to push me to grab my laptop. *Just to be sure*, I tell myself. *Just to know.*

I settle it on my lap and open a browser, my fingers hesitating over the keys.

African American child, Wren, New York, Missing.

I hit enter and hold my breath. The search results load. No results are found. I try again.

"Brooklyn New York Missing Children."

I click on the link for the Missing Children Organization and filter by what I can remember: dark skin, curly hair, bright green eyes, aged 3-4. SEARCH.

The page loads with a list of faces, but none match the child from my dream.

I let out a long breath, a wave of relief flooding through me. *Thank God.*

I hadn't realized how much tension I am carrying until now. It melts away, leaving behind a rare sense of calm, a lightness I haven't felt in... forever, it seems.

My phone dings with a message.

Thorne: Didn't see you at the coffee shop. All good?

I smile, feeling even more at ease.

Rose: Didn't feel like working today. Took day off..

Thorne: You feeling ok?

Rose: Yeah, honestly, I feel the best I have in a loooong time. Didn't want to waste a good day working.

And it's true. For the first time in what feels like forever, I actually feel good. Like myself again, like the heaviness has lifted. I don't know if it's the relief of realizing the boy was just a dream or if today just happens to be one of those rare, random, better days, but I'll take it.

It's almost unsettling to feel this okay. It's like my mind is bracing for something to go wrong again. But for now, I'll let myself enjoy it.

Thorne: Want to spend a good day together?

Rose: Absolutely. I'm craving a burger.

Thorne: Burger? You got it. Meet or pick you up?

Rose: I can meet in an hour?

Thorne: Same place?

Same place? I stare at the words for a second. I can't remember what place he's talking about. I brush it off, determined not to let anything spoil my mood. I'm having a good day.

Rose: Just to confirm, can you send me the address?

Thorne: Yeah, one sec.

A moment later, my phone pings with the location. I tap on the address, and Maps tells me I've been there less than two weeks ago.

I blink, confused. How? I don't remember ever eating there. I shake my head and push the thought aside. It doesn't matter right now. So I'm still missing days. What else is new? I mentally shrug, telling myself to save the worrying for a therapy day.

Rose: Great. See you in an hour.

I toss my phone onto the bed and close my laptop, standing up and stretching out the stiffness in my limbs. I feel good. I feel really good. And maybe today, just for once, everything will stay that way.

I take my time getting ready, savoring the way my mind feels clear for the first time in... I don't even know how long.

Stepping outside, I'm immediately hit by a freezing gust of wind that makes me gasp. When did autumn turn into the Arctic?

I return to my apartment, quickly deciding there's no way I'm walking. Not today, not in this weather.

I pull out my winter gear and tuck my chin into my scarf before braving the cold again, getting into my car, and cranking up the car's heat.

I drive to where the GPS tells me to.

I pull up to Jo's Burgers and manage to find a parking spot right outside the restaurant entrance. I spot Thorne immediately through the window. His tall frame is hard to miss.

He waves, sporting a goofy grin that makes my heart do a weird little flip.

I smile back, gripping the steering wheel. I don't recognize this place, but he does. And that's what matters.

After a deep breath, I step out of the car and make my way inside, the biting cold snapping at my heels.

"Hey, babe," Thorne says the moment I reach him, getting up from his seat to greet me.

He wastes no time rubbing up and down my arms, trying to warm me up. His hands are firm, but I can't help relaxing under his touch.

"It's deathly cold outside. I'm glad you drove," he says, still rubbing my shoulders.

"Yeah, me too." I laugh. "My fingers practically froze to the steering wheel."

Thorne takes my hands in his, rubbing them gently. I feel a pleasant warmth spreading from where his fingers meet mine. Then, he leans and blows warm air onto my fingers, sending a shiver that has nothing to do with the cold running through me.

He glances up at me, eyes sparkling with mischief, before planting a soft kiss on my knuckles.

"All better," he says with a wink, settling back into his chair.

I try to act nonchalant, but I can feel the heat rising to my cheeks as I sit across him.

He watches me, lips curling into a small smile like he knows exactly what kind of effect he has on me.

I tuck a strand of hair behind my ear and smile back, hoping he doesn't notice the way my stomach is doing actual somersaults.

"I ordered your favorite so you could dive right in," he says, gesturing to the plate in front of me.

I look at the burger and fries, trying to mask my confusion. *My favorite?* I think as I slide off my coat and scarf.

I don't remember ever having this before, but it looks incredible. "Thanks," I say, a bit uneasily.

But as I take the first bite, all my worries melt away.

Holy Canola Oil. This is the best thing I've ever tasted.

The flavors explode on my tongue, and before I even realize it, I'm doing a little happy dance in my seat. I take another bite, humming in delight, and catch Thorne watching me, smiling like he's completely enamored.

I cover my mouth with a napkin, laughing. "What? Don't look at me like that."

"Like what?" he says, leaning forward, his eyes twinkling. "Like I enjoy watching you fall in love with a cheeseburger?"

I roll my eyes, trying to suppress the smile aggressively, tugging at my lips.

"Hey, I can't compete with Jo's Burgers," he teases, shrugging dramatically. "I just hope I get that same look every now and then."

I snort, feeling the blush creeping up my neck. "You wish."

"Do I?" He smirks, his eyes dancing with playful challenge.

I bite my lip, looking away before my heart bursts out of my chest. The ease between us feels almost surreal as if we've been doing this for years, and I can't help but think how fast I've fallen for him. A stranger from the coffee shop. It's insane. But with the way he's looking at me right now, I'm starting to think it might not be crazy at all.

"So," Thorne says, snapping me out of my thoughts. "What do you want to do today?"

I lean back, wiping my hands on a napkin. "Literally anything. I just want to enjoy the day. What time do you head to the restaurant?"

He fakes a dramatic cough, clutching his chest. "I'm too sick to go in today," he says with an exaggerated wink.

I burst out laughing, shaking my head. "Oh, really? Convenient. Me too."

"What can I say?" He leans in, lowering his voice. "I'm a terrible restaurant owner when it comes to spending time with you."

"You better hope your boss doesn't hear that," I tease, knowing he doesn't actually have someone to answer to.

He raises an eyebrow, flashing me a wicked grin. "Don't worry he's seen you. He'll forgive me."

The way he's looking at me sends butterflies right to my stomach. It's too much, and not enough, all at once.

"Smooth," I mutter, unable to control my girlish grin.

"What was that?" he teases, leaning in closer. "I didn't catch that."

I roll my eyes. "I said you're smooth, okay?" I laugh, swatting his arm.

He grins wider, satisfied with himself. "I try."

Lunch wraps up with a back-and-forth of whose burger was better, but we both know mine was.

Thorne insists that his sweet potato fries were the real winner, but I catch him stealing one of my waffle fries when he thinks I'm not looking.

We laugh our way out the door, deciding to spend the day at the Science Center.

When we get to the Science Center, we immediately head to Rocket Park. Thorne insists on launching one of the model rockets, grinning like a little kid as he watches it soar into the sky. It's impossible not to smile around him, especially when his excitement is so contagious.

Afterward, we spend an embarrassing amount of time at the Bubbles exhibit, where we try - and fail - to create the biggest bubble. Thorne keeps blowing too hard, popping mine just as I'm about to win the imaginary bubble Olympics.

"Sabotage!" I accuse, pointing at him dramatically.

He raises his hands in mock surrender. "I would never. I'm innocent, I swear!"

"Sure, sure," I say, narrowing my eyes at him. "That's what all bubble-saboteurs say."

"I think I'm going to need a lawyer," he teases. "If you let me win, I'll make it up to you with a secret dessert later."

I pretend to think it over for a moment. "Tempting. But I don't play to lose, Thorne."

He grins, eyes sparkling. "Guess I'll just have to out-bubble you the old-fashioned way."

We continue laughing like idiots. Each too wrapped up in the fun to care about winning or losing anymore.

This is the best day I've had in so long, I think as we walk hand in hand to the next exhibit.

We wander into a temporary exhibit about communication, and his face lights up as he spots a display with working telegraph machines. "Come on," he says, tugging my hand and leading me over.

I raise an eyebrow as we sit at opposite ends of the table, each with our own telegraph transmitter. "So, what exactly are we doing?" I ask, curious.

"Well my sister and I used to play with one of these growing up. We'd send each other secret messages in Morse code. Got pretty good at it, actually." He smirks.

"Of course you did. You two had your own private spy network, didn't you?"

"Maybe," he says with a wink. "And I still remember all the codes. Want to give it a try?"

I look down at the laminated page in front of me, filled with letters and their Morse code translations. "You're on," I say.

All my blinking practice better pays off. I refuse to embarrass myself.

He taps out a quick message.

"Hey," the code reads.

I respond, "HI."

Thorne shoots back with, "u r cute."

I snort, glancing up at him. "Really? Telegraph flirting?"

He grins, not even a little embarrassed. "You know, classic and effective."

"THX," I send back, smirking to myself. "u 2."

I feel my cheeks heat up. Who flirts through Morse code? And why do I find it so dang charming?

I push my chair back, laughing softly. "Alright, enough of that. Let's—"

"Wait," Thorne interrupts, holding up a hand. "I've got one more message for you. Don't go yet."

I pause, curious, and lower myself back onto the stool. "Okay, what is it?"

He looks down, focusing as he types out the first code.
"I think."

I glance at the paper, translating the dots and dashes, furrowing my brow as I look back at him.

He's watching me closely, a smirk on his face.

He begins tapping out a code again.

"NO."

"I know."

My heartbeat quickens as I glance between the page and the transmitter, decoding each letter. *What is he up to?*

Then, he taps out the final message.

"I love you."

I freeze as I stare down at the page in front of me. My hands shake as I double-check the letters, just to be sure. *I love you.*

When I finally look up, he's giving me this shy, one-sided shrug, his eyes soft and vulnerable in a way I've never seen before. He bites his lip like he's not sure what my reaction will be. His half-smile tells me he's hopeful.

Something inside me bursts open. I'm on my feet, rushing over to him. He barely has time to stand, and I'm already in his arms, holding him tight.

"I love you, too," I whisper, my lips brushing his ear.

He lets out a breath, pulling me even closer, and I feel him smile against my hair.

For the first time, my heart races in a good way. Before I can second guess anything, I tilt my head up and plant a kiss on his lips.

The kiss is soft at first, like we're both still figuring out these new feelings between us. But then his arms wrap around me tighter and the kiss deepens. I don't care where we are, or that we are standing in the middle of an exhibit meant for kids — right now, it's just us, and everything feels perfect.

When we finally pull apart, I can't help but laugh softly, resting my forehead against his. "So... Morse code, huh?"

He chuckles, his hand still resting on my waist. "Hey, I told you it was effective."

"I'll give you that," I say, smiling up at him. "But next time, maybe just use words?"

Thorne's eyes twinkle mischievously. "What, and miss out on a chance to flirt with you through secret codes?"

I roll my eyes playfully. "You're impossible."

"Yeah," he says, pressing a quick kiss to my forehead. "But you love it."

33

CHAPTER THIRTY-THREE

I arrive home and flop on the couch. I remove the many layers as I run through the memories of today's official "Best Date Day Ever." We ended the night at a Korean BBQ restaurant, which I had never tried before but was delectable. Who knew cooking your own meats over a small table campfire could be so romantic?

After dinner, we picked up hot cocoa and took in the city's lights.

His sister called, and I tried to give them privacy, but instead, he pulled me closer to meet her via video call.

Georgie has the most beautiful silver hair I have ever seen on someone so young and has piercing blue eyes. We chatted for a few minutes and agreed that we would all talk again soon.

When he ended the call, Thorne looked at me and said, "She likes you."

I insisted that she was just being polite, but he swore I had to trust his brotherly intuition.

After sharing another kiss, we got in our respective cars and went our separate ways. I've never experienced this feeling before, but I can tell that I never want to be away from him for too long again.

I hop in the shower and let the hot water warm my bones. Today went better than I could've ever imagined.

Afterward, I brush out my hair.

As I dry my face with a towel, I hear my surroundings change. I look at the mirror, and Charlie's face stares back at me.

"Wake up, Junie."

I see his hands reach through the glass toward me.

Panicking, I step away quickly, slamming my back into the wall. *Ouch.*

I reach up to the back of my head and feel hot liquid. When I look at my hand, it's covered in blood. I stare at my hand, frozen, unable to explain what's happening to me.

Charlie's hands reach out for my shoulders, and I squeeze my eyes shut. He's lightly shaking me.

Just a dream. Just a dream.

When I open my eyes, I'm in The Room.

"Oh, good." Charlie smiles at me. "You have someone coming to see you soon. I wanted to make sure you were alert prior to them arriving."

Someone is coming here?

He brushes my hair and adjusts the bed so that I'm sitting up more. He's excited for whoever is coming to visit, and it's a strange atmosphere. The room is even cleaner than usual. He's been expecting company. This guest is important to him.

After he has me set up to his liking, he begins watering the plants and singing at the top of his lungs. He's really happy about today's events. I'm still riding my high from the date with Thorne. We can both be in a good mood today. I don't mind the change in routine.

After a while, the doorbell rings. Charlie claps a singular thunderclap. "She's here."

He grins the largest smile I've ever seen on this man's face. He makes his way to the door. Even though I can't see the action take place, I hear him say, "Georgie!" and I hear the familiar sounds of a long embrace.

Georgie? Thorne's sister?

She enters the room.

"Oh, my God! It's so good to see you," she says, wrapping my limp body in a long hug. It's the same woman from the video call.

I smile internally, knowing that my dreams are finally listening to me.

"Looks like she's happy to see me, too," Georgie says, looking back at Charlie.

"What do you mean?" He's dragging her luggage into the room.

"Look," she says eagerly, gesturing to my face. "She's smiling."

Charlie looks at me intently and walks straight toward me, his eyes locked on my face. "She…" He hesitates. "She's never done that before."

Charlie and Georgie share a look, and then he jumps up, wraps her in his arms, and spins her around, her legs lifting off the ground in his bear hug.

Both laugh as they celebrate.

I feel myself smile even more at the sight of these two. I don't quite understand their excitement, but it feels like my brain is celebrating my new love life with me. And I'm perfectly okay with this outcome.

34

CHAPTER THIRTY-FOUR

The sun is bright, and the air feels warm on my skin. I don't need my heavy winter coat today.

I breathe in deep as I walk the familiar route to the little cafe where Violet and I have our usual breakfast date.

The trees lining the streets are budding with delicate flowers, soft bursts of pink and white. I snap a picture and send it to The Daisy Chain. It feels like spring has arrived overnight, with the kind of day you want to bottle up and keep forever.

I smile, glancing at my phone. It's 9:28 AM. I am early, for once.

Rose: I beat u here! C U Soon Loser

I hit send and grin.

Violet is usually the punctual one, but I manage to get here first today.

I slip into the restaurant, choosing our usual booth by the window, and wave to the waitress with a smile. The place is quiet, except for a couple of regulars sipping coffee at the counter.

I slide into my seat, tapping my fingers against the table.

After a few minutes, I check the time. 9:42 AM. No big deal. She is probably stuck in traffic or something.

Rose: Just checking, r u on ur way?

My thumb hovers over the screen for a second before I hit send.

I stare at my phone for a beat longer, waiting for the dots to pop up, for the reply that would tell me she's around the corner or has just parked. But nothing comes.

I lean back, frowning. She has never left me hanging like this. Violet is always reliable, annoyingly so sometimes. Always showing up exactly on time, never late, never missing.

Rose: U there? - 9:59AM.

Rose: I'm getting worried, where r u? - 10:01AM.

My heart skips, the noise of the restaurant no longer comforting. I feel the first pangs of a panic attack.

I hit the video call button.

It rings and rings.

No answer.

My pulse quickens.

It continues ringing.

Still nothing.

I end the call and press Violet's number again—10:04 AM.

Still no answer.

Rose: Half hour late, is something wrong? - 10:06AM.

My fingers tremble as I hit the call button a third time, my breathing shallow. *Please, Violet. Answer.*

Nothing.

The restaurant suddenly feels too loud - plates clattering, distant chatter, the clink of glasses and silverware. I grip the edge of the table, swallowing hard.

> Rose: V ANSWER ME! I'M GETTING SCARED! - 10:14 AM.

I can't sit still anymore. My leg bounces under the table as I scan the room. *Where is she?*

I hit the call button again, desperate. 10:17 AM. Why isn't she picking up?

The edges of my vision blur.

She has to answer.

I tap out another message, my hands shaking so badly I almost drop my phone.

> Rose: U better be dead on the side of the road & not just ignoring me. - 10:19 AM.

I immediately regret that message, my chest constricting with guilt. 10:20 AM - Another call. No answer.

The clock ticks by, every second stretching painfully. My thoughts spin out of control. I can't stop myself from picturing her hurt somewhere or worse. What if something happened?

My phone buzzes in my hands, and I nearly drop it, but it is just an annoying "Spam Likely" Call. 10:21 AM. Still nothing from Violet. I squeeze my eyes shut, gripping my phone tighter.

> Rose: I didn't mean it Vi, please answer me. DO NOT BE DEAD!!! - 10:22 AM.

I stare at the screen. *Just answer, please.* I will V's name to pop up and see the dots start typing. But all I get is silence.

The hostess approaches me, her voice distant, muffled. "Ma'am, I'm sorry, but we need the table for other customers..."

I look up at her blankly, barely registering the words.

I nod, standing up on shaky legs. I hadn't even noticed how much the restaurant had filled up around me.

I walk outside, the sun no longer comforting. My body is cold all over. I pace in front of the cafe, my breath coming too fast, too shallow. My head is spinning, and my stomach twists painfully.

I sit on the bench to calm my nerves. My heart thuds in my ears now. I can barely hear anything else.

> Rose: U better have a very good excuse for flaking on me.

> Rose: LOL JK - 10:31 AM.

I hit the call button again. Nothing. 10:33 AM.

> Rose: I luv u. Plz answer me.

"Please answer me." I say the words as if that would somehow make her appear suddenly. Why won't she answer? Where is she?

In a last-ditch effort, I call Mei. The call goes straight to voicemail. Where are they?

My phone slips out of my hands, landing on the pavement with a dull thud. I don't pick it up. I just stare ahead, unfocused, feeling the world around me start to unravel.

The ringtone pulls me back to reality. I feel the pavement scrape my knuckles as I reach for my phone—Violet's name.

My heart jumps. *Thank God*. She is ok. She has to be.

I quickly push back my hair and adjust to look less frazzled before hitting the Accept Video Call button.

"Violet," I sign, my hands still shaking. **"Where have you been? I texted and called a million—"**

"Rose?" Her face is stern but concerned. **"Why aren't you here?"**

I blink, raising my eyebrow and tilting my head in a traditional ASL "Huh?" I point behind me to the restaurant. **"I'm here waiting for you, I—"**

"Rose, today's my wedding day."

The words hit me like a metal bat to my stomach, knocking the air from my lungs. **"What?"** I stare at her as she nods. **"That's not - V, that's not possible,"** I sign.

"You were supposed to be here thirty minutes ago." Her face is soft, and she's not signing with anger; she's just worried.

Thirty minutes ago? My mind scrambles to make sense of her words. Her wedding day. How did I forget? How could I forget something this important?

I feel a dizzying blur of thoughts crashing into each other, none of them sticking. How have I lost so much time? What day is it?

"I don't understand. I don't even remember—"

My signing is sloppy as tears streak down my face.

"Rose, I don't have time for this right now," Violet cuts me off, her hands shaking more now. **"But please, just... just get here, okay? I need *you*."**

She ends the video chat, and I just stand there, staring into noth-ing—*her wedding day*. I have to be there. I'm her maid of honor. How had I—?

I break into a run, feet slamming hard against the sidewalk as I make my way to my car, the world blurring past me. My thoughts race faster and faster, tumbling over each other in the chaos.

I fumble with my keys, throwing myself into the driver's seat. My hands shake uncontrollably as I start the car.

The world outside the windshield seems to spin, trees and buildings merging into a blur as I speed toward the venue.

The panic suddenly increases, my chest tightening, squeezing me tighter and tighter until it feels like my ribs will snap under the pressure.

I pull off onto the side of the road. I can't catch my breath. I can't think straight.

My hands slip off the wheel, slick with sweat, my vision narrowing to a tunnel. My pulse thunders in my ears, louder than anything else, louder than the engine's roaring.

I gasp for air, but it's not enough. My lungs are on fire, screaming for oxygen, but it's like there is none left. I am losing control.

My head pounds, a relentless numbness that only adds to my madness. Black spots dance at the edges of my vision, growing, spreading.

Not now. Not now. Not now.

My hands tremble violently as the edges of my world start to dissolve, fading into that awful, suffocating darkness. I want to escape.

No. No. Not now.

But it was too late.

The world around me disappears.

35

CHAPTER THIRTY-FIVE

When I open my eyes, the light is harsh, blinding, too bright. The familiar smell of The Room punches my gut. The monitors scream a high-pitched screech that sets my teeth on edge.

Charlie steps into my line of vision - his face pale, his eyes wide with panic as he rushes toward me, knocking over the medicine tray in his scramble to get to my bedside.

"Junie, stay with me," he pleads as he fumbles with the medicines. "Please, stay with me."

My heart hammers harder than ever. Each beat slams like it is trying to tear its way through my chest. The monitor echoes, the sharp, piercing beeps growing louder and faster.

"Please work," he mutters as he injects something into my arm. "Please work..."

The panic isn't just swallowing me whole; it's as if my body has decided to revolt. A violent jerk ripples through me, and then another, harder, faster. My muscles spasm uncontrollably, my arms and legs thrashing against the bed as if they have a mind of their own. I can't stop it. I can't stop any of it.

I can still hear the screech of the heart monitor in the background, the beeping turning even more erratic. My head slams back against the pillow, and my teeth are clenched so tight that I think they will crack.

Through the haze of flashing lights behind my eyes, I catch a glimpse of Charlie. His face is drained of all color, frozen for a moment in sheer terror. I see him panicking, his hands fumbling with syringes as he stares at me, completely unsure of what to do.

"Junie!" His voice breaks, trembling with desperation. He drops a vial, curses, and grabs another. "Hold on, just hold on - please."

My body jerks violently, each spasm worse than the last. The air is thick. My breath comes in short, uneven gasps barely filling my lungs.

Then I feel a needle plunge into my arm - another injection.

Charlie's fingers shake as he empties the syringe. I watch his wide eyes. He frantically whispers, "Come on... come on, work..."

Slowly, the seizing starts to ease. The violent tremors become smaller jerks, my body fighting to regain control.

The tightness in my muscles begins to fade, leaving me weak and sore. My entire body feels like gelatin, drained of every last ounce of strength.

The room sways around me, blurry, shifting. The tiredness hits me hard, pulling me under faster than I can fight it. I try to focus on Charlie's face, but my eyelids feel impossibly heavy.

The last thing I feel is his hand on my cheek, his eyes sharp with worry. He pleads with me, but it is fading, his voice slipping further and further away.

My vision blinks out.

$$36$$

CHAPTER THIRTY-SIX

When I open my eyes, the cold grip of fear immediately seizes me. I blink, once, twice - disoriented. Where am I? I'm still shaking as I take in my surroundings.

Violet's wedding.

The sun streams through the tall windows, casting warm beams onto the aisle, chairs adorned with lavender and navy flowers, and a soft melody playing in the background.

I stand in the middle of it all, right where I'm supposed to be. But I am not... This morning, I had completely forgotten this day even existed, and now I am here. Fully dressed. Fully prepared.

I barely have time to breathe before I feel Thorne's hand gently slide around my waist, his lips brushing my cheek. "You look beautiful," he whispers.

For a moment, I cling to that calm.

"Not so bad yourself," I manage, offering a weak smile as I straighten his tie.

Inside, I'm still spiraling. My mind swirls with fragmented thoughts, barely clinging to reality. I feel like I'm sleepwalking through a dream, the seams of my world unraveling, and I can't catch the threads. But Violet... I have to be here for her. *Focus. Just focus on her.*

With shaky breaths, I make my way to the bridal suite, and when I see her, I almost lose it. Tears instantly spring to my eyes.

Violet stands in front of the mirror, glowing, her smile soft and radiant, dressed in the most breathtaking gown I've ever seen.

"Oh my God..." I whisper, unable to stop the tears from falling.

Mei, who is fixing Violet's veil, grins over her shoulder, her eyes as glassy as mine.

"Right?" Mei says. "She's a literal goddess."

Violet turns to face me, her hands nervously fidgeting. **"Stop,"** she signs. **"You're going to make me cry before I even make it down the aisle."**

I rush forward, wrapping my arms around her. I look her in the eye, and I am heavy with emotion. **"I'm so proud of you."**

I force myself to remember every detail of this moment. **"It's always been you and me against the world. I wouldn't have it any other way."**

We squeeze each other tight, the weight of everything we'd been through heavy between us. Just the two of us - no, the three of us - forever, no matter what happens.

I pull Mei into our embrace, the tears flowing freely now.

Mei joins our sobbing, laughing through her tears as she tries to keep her makeup from smudging.

After a moment, Violet pulls back, wiping her eyes with the back of her hand. **"Ok, FISH!"**

She laughs. **"We need to retouch our makeup before the ceremony."**

Violet dabs her face with a beauty blender, sniffling, trying to compose herself.

She turns to me. **"Can you go check on Cam? Make sure he's not freaking out?"**

I nod, giving her one last squeeze before heading toward the groom's suite.

When I knock on the door, Cam opens it looking like a mess. His usually neat curls are wild, his eyes wide with panic.

"I forgot my hair stuff at home," he says, running his hand through the frizz. **"I look like a disaster. I can't marry Vi looking like this."**

"You're marrying my sister, period," I reassure him, though his hair is definitely... a problem. **"Give me two minutes."**

I rush out to find Thorne. He's lounging by his car, but as soon as he sees me approaching, his posture straightens.

"I need a huge favor," I say, slightly out of breath. "Cam forgot his curl cream. Can you run to the pharmacy and get some? Like, now?"

His lips curl into his mischievous smile, and he gives me a mock salute. "Aye, aye, Captain."

I laugh, the tension easing from my shoulders. "You're my hero," I tease, fanning myself dramatically.

Seventeen minutes later - yes, I counted - Thorne returns, his arms full of every type of curl cream imaginable. I stare at the vast selection. "What the—?"

I burst out laughing. "You didn't have to buy the whole store!"

He shrugs sheepishly. "I've never dealt with his hair type before. I asked a worker for help, and she asked me if his hair was a level two, three, or four, and I have no idea what any of that meant. So I just got it all."

I kiss him on the cheek. "You're ridiculous," I say, but my heart swells with affection.

I grab the products and race back to Cam, emergency averted.

Everyone looks absolutely beautiful, and we all take our places as The Wedding March begins to play.

Thorne and I make our way down the aisle, and he gives Cam a thumbs-up as we take our designated positions. Then Mei and Cam's childhood best friend Max come down behind us. Finally, the doors open and reveal Violet.

Cam immediately cries upon seeing her. She is the most beautiful bride I've ever seen, so his reaction is definitely warranted. Their eyes are locked on her the entire journey to him.

Her dress softly rustled with each graceful step. She glows from within from love and anticipation.

The ceremony begins, and it is... perfect. Absolutely perfect. Watching it unfold in ASL, every gesture is a painting in motion, each sign its own form of poetry.

When they exchange vows, their hands say more than spoken words ever could—each sign, each gesture brimming with emotion, a promise not only said but felt.

The minister asks, **"Who gives this woman to this man?"**

Mei and I stand together proudly. **"We do,"** we say in unison.

When Vi asked us to give her away, we were shocked but beyond happy to have that privilege.

The moment Violet and Cam seal their new commitment with a kiss, the world seems to pause. The tenderness in their embrace lingers; a quiet intimacy that makes the air shimmer around them. It is more than just a wedding; it is a work of art, alive and breathing in their own language of love.

As I ride with Thorne to the reception, a sickness gnaws at my gut. How much have I actually been present for? Did I even help with the reception? I feel like I'm free-falling, unsure of what moments I've been a part of and what I've lost to the void.

We step into the art studio, and the sick feeling fades. The place is stunning. Every detail - from the cake to the flowers to the art displays - is perfect. I hadn't ruined it.

Violet finds me halfway through the night, pulling me in for a hug. **"Thank you. For everything."**

I squeeze her tight. **"You deserve even better than this."**

She grins. **"Stop! I'll cry again. Come on, let's dance."**

We sway together in a slow circle, my fingers tapping out the beat on her back so she can stay in time with the music. When the song ends, she nudges me with her elbow. **"Go grab your man. It's your turn."**

I find Thorne easily in the crowd and pull him close. The room feels like a dream as we dance together under the dim light of the disco ball. The night is painted in hues of purple, each second stretching into something infinite and beautiful.

I catch Thorne's eyes, and for a moment, everything else falls away. It's just us—just this.

I stare into his dreamy eyes and notice he's tapping his finger on my back in a pattern, and it clicks—Morse code. My heart skips a beat.

.. / .-.. --- ...- . / -.-- --- ..- (I love you).

I smile, tapping back my silent reply on the back of his neck without hesitation.

.. / .-.. --- ...- . / -.-- --- ..- / -- --- .-. . (I love you more.)

I'm amazed for a moment at how much my Morse code skills have improved. My practice in The Room must really be paying off.

I push that thought immediately away. None of that has any place here.

The connection between us feels almost electric, a language only we can understand. It's so intimate, so tender - this wordless exchange under the sparkling lights.

We hold each other a little closer, savoring the moment, the music, the warmth between us. Just as the song nears its end, Thorne pulls back, his hand sliding from my waist to cradle my cheek. His gaze locks with mine, deep and intense, and I can feel the world tilt on its axis.

He blinks slowly and deliberately. The rhythm is different this time, and it takes me a second to decipher the message. It takes my breath away.

-- .- .-. .-. -.-- / -- . ..-.. (Marry me?)

37

CHAPTER THIRTY-SEVEN

I know where I am immediately, but I keep my eyes closed. If I don't acknowledge The Room, maybe I can stay in the beautiful memory of Violet's wedding just a little longer. It feels like forever ago and like yesterday, all at the same time.

Thorne's proposal still plays in my mind as it happened in slow motion and was suspended in time.

We were on the makeshift dance floor, twinkling lights above us, my lavender dress swirling as we moved. By the time I successfully deciphered his secret message, I hadn't even realized everyone had stopped dancing, their eyes fixed on us, beaming.

When I looked back at Thorne, he was already on one knee.

My heart caught in my throat as I worried. *What if Violet feels like I am stealing her moment?*

But when I looked around, everyone was already smiling and waiting.

Thorne, looking up at me, whispered, "Don't worry, I already asked Vi."

Tears welled up in my eyes as I turned to my sister, and there she was, her face radiant, signing **"yes"** with such joy, urging me to not leave him waiting.

I said yes, of course. How could I not? The man of my dreams, in the most perfect moment, surrounded by our closest family and friends.

Thorne swept me up, twirling me around as laughter and applause filled the air, my dress floating like a soft cloud around us. The night became a blur of happiness, love, and pure magic. It felt like something out of a storybook, a moment I could relive over and over in my mind forever.

But here, in The Room, that warmth and light evaporate as soon as the memory fades. I don't want to be here. I never do, especially not after such a perfect moment, one where love filled every corner of my world. There's nothing here that can even compare.

I pretend to be asleep as I feel Charlie's hands moving me, changing my clothes. It doesn't scare me like it used to, but it still makes me wildly uncomfortable. I hate it every time it happens—being in such a vulnerable position, completely at his mercy.

I focus on keeping my eyes firmly shut, waiting for that moment of relief when it's over.

When I feel the blanket pulled back over me, I exhale softly, my muscles relaxing. Even though I no longer fear being hurt by Charlie in these moments, the relief is immediate the second I know I'm dressed again, tucked back into this hospital bed.

There's something warm against my leg, soft and vibrating with a low purr. I blink my eyes open, curiosity momentarily replacing the tension.

"Hi there," Charlie says gently.

He's smiling—actually smiling.

Once again, the happiness of my real life has created a pleasant atmosphere in my dreams. I can't complain about that.

I glance at the source of the warmth on my leg, expecting to see the cat that's purring so heavily, but I'm met with disappointment. The cat is hidden beneath my blanket, just a large, misshapen lump shifting with its movements, the steady hum of its purrs the only sign that it's really there.

Guess you're shy, I think.

I find comfort in the fact that it's there, though unseen but present, a strange contrast to the usual coldness of this place.

"Device Connected," I hear a robotic voice say.

Moments later, The Room is filled with music. I think I may be right. The mood of The Room is determined by my state of mind because I love this song. Internally, I hum; the beat makes me want to dance. I wish I wasn't paralyzed in this dream world.

Charlie is watering the many (and ever-growing) collection of plants, and internally, I smile as I see him sway to the music. I've never felt a connection to this strange man before, but somehow, this scene feels... normal? I can't explain it.

He's singing along to a Vincent Lima song as he goes about his work.

I would've never guessed it by looking at him, but Charlie can really sing. I'm glad my mind is taking it easy on me tonight. This isn't so bad.

When the music reaches the height of the chorus, Charlie walks toward me, grabbing my limp arms and swaying them back and forth, almost like we are dancing together.

The song ends, and he kisses my unmoveable hand. "You make a wonderful dance partner, my dear," he says with an exaggerated bow.

He sits on the edge of the bed, scrolling through his phone for the next song choice.

A slower song starts that I don't recognize. Charlie turns to face me again. "They called it progress, Junie."

His face is lit up with excitement, but I have no idea what he's talking about. That's not abnormal. I rarely understand what's happening here.

"The results were positive," he continues. "Everything I've done, everything *we*'ve done," he emphasizes, "*we*" like I've done something more than just lay here like a dead body. "It's paying off. It's the best news I, we, could've ever received."

Again, with the "we."

I still don't understand what he is going on about, but if he's happy and it makes this room a better place to be, then I'm gonna be happy about it, too.

"We are going to try something new," he says excitedly. "No physical therapy today, don't worry."

Charlie gently moves my legs to one side of the bed. It causes the cat to scurry and run out of the room. I didn't get to see it, but I saw the fluffy white tail running away.

He leaves for the briefest of moments and returns with a large box. He sets it on the newly created space on the bed now that my legs and the fat cat are no longer in the way.

Charlie pulls each item out of the box like Vanna White, presenting it to me like I've won some kind of lottery.

The first item is a baby's hat, like the striped kind they put on newborns in the hospital. He holds it out to me and then wraps my hand around it. If this is supposed to spark some emotional reaction, it's lost on me. But it does make me wonder if Junie has a kid, what other significance would a baby's hat have?

Charlie returns the hat gently back in the box and pulls out a photo frame. "He was so little," he says as he turns the picture toward me.

I try to squint to see the photo clearer, and apparently, Charlie can tell because he brings the image closer. It's a beautiful, dark-skinned baby. The photo is from a local hospital.

I glance back down at my arms. If this is Junie's baby, then Charlie is definitely not the father.

I don't have time to contemplate it more. Charlie is moving on to the next items in the box. He's unrolling a large poster and stares at it for a moment. "This would look nice in here, actually. Let's hang it up."

He heads toward the kitchen, disappearing, and then he's back with those sticky, no-damage picture-hanging things. He blocks my view with his body as he hangs the poster right in front of my line of vision above the TV stand.

"Ta-Da!" he says dramatically, jumping out of the way.

It's beautiful. Now that I can clearly see, it's not a poster. It's a painting.

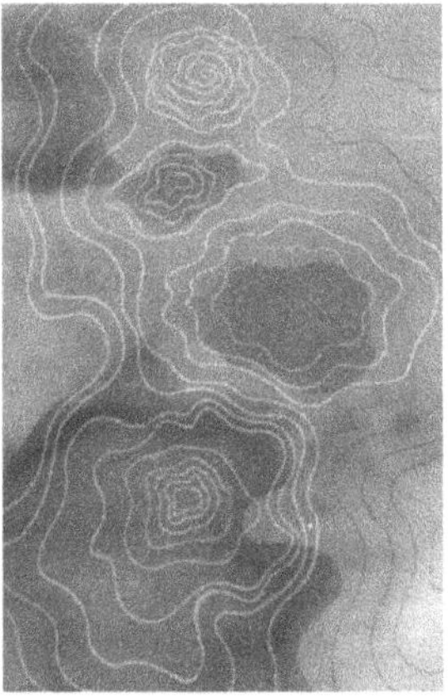

Violet would love this piece. She would die to have a piece like this in her studio. I can't explain it, but emotions are welling up inside me. I stare at the abstract streaks of purple, red, and pink and feel overcome by a strange nostalgic feeling. A tear rolls down the side of my face.

"Oh, don't cry," Charlie pleads. "It's meant to make you happy, not sad."

He wipes the tears from my face. I wish I could explain to him that I'm not sad, but I also wouldn't know how to explain the feelings in my chest.

Charlie gently squeezes my hand. As he turns back to the box, he mutters, "I think this is working."

Now, I'm hit by a certain kind of sadness. If all of this is supposed to help Junie remember something, it's all pointless. Junie isn't here, and I don't have a connection to any of this. Even worse, if this world is just something my subconscious has created to deal with my childhood trauma, then I'm more confused and have more questions than answers. This box holds memories, memories that don't belong to me.

"Hey," he says excitedly. "Remember this?"

He holds up a light pink box and tilts it to show me the top. It says, "Belated Wedding Gift! Don't blame me. You're the one who moved up the date."

There's a winky face at the end. Somehow, this calms my nerves, reminding me this is just a dream. Of course, I'd dream about wedding gifts. Marrying Thorne is the only thing on my mind 24-7.

Charlie opens the box and inside is a beautiful mahjong set. I've never played the game, but I can certainly admire the craftsmanship.

He looks down at the box, and his cheeks turn a bright red.

Charlie looks up at me, and our eyes lock. "And you said Strip Mahjong wasn't a thing," he says with an embarrassed laugh. "But I beat you enough times to prove you wrong."

I don't know if I have the ability to blush in this body, but the heat spreading across me feels like I can.

I look down at my hand, but there's no wedding ring. Internally, I chuckle at the plot hole my own brain has created. I'm not married > I've never received wedding gifts > hence, I've never played any type of "Strip" Anything with this man.

Charlie tucks the box away, and now I'm playing my own game. "Spot the Plot Holes." That's how I know when I'm dreaming, things don't line up and make sense. Let's see what else I'm making mistakes on.

Next, he pulls out a baseball cap. He's already laughing before he shows me the front. "Oh, man," he says, wiping a happy tear from his eyes. "I've never been more disgusted or attracted to you than the day you won this."

Now I need to know what's on that hat.

He puts the hat on his head, "What do you think?"

It's a blue hat with a burger graphic and battle flags crossed behind it. "I Came, I Ate, I Conquered." It's from a Jo's Burgers eating competition labeled 2021.

Another plot hole! Firstly, I could never win an eating contest. The thought of it makes me gag. Secondly, it's 2019, so I can't even begin to explain my brain's reasoning for that error.

Charlie makes his way through the rest of the items, and time passes quickly enough.

I find a few more plot holes, like a photo of people I've never seen before, and there is even a picture of my apartment. My real apartment. But the apartment is completely empty, and my brain hasn't bothered to fill the photo with furniture. My brain is lazier than I realize, which is oddly amusing to contemplate.

Charlie loads most things back in the box but puts some out for display on the TV stand. The trinkets he decides to keep on display make sense. It gives this sterile room a more homey feel. For a moment, I wonder if all of these things will still be here the next time I'm back in The Room.

He is back on his phone, searching for a new song. As soon as it starts, I recognize it immediately.

Charlie sways like he's dancing with an invisible spirit. I close my eyes to enjoy the song. My mind is being nice to me today.

In my mind's eye, I'm back on the dance floor with Thorne. I'm still his girlfriend, moments from becoming his fiance. I'm almost experiencing an out-of-body feeling, watching Thorne and I dance together from outside myself. *Thank you, brain*, I think.

My eyes are closed as I sing the song in my mind.

I love you, Thorne. I'm going to come home to you as soon as I can.

Thorne is what's real. He is my home. This room is not my prison; it's to remind me what's most important. *I love you. I love you. I love you, Thorne. Thank you brain.*

I open my eyes, feeling a peace that I have never experienced here before.

Charlie stares at me wide-eyed. What's happened?

"Junie?" he says, full of emotion.

I follow his line of sight to my right hand and see that, somehow, I am tapping two fingers against the blanket to the beat of the music.

I am moving.

38

Chapter Thirty-Eight

I slide into the booth, my heart racing with excitement and nerves as I settle in next to Violet and Mei. The cozy atmosphere of Thorne's restaurant envelopes us, the table illuminated by soft lights that glint off my new engagement ring. My fingers fidget with the band as I catch sight of it, the sparkle reflecting all the love I feel around me.

"Wow! Rose, it's beautiful!" Violet's eyes sparkle as she gestures toward my ring with exaggerated flair.

"Do you have a date yet?" Mei signs, her hands moving gracefully.

I shake my head and feel my cheek ache in response to my wide smile. **"Not yet! We want to keep it low-key, maybe a small spring or summer wedding. You know, something intimate."**

Thorne catches my gaze from across the table, and my heart does a little flip. He has that look in his eyes—the kind that makes me feel like I am the only person in the world. It's admiration and awe, and I can feel the warmth radiating between us.

I quickly shift my focus back to the girls, though it's hard to ignore the way his eyes linger on me.

"Okay, but what about the honeymoon?" Cam interjects, leaning forward with a teasing grin. **"You must have a destination in mind?"**

I laugh, feeling giddy. **"I've been thinking about Italy or maybe Scotland."**

Violet jumps in, her enthusiastic signing infectious. **"Cam and I went to Krabi, Thailand, for our honeymoon, and it was incredible! We** visited the Ao Nang Elephant Sanctuary. You would love it, Rose! We got to feed, bathe, and play with rescued elephants!"

"I can't believe you guys didn't take me!" I mock-pout, throwing my hands up dramatically.

The girls giggle, and I glance at Thorne, who is clearly imagining our future together.

Violet leans in, her eyes mischievous. "But let me tell you, the hardest part of marriage is definitely not having the bed to yourself anymore!"

Cam shoots her a smirk. "That's not what you said last night," he quips.

The table erupts with laughter.

Violet's cheeks transform to crimson, and she swats Cam's arm. "You're terrible!" she signs, half-laughing, half-embarrassed.

Mei waves dramatically to calm us down. "Settle down, you two! This is a *family* dinner," she teases.

"Family, yes," Cam shoots back, raising an eyebrow. "No one said anything about it being family-friendly!"

"Guys, come on!" Violet's signing more serious now, her face still red, but she's laughing along with the rest of us.

"Just teasing, Vi," Cam says, reaching across the table to hold her hand, their fingers intertwining.

The warmth radiates from their connection, and I feel a swell of happiness for them.

The waiter brings out our beautiful dinner: pan-seared duck, fennel, mashed potato purée, crispy Brussels sprouts with shallots, and a divine cherry sauce. My mouth waters at the sight, and we all take a moment to savor the feast laid before us.

The rich flavors blend together beautifully, and we fall into a comfortable silence, relishing the exquisite meal.

Then, Mei waves to get our attention. **"I have some news,"** she signs, her expression serious yet excited.

All eyes are on her, and I feel anticipation and concern wash over us.

"I'm going home to China for a few months to help my grandparents move condos," she confesses. A hush falls over the table.

"I promise I'll be back in time for the wedding!" she adds, swearing with her fingers.

While I am excited for her to travel and help her family, I don't want her to go. The thought of not having Mei around for the next few months feels heavy, a void I'm not sure how to fill.

We all hug tightly, a comforting embrace that speaks of our bond and the memories we share.

"But tonight's not about that," Mei signs, breaking the hug with a bright smile.

She raises her wine glass high, her spirit undeterred. **"Tonight is for celebrating Thorne and Rose!"**

Our glasses meet with a clink, the sound resonating through the air like a promise of our friendship.

We settle back into laughter and easy conversations, the camaraderie feeling like a warm blanket around us. I can't describe a more perfect night, the five of us together, filled with food and love.

Throughout the night, Violet and Cam share the photos from their honeymoon. They are not kidding. Krabi is beyond gorgeous. The white beaches, the clear blue sea, the green mountain cliffs. Every photo is breathtaking.

Violet shows photos they have taken with the rescue elephants at the sanctuary. She explains that it costs the sanctuary thousands of dollars to save these elephants from work camps. But once they are rehabilitated, they live a life of luxury.

I gesture to Thorne, asking what he thinks about Thailand instead of Europe.

"I'D GO ANYWHERE WITH YOU," he says in response.

My life, my love, my family, and even my dreams are all falling perfectly into place.

39

Chapter Thirty-Nine

The day to drop Mei off at the airport comes too quickly.

"Promise me you'll be back in time for the wedding?" I say, practically begging for reassurance.

"Of course," she says confidently. "I wouldn't miss it for the world."

Violet and Cam have to drive to Pennsylvania for his grandfather's funeral, which Mei understands. But now it feels strange standing in the airport drop-off lane without Violet here.

We embrace for a long time, and then I pull Mei's luggage out of the trunk.

"You sure you have everything you need?" I ask.

"I'm only going to be gone for ten weeks," she says. "If I run out of something, I'm sure I can get it over there. Most of our products here are from China anyways."

She's right, of course. Mei's not going to the middle of nowhere. She's going to the ninth most populated city in China and will be surrounded by 11 million people. If she runs out of toiletries, there's bound to be a convenience store nearby to hold her over.

"I'm going to miss you so much," I say as tears fill my eyes. "We've never been apart for this long in our entire lives."

"I'm going to miss you too," she says, clearly trying not to get emotional. "I'll video call you and Violet as much as I can, and I'll bring back gifts."

"Oooh," I joke. "I'll take one of those red envelopes that are stuffed with cash."

She scoffs at me. "Yeah, right. I don't even get those. The best I can promise is a fortune cookie that says something cryptic like 'Cash will come your way when you least expect it.'"

We both laugh, trying to avoid how sad we feel.

The time comes when we can no longer extend our goodbyes, or Mei will risk missing her plane. We hug once more, and I watch her walk through the sliding doors.

I sit in my car, watching her approach the check-in counter through the window. I'm really going to miss her.

Repeated honking pulls me from my thoughts. I look in my rearview mirror, and the guy behind me is blaring his horn and giving me a middle finger out the window. He points to the sign, "DROP OFF PARKING ONLY - 5 MINUTES."

He yells profanity, telling me to get out of the way.

"Alright! Alright! I'm moving!" I yell out the window as I shift into Drive.

I head to Sam's to get started on my work, but I know it's going to be a struggle. How can I focus when my best friend is flying to the other side of the earth?

40

CHAPTER FORTY

I wake up to the sharp tug of electrodes pulling at my skin. It takes me a second to understand what's happening.

My body twitches—jerks, really—involuntary movements that make my muscles ache and pulse. I can hear the low hum of the machine next to me and feel the mechanical buzzing through my limbs.

This isn't right.

The Room feels more oppressive than last time, the lights casting long shadows. Panic rises in my chest as I struggle to focus. I'm supposed to be happy. I'm supposed to be living my life, marrying the man I love, and planning my future. But I'm here, and I am in pain. I know I'm upset about Mei leaving, but I don't think I should be electrocuted for it.

I close my eyes, trying to remember what my therapist said: Break the barrier. Communicate.

I try to move like I did last time I was here, but the electricity running through my muscles makes that impossible. My heart pounds as I snap my eyes open, focusing on the only thing I can control: my eyelids.

... --- ...

S-O-S.

I blink over and over, willing Charlie to notice. I need him to understand. I need him to save me.

His face, blurry at first, slowly sharpens as he leans in closer, watching me. For a second, I think he might actually understand me—really see me.

"You're not in danger, Junie," Charlie says quietly, his voice calm. "It's just FES. Functional electrical stimulation. It's supposed to help your muscles make progress. You moved on your own, remember? This is just to help speed the process along. It won't hurt you."

It's already hurting me. My muscles jerk again, twitching violently under the electric pulses.

My eyelids flutter from the strain, but I keep my gaze on him. He understands me, and yet... nothing changes. He's still there, overseeing it all like everything is fine.

Exhaustion overwhelms me as the machine keeps going, pulsing through me until it finally stops. I sag, heavy and limp, like I've been drained of every ounce of strength I had left. My muscles are sore as if I've just run a marathon, and I've never experienced anything like this before.

Suddenly, Charlie is over me, and he brushes my hair out of my face. "You're doing so good, babe."

He starts removing all of the electrodes from my body. "You're getting so much stronger. You'll be up and running in no time."

I actually roll my eyes like that would happen.

Charlie applies an ointment to every spot an electrode was. Now that I'm more settled, I glance around the room. All of the trinkets that he set out last time are still on the TV stand. The painting is still displayed above it.

He massages my muscles, and I must admit that it feels really good. I feel a slight buzz running through my limbs, as if my whole body has fallen asleep, but the pressure is comforting.

The last time I was in this bed, I had found so many plot holes during our little game of "Memory Lane." Now, with this new experience, I am left wondering what the purpose of this new therapy is.

Charlie is so close to my face that I try to take one last effort to communicate, a shot in the dark to bring an end to The Room.

.... . .-.. .--. (HELP)

"Are you in pain?" he asks.

I am filled with hope. He understands me.

"They said most people don't feel any pain with FES, just some temporary soreness."

He looks through the vials on the medicine tray. "I followed all the instructions, but maybe I had it set too high."

Charlie prepares a syringe, flicking the air bubbles out of the liquid. "I'll turn it down next time, I promise."

He plunges the needle into my IV port.

I don't know if my therapist is right; if communication unlocks the prison door. But I do know that time is just about up. I have about five minutes before my world will go dark. He dosed me with the good stuff.

41

CHAPTER FORTY-ONE

DR. J. WIESE - PSYCHOLOGIST

Dr. Wiese's office feels brighter today. I can feel the warmth of the sunlight on my back as I sit in my usual chair, my hands resting lightly on my lap. For the first time in a long while, I feel like the worst is behind me.

"You seem different today, Rose," Dr. Wiese says, her perceptive eyes scanning me with curiosity and warmth. "There's something in your demeanor that I haven't seen in a while. What's changed?"

I can't help the small smile that tugs at my lips. "I think...I finally made progress in The Room."

Her brows raise slightly, but she doesn't interrupt, letting me explain in my own time.

"I was able to communicate," I continue. "I blinked out 'help' in Morse code to Charlie. And he answered me. I really think he understood me."

Dr. Wiese leans forward slightly, her expression a mix of intrigue and encouragement. "What did he say?"

"He asked if I was in pain," I say, exhaling a shaky breath. "And he said he's trying to help me. I don't fully understand what that means, but for the first time...it felt like I wasn't just trapped forever."

Dr. Wiese nods. "That's significant. This is a great first step in understanding the things that your subconscious is trying to tell us. You said he wants to help you—what do you think that help might look like?"

I pause, considering her question. "Maybe it's about letting go," I say slowly. "Or facing things I haven't wanted to face. Either way, it feels like I'm getting closer to some kind of answer. And for the first time, I'm not as scared of what that might be."

Her smile widens slightly. "You've been doing so much work to process your grief, your past, and your sense of self. Maybe this communication is a reflection of that—your subconscious telling you that you're ready to heal."

"It feels that way," I admit. "For so long, The Room has been this place of fear and confusion. But now...I don't know. Maybe it's not just a nightmare. Maybe it's something I need to go through to get to the other side."

"That's beautiful," she says softly. "And I think it's a testament to your resilience, Rose. Even in the face of these terrifying experiences, you've found a way to connect, to understand, and to grow. That's remarkable."

For a moment, we sit in comfortable silence.

"Do you think this means I'm almost done with The Room?" I ask hesitantly.

She tilts her head, considering. "It's hard to say. Healing isn't always linear, and sometimes, we revisit things before we're truly ready to let them go. But from where I'm sitting, it sounds like you're closer than ever to finding peace with it."

Her words give me a glimmer of hope, and I cling to it tightly as I leave her office after our session.

As I walk down the street, I let my thoughts wander. If this really is the beginning of the end of The Room, what comes next? Can I finally leave behind the nightmares that have haunted me for so long?

I look to the sky and let the sun warm my face. I take a deep breath, the fresh air filling my lungs.

Maybe these nightmares will lose their grip. And when they do, they will leave behind something even stronger: the hope of waking up to something better.

$$42$$

Chapter Forty-Two

I prop my phone against the coffee maker, stirring my cereal with one hand and glancing down at the screen as Mei's name pops up. I smile —I haven't heard from her in a few days, and I've been missing her more than I care to admit.

The video call connects, and I'm about to crack some joke about the time difference when I freeze.

Mei's crying. Her face is blotchy, her eyes red and swollen, and she's trying so hard to compose herself, but it's obvious she's been sobbing for a while.

My stomach drops. "Oh my God, what's wrong?" I ask, the cereal instantly forgotten.

She shakes her head, struggling to get the words out. "I... I don't think I'm gonna make it back for the wedding."

My breath catches. "What do you mean?"

Her chin trembles as she wipes her tears, trying to keep it together. "It's really bad here, Rose. So many are sick. The hospitals are overrun, and death... there's just so much death."

I blink, trying to wrap my head around what she's saying. The usual bustling energy in her face is replaced with a heavy kind of emptiness, like she's carrying something far too big for her to bear.

"What are you talking about?" I ask.

Mei takes a deep breath, her eyes hollow as she speaks. "Wuhan is officially in lockdown. We can't leave. I can't board a plane. I'm stuck here."

The words hit me like a punch to the gut. "You're scaring me, Mei... What's happened?"

She looks away from the camera for a second, her lips trembling as she tries to find the words. "There's some virus... It's spreading fast all through China. Everyone is getting sick. I mean, everyone."

For a moment, I can't breathe. "Are you staying safe?"

The question feels ridiculous the second it leaves my mouth. Of course, she's not safe. If she is safe, she wouldn't be crying like this, sounding like she's breaking apart piece by piece.

"I don't really have a choice," she says flatly.

Mei wipes her eyes again, but the tears keep falling. "The borders are closed—no one in or out. We're stuck here. Everyone's been ordered to stay inside—only one person can leave the house for essentials, and even then, it's dangerous."

I can't stop staring at her, trying to read between the lines of what she's saying. Mei's eyes are wide with fear, and for the first time since I've known her, she looks utterly lost.

"There are checkpoints everywhere," she continues, her voice shaking. "The police check your temperature, your health status, and they've set up these... these makeshift hospital tents in the streets because there's no more room in the hospitals. You can hear the sirens all day, and there are drones flying overhead to make sure no one's breaking the rules. It feels like we're trapped."

A cold shiver runs down my spine. This sounds like something out of a dystopian novel, not real life. I watch her eyes as they dart around like she's constantly on guard.

Mei looks exhausted. The usually vibrant person I know, the one who smiles through every challenge, is being swallowed whole by something darker than I can understand.

"I... I don't know what to do, Rose," she whispers. "They're saying we might run out of food soon. Families are being told to ration what they have because no one knows when things will get better. I'm scared. I'm so scared."

It feels like a knife twisting in my chest. I don't know how to respond. I've never seen her like this—so vulnerable, so small. I wish I could reach through the screen and hug her, tell her that everything's going to be okay, but the words stick in my throat.

Still, I try. I have to try. "Mei, it sounds like the government has things under control. They're locking everything down for a reason. I'm sure it'll blow over before you know it. You'll make it. I have no doubt that you'll be back in time for the wedding."

Even as I say it, I feel how pointless the words are. They don't match the reality I see on her face. She's living a nightmare, and all I have are empty reassurances.

Mei gives a shaky smile, but I can tell she doesn't mean it.

"I hope so," she whispers, her voice barely audible. "I really, really hope so."

Her gaze drifts off-screen for a second, and I can see her trying to pull herself back together to be the strong, unflappable Mei I've always known. But there's no hiding it now. She's scared, and I am too.

No matter what I say, I can't protect her from this. I can't even fully understand what she's going through. All I can do is sit here, miles away, and pray that she'll be okay.

Deep down, I feel this sinking dread settling in my bones. Something about this doesn't feel right. Something tells me that this isn't just going to blow over. I watch as Mei wipes away another tear, her hands trembling slightly.

This virus... this lockdown... it might be bigger than anything we've ever faced. I hope it goes as quickly as it began.

43

CHAPTER FORTY-THREE

*N*o. No. No.

  I communicated! Charlie understood me. I thought I was done with this.

I am frustrated. I am tired. My best friend is stuck in China, living in the "Based on a True Story" edition of the movie Contagion. My wedding is getting closer and closer. I have so many other things to worry about. I shouldn't be here.

"Oh, you're up!" Charlie says excitedly before I can even see him. "I have some new things for us to try."

I'm not a guinea pig, Charlie. I don't want to play your stupid games.

"I recognized your blinking," he says, far too overjoyed for someone stating the obvious. "I'm hoping I wasn't just imagining it, so we are going to test it."

I stare at him. I am not in the mood for this today.

"I'll ask you some questions," he says eagerly. "If the answer is yes, blink once. If it's no, blink twice. Got it?"

Blink.

"Do you know where you are?"

Blink.

"Oh, good." He sounds shocked by that answer. "Do you remember who you are?"

Blink. .-. --- ... . ROSE.

"Junie," he sounds like he's going to burst into a sob. "You came back to me."

.-. --- ... . ROSE, I blink again.

I'm not Junie. Can't he see I'm not Junie? .-. --- ... .

He clears his throat, trying to recollect himself and push away his emotions. "Are you in pain?"

Blink. Blink.

"Can you move?"

Blink. Blink.

"Do you remember what happened to you?"

Blink. Blink.

He sighs, dropping his head into his hands. My answer disappoints him, and I don't know why. His shoulders tremble. He's sobbing.

"Do you remember me?" His voice breaks my heart. I hesitate. He's already so broken. I don't think he's a bad guy. I don't want to hurt him more than he already is. But I can't lie, I don't know him from Adam.

Blink. Blink.

He nods so slowly that it's almost painful to watch. The tears have stopped falling, and a new emotion has taken over. Charlie clears his throat again. "Excuse me."

He steps away from the bed and heads toward the bathroom. Before closing the door, he makes eye contact with me one last time. Charlie blinks as more tears suddenly fall from his eyes, and the door closes, leaving me all alone. The door lock clicks, followed by the most painful-sounding howl coming from behind it.

I now know what the sound of a heart shattering into a million little pieces sounds like, and it will haunt me for the rest of my life.

44

Chapter Forty-Four

Dr. J. Wiese - Psychologist

Suddenly, I'm sitting in my therapist's office. It takes a minute for me to reorient myself. My body still feels heavy, like I'm dragging the weight of The Room with me. I shift uncomfortably in the chair.

My therapist sits across from me, her hands resting gently on her notebook. She's waiting, giving me space to speak, but I don't know where to start.

"You were wrong," I blurt, the words tumbling from my mouth before I can stop them. "I communicated with him again—Charlie, I mean. We had a full conversation just by blinking. He knew what I was saying, but it didn't change anything. I'm still... stuck. It didn't matter."

Dr. Wiese nods, her expression soft but focused. "That must have been incredibly frustrating for you. Remember how I stated healing isn't always linear? This is still progress, even if it doesn't feel like it right now."

I let out a harsh laugh, shaking my head. "Progress? I had to break an imaginary man's heart. I was left entirely alone while he sobbed in the bathroom. That's not frustrating or significant. It's borderline torture."

"It's hard when the people around us don't respond the way we expect or hope," she says with a steady voice. "But what you did was a breakthrough. Progress doesn't always happen the way we want it to or as quickly as we'd like."

I want to scream. Her assurance feels hollow, like a promise that's been broken a thousand times.

"It feels pointless," I mutter. "I'm fighting to get through to him, but I'm still stuck. The Room keeps dragging me back, and I can't break free."

Dr. Wiese pauses, her eyes searching mine. "Maybe it's not just about getting through to Charlie. Maybe it's also about finding a way to regain your own control. To find some peace, even when things feel out of your control."

I shake my head, my frustration boiling over. "I've had some peaceful nights in The Room. I even moved two of my fingers at one point," I say while holding up my pointer and middle finger, reenacting the way I tapped to the beat. "After I got engaged to Thorne, The Room wasn't so scary anymore. I have a sense of control now, but it's not changing anything."

She looks at me with that patient, understanding expression she always wears. "It's not going to happen all at once, Rose. But you're stronger than you think. You've already made progress, even if it doesn't feel that way."

I don't know what to say to that. I don't feel stronger. I feel... tired. Exhausted in a way that sleep can't fix. I nod mechanically, signaling that I've heard her, but the words don't sink in.

When I leave the office, I'm still carrying the same weight on my shoulders. Nothing feels lighter. Nothing feels resolved.

The city buzzes around me, the traffic and people moving past in a blur, but I feel detached like I'm stuck in slow motion while everything else speeds by.

I take a deep breath, but the air feels heavy and thick. Nothing's changed. And that's the scariest part.

45

CHAPTER FORTY-FIVE

MARCH 2020

I don't want to get up. I don't want to face the world today. The wedding is less than a week away, and Mei is still trapped in China.

Every day, she sends messages, letting me know she is okay, that she is following all the rules, and that things will get better soon. But it isn't enough. She should be here, not stuck halfway across the world with no way back. I flick on the TV, desperate for a distraction from the endless pit of disappointment gnawing at me.

"Breaking news: Governor Andrew Cuomo has passed the 'New York State on PAUSE' executive order."

The words hit like a freight train. I freeze as the news anchor drones on about lockdowns, social distancing, and the rapid spread of COVID-19. Everything is shutting down.

My mind goes blank, the droning of the TV fading into white noise. I can't move, can't think.

I'm not 100% sure how long I disassociated, but my phone rings, jolting me back to the present. Thorne.

I barely have the strength to answer, but I do. "H-hello?" I say.

"Baby, did you see the news this morning?" His concern is palpable, like a warm hand reaching out to me through the phone.

"Yeah…" I whisper, and suddenly, everything I've been holding inside for weeks spills out. I burst into tears. Ugly, messy, overwhelming tears.

"I know. I'm so sorry." Thorne soothes.

I sense how much this pains him. "I've been getting messages from all the vendors. We're getting the deposit back on everything." He tries his best to sound hopeful. "That's good news, right?"

"Yeah," I choke out. "That's good."

"You home?" He asks.

"Still in bed. I was trying to get some work done, but I'm too distract-ed," I admit.

"I'm coming over." He doesn't ask. He has already decided.

I try to protest, but he cuts me off. "I'm already on my way."

I drag myself out of bed, forcing myself into the bathroom to brush my hair and teeth—anything to feel remotely human.

I throw on fresh pajamas and a sports bra. I'm not ready to let Thorne see me in that raw, unfiltered state.

After unlocking the door, I crawl back into bed and text.

> Rose: *Doors unlocked. Let yourself in.*

An hour later, the door creaks open. His familiar footsteps pad down the hall. There he is, standing in my bedroom doorway with a paper bag from Jo's Burgers and two banana milkshakes in hand.

"I thought you could use some snacks," he says, holding up the bag with a sheepish grin.

"You've never looked sexier," I joke, and for a moment, the weight of my agony lifts.

We both laugh.

He makes everything feel lighter.

Setting my laptop aside, I officially give up on getting any assignments finished today. We tear into the food, tapping our burgers together in half-hearted cheers. It feels absurd, but in this moment, it's comforting.

"So," Thorne begins cautiously. "What do you want to do about the wedding? We could postpone if you want until—"

I kiss him, interrupting his words. A kiss that says everything I don't have the words for.

As I pull away, I whisper, "I don't want to wait. I'd marry you today if I could."

He looks at me, his eyes gleaming with that mischievous spark I love so much. "What if we did?"

"What?" I blink at him, unsure if he's serious.

"Let's get married today," he says, his excitement growing. "We already have the marriage license. Cam has his officiant license. The restaurant's closed for the foreseeable future... We can just do it there. Have a nice dinner, just us, Vi, and Cam. Mei and Georgie could join on Zoom. It'll be like they're really here."

I stare at him, processing his words. "Are you serious?"

He grabs my hands, his smile wide and sincere. "I want to marry you. You want to marry me. Why wait?"

I look around my room, my heart pounding. A last-minute elopement definitely isn't what we had planned, but... it feels right. If I'm going to be locked down, I'd rather have Thorne with me through whatever comes. I can feel the fear and hopelessness melt away, replaced by something warm, something hopeful.

"I say... yes." I say, filled with excitement. "Let's do it."

We spend the next thirty minutes calling everyone—Violet, Cam, our family, sending out Zoom invites, coordinating it all. By the time I make it through our guest list, my phone battery is at 14%, but my spirits are soaring.

"Violet's on her way," I tell Thorne. "She's gonna help me get ready."

He kisses my forehead gently. "I'll go grab my suit and meet Cam at the restaurant. I'll see you soon, Junebug." He winks as he exits, leaving me breathless.

The doorbell rings. I look through the peephole and see Violet.

As soon as I open the door, we hug tightly, and neither of us needs words.

She signs, **"Thorne's best idea yet!"**

I nod, tears of joy filling my eyes as we head to the bathroom to start getting ready.

Violet slides into her satin sage green dress, glowing as I put my hands on her belly.

"Eighteen weeks already," she signs proudly, her smile radiant.

I lean down and whisper to her stomach, "I can't wait to meet you."

Violet raises an eyebrow, signing, **"What did you say?"**

"It's a secret," I respond with a teasing wink.

Finally, we are ready. I stand in front of the mirror, and my simple yet elegant blush pink wedding gown hugs my curves in all the right places. This day has not followed anything I had imagined for my wedding day, but at this moment, I feel absolutely beautiful.

We arrive at the restaurant, and as I step inside, I'm blown away. The tables are lit with candles, the lights dimmed just perfectly. It feels like a dream. A perfect, intimate dream.

Thorne waits for me at the far end of the dining room, his smile wide and full of love. I can hardly look at anything else.

We say our vows with Cam officiating, his words steady in both speech and sign. The world fades away, and all that exists at this moment is us.

When Cam finally says, "I now pronounce you Mr. and Mrs. Thorne," we kiss, and I'm struck by the realization that this is how our wedding is meant to be.

Our guests on Zoom erupt into applause, their tiny faces lighting up the screen in neat little squares. But it's Mei's face that catches my eye—her smile trembling just a bit, her eyes glistening.

At this moment, I feel everything that has been stripped away from us by distance and circumstances.

My best friend, my sister in spirit, who is supposed to stand beside me today, is thousands of miles away. But as our eyes lock through the screen, none of that matters. She is always with me, even when she's out of my reach. I can feel that now.

"Rose," Mei whispers. "You're glowing."

Tears blur my vision as I try to smile back, my throat tightening. **"It's not the same without you,"** I manage to sign, knowing she can still see me clearly even through her teary eyes.

"I know," she signs back, her fingers moving gracefully despite the obvious ache in her heart. **"But you're still the most beautiful bride I've ever seen."**

I blink rapidly, trying to hold back the flood of emotions. **"I MISS YOU SO MUCH,"** I say, my hands trembling now.

"I'M RIGHT HERE," Mei holds her hand up to the screen as if she can reach through it and hold mine. "I'M ALWAYS WITH YOU. TODAY, TOMORROW—FOREVER."

That is the final nail in the coffin. The tears spill over, and I bite my lip to stop the gasp that threatens to escape.

I touch the screen, wishing more than anything that it is her hand I am holding instead of this cold piece of glass.

"I love you," I sign one last time before I pull away.

She smiles, nods, and mouths, "I love you too."

Thorne gently squeezes my shoulder, grounding me as I dab my face, attempting to save the last remnants of my makeup. This definitely isn't the wedding we had planned, but it is ours—and it's been perfect in every way.

After a while, we thank our guests and say our goodbyes, the Zoom meeting disappearing with a click. Then it is just the four of us—Thorne, Cam, Violet, and me—alone in the soft glow of candlelight. The restaurant feels magical like a scene pulled straight from a fairytale.

We sit at one of the tables, the flickering candles casting warm shadows across the walls. The aroma of the food Thorne and Cam have prepared fills the air, but I can barely focus on anything besides the man sitting across from me.

Thorne keeps stealing glances at me between bites, his lips quirking into that little smile that makes my stomach flutter every time.

"I don't think I've ever seen you this quiet," I tease, kicking his foot lightly under the table.

Thorne chuckles, his eyes sparkling. **"I'm just admiring my wife. Is that a crime?"**

"Your wife, huh?" I bite my lip, feeling the heat rise to my cheeks. **"I think I could get used to hearing that."**

He leans forward, resting his chin in his hand, looking at me like I am the only person in the world. **"You're gonna be hearing it for the rest of your life."**

After dinner and eating our slices of cake, Violet and Cam exchange a knowing look. The kind that only people who know you better than you know yourself can share.

"I think we'll leave you two lovebirds to it," Violet signs with a smirk, standing up and pulling Cam with her. **"Enjoy your first night as Mr. and Mrs."**

Once they leave, the restaurant seems so quiet, but in the best way. Just Thorne and me bathed in the candlelight like the world has narrowed down to just us.

Thorne reaches across the table, taking my hand in his. His thumb traces gentle circles against my skin, sending shivers down my spine. "I still can't believe I get to call you my wife," he murmurs.

I squeeze his hand, my heart swelling with so much love I don't know what to do with it. "I can't believe I get to call you my husband," I whisper back. "I've been dreaming about this day for so long, and now that it's here, it doesn't feel real."

He stands, pulling me into his arms without a word.

We sway gently to the music playing in the background, his hands resting on the small of my back, mine around his neck.

I bury my face in his chest, breathing him in, letting the steady rhythm of his heartbeat calm the storm of emotions inside me.

"You know," I say. "You're not getting rid of me now."

"Good," he whispers into my hair, his lips brushing my ear. "Because I never want to spend another night without you."

I pull back just enough to look at him, our faces inches apart. "I guess that means we should head home then, right?" I tease.

His eyes darken, and a slow smile spreads, dimpling his cheeks. "Are you sure you want to leave? We could stay here, have the whole place to ourselves..."

I pretend to consider it, biting my lip. "Tempting. But I think I have a better idea."

"Oh?" His brow arches in that sexy way that drives me crazy. "And what might that be, Mrs. Thorne?"

I stand on my tiptoes, my lips brushing his ear. "How about we go home, and I show you exactly how much I love being your wife?"

Thorne groans, his hands tightening on my waist. "You really know how to torture a guy, don't you?"

I laugh, pulling him toward the door. "Come on, husband. Let's go home."

As soon as we enter the apartment, Thorne turns to me with that mischievous grin that always gets me in trouble.

I raise an eyebrow. "Why are you smiling like that?" I ask, feeling suspicious.

"No reason," he says, but the twinkle in his eye tells me he's full of it.

Then he takes off his tie and steps behind me, sliding the silk over my eyes.

I laugh, my hands instantly going to cover his. "Oh, so this is how our wedding night is going to start?"

He chuckles, low and teasing. "Not exactly, but you'll see. Hands out."

I hesitate, loving the way he's practically vibrating with excitement. "I don't know," I tease, smirking even though he can't see it. "I'm not sure I'm into blindfolds and mystery surprises. Is this your way of introducing me to your weird kinks?"

Thorne leans close to my ear, his breath warm on my neck. "I promise you'll enjoy this one. Now stop stalling and do as I say, Mrs. Thorne."

Mrs. Thorne. God, I can get used to hearing that.

"Is that any way to talk to your wife?" I tease back, but I extend my hands anyway.

His fingers brush against mine briefly, and then something soft is placed into my palms. Instantly, I know.

I rip the blindfold off and gasp, "Dolly!"

The kitten blinks up at me with wide, curious eyes, and my heart practically explodes. "How did you—"

"I might've made a quick stop at Sam's earlier. Consider it a wedding gift," Thorne says, trying to play it cool.

I see he's just as pleased with himself as ever.

I stare down at the fluffy ball of fur, then back up at him, utterly overwhelmed with love for this man. "You really do know how to sweep a girl off her feet, don't you?"

He shrugs, grinning. "I figured if I was locking you down for life, I should probably get you a kitten to seal the deal."

I laugh and kiss him again, this time deeper. Dolly wriggles in my arms, and I gently place her down before pulling Thorne even closer. I hold onto his collar as if I'm afraid he'll float away.

"Well," I say, glancing toward the bedroom door, giving him a mischievous look of my own. "Now that I've gotten my surprise, I think it's time for yours."

Thorne raises a brow, his hands already on my waist. "Oh? And what would that be?"

I give him a playful grin as I lead him toward the bedroom. "Let's just say it's a wedding night you won't forget anytime soon."

He chuckles darkly, stepping ahead of me to open the door. "I'm counting on it, Mrs. Thorne."

46

Chapter Forty-Six

*R*egain *a sense of control. Communicate. Move your body. You are in control.*

I repeat these thoughts a few times before committing to opening my eyes. I'm scared to see Charlie after the last time. I don't think he'd hurt me in a million years; he's proven that much. But I think my communication goals may have broken his spirit, and I don't know how he'll treat me after something like that.

I glance around the room, and it is dim, with no lights on and no sun streaming through the windows. I squint into the darkness, but I think I'm alone. It's eerily quiet here too.

Occasionally, in the distance, I hear the jingle of the bell on the cat's collar, but other than that, it is deathly still.

I may as well take advantage of my time alone and try to find my sense of control. I don't believe it will help at this point, but I've got to at least give it a shot.

There's no one here to communicate with, and I already have communicated with Charlie so much that I no longer believe that's part of the solution.

You have to move.

I try to move my fingers the same way I did that first time. I focus all my energy, all my strength. I even send out a little prayer that this will work.

Nothing. Not a single movement.

I take a deep breath. I'm not going to give up. I can feel a slight voluntary muscle contraction course through my body. A spark of determination fuels me and is strengthened when I realize I'm able to morph my face into a small smirk. I'm doing it. I have never felt more empowered.

I'm hyper-fixated on my toes, urging these piggies to go to the market, or anywhere they wanted, really, when Charlie comes bursting through the door. He has a frantic mania about him that actually concerns me.

"So I talked to the doctor," his words spill a mile per minute. "She said we need to find what you can control, and maybe we can unlock this whole thing."

Ironic. My doctor said the same thing, I think. What a coink-a-dink.

"So what should we try first?" He looks at me with puppy dog energy, like a newly adopted pet seeking his owner's acceptance.

I don't think I can give him what he's looking for.

"I got these flashcards," he says, holding them in the air. "They're for little kids, but I thought we could use them to check what you remember."

Charlie pulls out the first card with a red apple.

Oh boy. This is going to be fun.

"Is this a red apple? Remember, once for yes, twice for no."

Blink.

"Ok, awesome."

The next card has a Dalmatian on it. "Is this a chihuahua?" he asks.

Internally, I chuckle. Blink. Blink.

This continues on for way too long, and my eyes are burning from the effort.

Charlie grabs a paper and pen and jots stuff down. "Ok, so we've determined that you have really good recognition skills. That's such a big first step."

I've been able to identify these objects since I was four, Charlie. This is not a big step. A preschooler could handle this.

"Let's check movement," he says, clearly optimistic. "You moved your fingers last time. Can you do it again?"

Blink. Blink.

"I'm sure you can! Let's just try."

Nothing.

He slips his hand into mine. "Try squeezing."

Nothing.

"Even just a little bit."

Still nothing.

"I know you can do this, Junie." I hear his disappointment. His hope is slowly fizzling out.

You have to gain control. You know it. Charlie knows it. Now do it.

I can't squeeze his hand. But my head rolls to the side, and I look at him from a different angle now. *I did it! I moved!*

It isn't exactly what I aimed for, but I did it!

Charlie is ecstatic. He jumps around the room and returns to my bedside. He grabs my face and plants about a thousand little kisses all over it.

I saved the day with a simple head movement. If that's not control, I don't know what is.

He scribbles in the notebook, writing who knows what about my "progress." Once he's done, he sets it to the side.

"Ok. You're doing great!" he assures me. "Let's test your memory next, ok?"

Blink.

He wanders to the bedroom. I am not certain it's a bedroom since I can't move past this room, but something about this apartment's layout feels familiar.

Charlie appears in the doorway a moment later, holding a photo album.

He sits on the edge of the bed and opens the book. "You're doing really great, ok?" he says shyly. "If you don't remember, it's alright. We'll keep working on it."

Charlie holds up a picture of an old man. "If you recognize something in the photos, blink once. If not, blink twice."

Blink. Blink.

His shoulders sag. "That one might be for the best, honestly."

The next photo is of a woman. It looks older and yellowed around the edges. There's something familiar about her, but I can't put my finger on it.

As if reading my mind, he moves the Polaroid closer. It looks just like Dr. Wiese, but maybe fifteen years younger. She's holding an infant in her arms, and a toddler is pulling on her floral dress.

Why would he have a photo from my therapist's Wonder Years?

Blink.

"Great! Who is this?"

-.. --- -.-. - --- .-. / .-- .. . . (Doctor Wiese)

"Really? A doctor?" Charlie looks at the photo in a sort of awe. "You never told me your mom was a doctor. I guess that's where you get your desire to take care of everyone from."

He looks at me and brushes my hair back gently. "I'm sorry you didn't get a chance to really get to know her. I would've loved to have met Joy. She sounds like a powerful woman."

Charlie tucks the Polaroid back into the box. "I mean, she raised the two most amazing women in the world, even if it was only for a little while. So I'm guessing she had to be amazing."

Joy. That was my mom's name. How did I never notice Dr. Wiese's first name was the same?

"Here's one of my favorites," he says as he shows me a photo of that child. What was his name? Glenn... something. No, Wren. Doesn't matter, though. I don't actually know him. Just an NPC that I know nothing about.

Blink. Blink.

That one hurt him. I don't understand the importance of this little boy, but not remembering him did a lot of damage.

Charlie quickly moves on to the next photo.

It's Sam. I know, Sam! From the coffee shop.

Blink.

"Really?"

Blink.

... .- – (SAM).

"Yes!" He actually screams. Charlie's so excited.

He flips to the next photo.

I'm confused because it's definitely Mei's restaurant, but it's the wrong color on the front. Mr. and Mrs. Wong are in the photo, so I know it's the right place, but I don't ever remember them repainting the place.

Blink.

His excitement grows.

The next few photos I recognize from Violet's honeymoon in Thailand.

Blink.

Blink.

Blink.

Then Charlie shows me a group photo of about twenty different people. Some I recognize, some I don't know at all. The strangest thing is that I spot myself in the photo. How? I don't know where or when this picture was taken.

"Do you recognize anyone?" he prompts.

Blink.

"Who?" Charlie asks.

.-. --- ... . (ROSE).

He points me out in the photo. How does he know me? I feel a small flare of panic set off in my stomach.

"Who else?"

I look at all the faces, and I feel strange. Thorne's sister is in this photo. I've never met her in person. How is this possible?

Blink.

--. . --- .-. --. . . (GEORGIE).

"Great! Anyone else?"

I end up pointing out Violet, Cam, a guy named Roy from the newspaper that I spoke to a few times, Frank, the head chef at Thorne's restaurant, and Jaye from Violet's art classes. There's no explainable reason why all of these people would be together in a photo or why I would be in a photo without Thorne, so I have to chalk it up to dream logic.

My brain has taken a bunch of people I know well enough, including some I've never seen before in my life, mixing them together and putting them in a photograph to trick my memory.

Charlie points to a woman. "Do you remember her?"

Is this Junie? I've never seen her before in my life.

Blink. Blink.

He seems saddened but not terribly so. I guess it's not shocking that I don't recognize every face.

Charlie looks at me, barely holding back tears. "Do you remember me?"

I don't want him to ask that again. How do I explain that he's not real, that none of this is real? How do I tell him he doesn't exist, so how can I possibly remember a figment of my imagination?

Blink. Blink.

He pats my knee and stands. All the excited energy he had is now completely zapped from his body. "Really great work today." He almost sounds proud. "The doctor will be so excited to hear about your progress."

Charlie walks toward the hallway, and a door slams shut.

I don't know why I don't wake up after that, but I end up spending what feels like a couple of hours alone.

I stare at the wall for a while and decide I should keep trying to gain control. So I practice moving my toes, fingers, face, head, all of it. Sometimes, my body listens, but most of the time, it does not.

I use all my energy, attempting movements until my brain turns to soup from exhaustion. It is time to wake up.

47

CHAPTER FORTY-SEVEN

The next few weeks of getting settled as a newly married couple amid a global pandemic are interesting, to say the least. Even though Thorne and I have been together for over two years at this point, there are still so many things to learn about a person that can only be done by living in forced proximity to him.

We both have emergency survival kits already, so running out of food or water is never a worry for us. Still, during The 2020 Great Toilet Paper Shortage, we have a few arguments about who will get the last square when we get down to the desperation point.

Thorne had shut his restaurant down completely the week of the wedding but eventually reopened for To-Go service when the money started to dry up.

During the day, I busy myself with work and have earned several promotions during this difficult time.

In the evenings, I head to the restaurant and help with the dinner rush orders. Everything is a team effort, and we've grown closer because of it.

Thorne and I gained the famous COVID-19 fifteen pounds, and Thorne's physique has slowly transformed from Gym Bro to Dad Bod, but I have no complaints about that.

After a year of surviving during the end of the world, appearances really don't matter so much anyway.

During this time, I found out that my handsome husband has been lying to me. He would sneak away to the bathroom for a forty-minute shower and return smiling like a new person afterward every few weeks. Due to the world's circumstances, he isn't able to keep his secret forever.

When I found out, I had the worst stomach ache in history... from laughing. It turns out that Thorne's luscious black hair comes in a box from Walgreens.

When he decides that a trip to the pharmacy is no longer worth the risk of a deadly illness, he has to fess up and come clean.

Unbeknownst to me, his hair changed early, like that of his sister Georgie. It's a family gene.

Thorne doesn't want people to think he is old, so he's been dyeing his hair the same shade of black since he was seventeen in high school to cover the grays.

He's only thirty-two now and has a full head of the most beautiful black and silver hair. I'm actually jealous. It would take so much bleach and dye to get my hair to the same shade as his and Georgie's, except I'll have maintenance and fried hair to deal with.

Throughout the past three years of COVID-19, my hubby has worried many times that he has become something I never agreed to. Our bodies, our hair, and even our personalities have changed somewhat. Still, there is no one else I would have rather spent these years cooped up in our small apartment with.

It isn't all flowers and sunshine. We have problems just like every other couple. There are arguments and disagreements, sure. We are living through the most stressful events in recent history.

Every step outside is a risk, a life or death situation. We both lost a lot of loved ones to an illness that spread faster than anyone could have ever imagined.

I didn't get to say goodbye to my father. I think there will always be a part of me that regrets that. He died alone in a hospital on a ventilator seven weeks and three days before the vaccine was released to the public. I can't toss a stone into an NYC intersection without hitting someone who has lost someone dear to them. Most of us don't even get a chance to say goodbye.

Violet had her baby at an overrun and understaffed hospital. She was completely alone during her delivery due to the hospital not allowing visitors. I will never forget how strong she was to go through that alone, to not even have someone who speaks her language in the room with her. Still, eleven hours later, she delivered the most beautiful boy the world had ever seen. He has his daddy's hair and his mommy's eyes. Who knew that a little bundle weighing 7 pounds, 8 ounces named Maverick St. Wren Kingston could completely steal your heart and change your worldview?

I didn't get to meet him until he was already eleven months old due to the New York Quarantine Protocols. Still, I Facetimed with my sister and her family at every opportunity.

Time moves quickly. Days, weeks, and months even blur together like memories of a life I watch from the outside.

The only good thing about time slipping away from me at rapid speeds is The Room has stopped controlling my dreams as much. Maybe the real-life horror film we are all living in is enough to stop the nightmares from being so persistent.

Even when I go for months without a visit to The Room, somehow, I can still feel Charlie not so far away. He is always there in the back of my mind, haunting my memories. I'm not sure I'll ever be able to rid myself of him completely.

48

Chapter Forty-Eight

I put the finishing touches on my makeup, admiring the way the bold red lip color pops against my skin. There's something about getting ready this morning that makes me feel lighter as if the universe is finally giving me permission to exhale.

After all these months, Mei is finally home. I can't stop smiling as I stare at my reflection in the mirror, twisting the lipstick cap with a satisfying click.

"Remember, we are eating at Mei's tonight!" I call out into the apartment, excitement bubbling in my chest.

I can't wait to see her, to hear her voice in person instead of through a screen.

Thorne appears in the doorway, leaning casually with his arms crossed, a small smile tugging at the corner of his lips. "You girls should go. Cam and I can stay home with Mavey," he suggests.

I shoot him a flirty grin, holding up the lipstick like a weapon of persuasion. "And why would we do that?"

"It's been forever since the three of you were together," he replies coolly. "Plus, Cam could use some bro time."

"Yeah, I guess Vi could use a mommy break. She's been running on fumes," I say.

Violet would never admit it, but she needs the night off.

I grab my phone and text her, and the response comes almost instantly.

"She agrees," I say, leaning up to kiss his cheek. "That's from Vi."

His laugh is soft, and I float around the apartment, joy and disbelief coursing through me. I can't believe that tonight I'll be sitting in the same room with my three favorite people, that the long stretch of distance and missed moments will finally end.

"I've missed them so much," I whisper.

"After dinner, maybe we'll meet you at Cam's so Mei can meet her new nephew," I offer.

Thorne nods, his eyes crinkling at the edges. "Good idea."

I graze the roughness of his scruff. "You gonna shave before heading out?"

He rubs his chin, considering it for a moment. "I don't know. I think I'd look pretty good with a beard."

I lean in, just about to kiss him, but stop short with a teasing smirk. "Guess you just don't want any more kisses from your loving wife, then."

Thorne groans in mock defeat, heading toward the bathroom.

I can't help but grin when I hear the familiar hiss of the shaving cream can.

Moments later, he returns, freshly shaven, and immediately rubs his smooth face against mine.

"You're going to ruin my makeup!" I squeal through laughter, gently shoving him away.

"Fine, fine," he teases, backing off with a mischievous glint in his eyes.

He grabs his wallet, phone, and keys, moving toward the door. "I have to go to the restaurant and process our deliveries. Then I'm going to pick up some pizza and beers on the way to Cam's."

"Sounds good," I say. "I am going to Sam's to get some work done, then I'll head over to Mei's."

I glance at my phone, but before I lose myself in the distraction, Thorne lifts my chin gently, guiding my eyes back to his.

"Have fun tonight," he says. "You deserve it."

I smile up at him, feeling my heart swell. "You too, baby."

We share a soft, lingering kiss, and then he presses his forehead against mine. It's such a small gesture, but it's us. Our rhythm. Our way of reminding each other that we're still here, still together.

"See you soon, Junebug," he whispers before walking out the door.

49

Chapter Forty-Nine

The ground feels unforgiving—rough, hot, cold, all at once. I don't know how I ended up here, sprawled face-down on the asphalt, but it is scraping against my skin, and the taste of iron fills my mouth.

Blood.

My blood.

I blink, trying to make sense of the chaos around me. Flames lick at the night sky in the distance, painting everything in a fiery glow, and the heat radiates over me, but somehow, I'm still cold—shivering, trembling, like my body can't decide if it's burning or freezing.

My head pounds, each throb sending waves of nausea through me.

I lift my hand, my muscles screaming in protest, and manage to bring it to my face. My fingers come away slick with blood. What happened?

I try to piece it together, to rewind the events in my mind, but everything is jumbled—a blur of lights and sound, Mei's laughter, the screech of tires, and then... nothing.

Nothing but pain.

I force myself to move, to push up from the ground, but my body refuses. I can't feel my legs, my arms are too heavy, and every breath feels like a knife plunging into my chest.

Panic surges through me, clawing its way up my throat. I glance across the pavement, desperate for some sign of life, and that's when I see her.

Violet.

She's lying just a few feet away, her face smeared with blood, a jagged gash slashed across her face. Her eyes are closed, but her expression looks almost peaceful, as if she's just resting, and none of this is real.

No. No, no, no. "Vi-" I croak.

The effort sends white-hot pain shooting through my chest. I try to reach for her, my fingers scraping uselessly against the pavement, but my body won't cooperate. I can't move. I can't get to her.

"Vi!" I try again, louder this time.

A shadow looms over me, blocking my view of her, and panic explodes in my chest. I can't see her anymore. I can't see if she's breathing. I need to know if she's okay—she has to be okay.

"Ma'am, stay still." An EMT kneels in front of me, their voice calm but firm.

"No, my sister, she's deaf—"

My words come out in a rasp as I try to push him away to get past him to Violet, but the EMT holds me in place.

"We're going to flip you onto a backboard now. You need to stay calm."

His words barely register. I can't think about anything but Violet and Mei—*where's Mei?*

They lift me, the motion sending a fresh wave of agony through my body.

My vision blurs, the world tilting and spinning, but I manage to choke out the words, "My sister. Mei. Please."

"We're getting you to the hospital," an EMT says, their voice distant like it's coming from underwater. "Just stay with me, okay?"

But I'm not with them. I'm not even here. My mind is stuck on that one moment—Vi's smiling face, Mei's laughter, the warmth of their presence so close, now ripped away.

The sirens scream around me, drowning out everything else.

I hear people shouting, but I can't focus on any of it.

The night sky is smeared with blue and red lights. The stars should be there—bright, beautiful—but they're gone, drowned out by the chaos.

Somewhere in the distance, I hear the faint notes of Violet's song. She's okay. She has to be.

Black and yellow, black and yellow, black and yellow.

But I can't see her. I can't see anything anymore.

Darkness creeps in at the edges of my vision, and my body feels like it's slipping from me and floating away. The pain is fading, numbing, as if my mind is retreating somewhere far from this broken, twisted reality.

"Stay with me," the EMT urges again, but it's fading now too.

My last thought before everything goes black is of Violet, her face smeared with blood and Mei's laughter echoing in the distance. The memory of them—so close, yet so far.

And then—nothing.

The world goes silent.

50

Chapter Fifty

I'm floating, drifting in a haze of confusion and pain. The fluorescent lights above flash like a strobe, blinding me as I'm rushed down a cold, sterile hallway on a gurney. *Where am I? What's happening?*

I try to express my fears, but no words come. My throat is dry, and a sharp ache gnaws at my chest. Everything hurts.

I attempt to move, but a brace holds me tight, immobilizing me, and the realization sends panic surging through my veins.

The world around me is a blur—shadows darting in and out of my vision, faces I can't make out.

A woman's voice cuts through the fog.

"What do we got?"

I want to scream, to ask her what's going on, but all I can manage is a faint, muffled sound.

A man responds, clinical and detached, "Female, aged twenty-five to thirty. EMS arrived on the scene and found the patient responsive but confused. Suspected head trauma due to visible contusions on the forehead. The ambulance crew administered spinal immobilization and placed the patient on oxygen at 4L via nasal cannula."

His words wash over me like cold water, each sentence a reminder of the darkness I can't escape.

"What were the vital signs at arrival?" the woman asks.

"BP: 138/85. Heart Rate: 100 bpm. Respiratory Rate: 18 breaths per minute. Oxygen Saturation: 96%. Temperature: 37°C. GCS: 6. Eye: 3, Verbal: 1, Motor: 2."

I cling to those numbers, desperate for something familiar.

The gurney suddenly stops moving, and someone lifts my eyelids. I squint against the blinding light, but I can't see the woman's face—just a silhouette against the glare.

"Pupils: Equal, round, and reactive to light," she says.

I feel something tugging at my shirt, then a cold touch against my chest.

"Heart sounds normal but tachycardic," she continues, the coldness shifting to my ribcage. "Airway patent, breathing spontaneously, lungs clear bilaterally."

Then, a sharp jab pierces my arm, followed by another in my leg. I wince, but I can't react; my body won't obey.

"Full body paralysis noted, no voluntary movement in limbs. Multiple abrasions noted on the forehead and upper body," the man adds.

"Let's get a CT of head and neck, X-rays of chest and extremities, and some blood work. CBC, BMP, and a coagulation panel," the woman orders steadily.

I can sense the urgency beneath her calm exterior.

The world fades in and out of darkness, and I realize I'm struggling to maintain consciousness.

I'm poked and prodded like livestock, and strangely, I long for Charlie to be the one to take care of me. He has always been much more gentle and less rushed than the various medical staff rushing to and from my bedside.

After what feels like hours of tests and scans, I am exhausted as I'm rolled into a dim and cold room.

Thorne rushes into the room, still wearing the same clothes I kissed him goodbye in this morning. I try to say something, but I can't produce any sounds.

Over the next few hours, he sits for a bit and then switches to anxiously pacing the room.

I want to stay present for him, but I can't help when my eyes flicker shut.

My eyes are closed, but I feel a strange sense of relief knowing I'm in The Room. The beeping of the machines now calms my brain like white noise.

I hear Charlie walking around, so I open my eyes and search for him. But I'm not where I thought I was.

The room is dark, and I'm alone. The footsteps I thought were Charlie's were just staff passing by in the hallway.

My skull feels like it's caving in, and I can barely gather my thoughts. *Where is Thorne? Did he leave me here?*

Thankfully, before I have time to panic, he returns with a doctor. I recognize her as the woman who ordered my tests upon arrival.

"I want to discuss your wife's test results with you," she says, ushering him into a seat.

Her words are formal and serious, but she delivers the bad news with ease. "The accident has caused damage to specific parts of your wife's brain. Upon arrival, we did an MRI, and it showed evidence of a moderate brain stem injury, particularly in the ventral pons region."

"What does that mean?" Thorne asks, but he sounds desperate. "She'll get better, right?"

"At this point"— she shifts her soft gaze between Thorne and me— "it's hard to say. She has significant edema surrounding her brain stem. Due to the swelling, we can't tell if there's any permanent damage yet. We need to watch her for at least forty-eight hours and see if the swelling starts to subside."

Thorne breaks into a painful sob that crumbles the dam of my own emotions. I want to scream. I need to know where Violet is. I need to get out of here.

"We'll continue to run tests every few hours to keep up with her progress," the doctor says hopefully. "Until we have more answers, you can keep talking to her, keeping her alert. Her scans show that she's retained at least a level of cognitive awareness. Take comfort in knowing that she knows who you are."

"Comfort," he says, defeated.

He walks to my bedside and lightly grabs my hand. "I'll be here no matter what."

Thorne talks to me, but I can't make out what he's saying. I have the worst headache of my life, and it's taking all my effort not to throw up. I don't know how to describe a feeling that is the worst pain possible but also completely numb at the same time, but this is it.

My vision fades, and all noises blend into the background. I know this feeling. I know what's coming.

My muscles contract, and my jaw clenches down tight. The same thing has happened previously in The Room. I'm having a seizure.

I start convulsing hard as my body slams on the bed.

In the distance, I hear Thorne's panic as he yells into the hallway for help.

"CODE BLUE, ROOM 312, CODE BLUE."

I can't hold on anymore. I'm too tired.

Where am I? It's pitch black, and I feel cold. *Am I dying?*

"Hey, buddy!" I hear my husband's voice break through the silence.

Immediately, I call out to him.

"I'm here!" I scream, my throat hoarse. "Where are you?"

He draws closer and closer.

"I can't see you. I'm lost, Thorne."

He's talking to someone, he can't hear me.

"I'm here," I say, more defeated this time. "Don't leave me."

I sit in the abyss of darkness and cry harder than I have in a long time.

I'm still surrounded by darkness. I don't know how long I've been here in this state of "in-between." Sometimes, I hear people talking. Other times, I'm completely alone with just my intrusive thoughts for company.

Time is not my friend. I know that now. Has it been hours? Days? Weeks? I can't tell anymore.

From the darkness, I hear a child playing. I reach out into the blackness that surrounds me. I need to find someone, something, to get me out of here.

The child laughs, and I can tell I'm getting closer.

Then I hear Thorne again, recognizable immediately. "Yeah, your auntie is taking a long nap," he says.

He sounds exhausted. I can tell he's putting on a brave face.

"She'll be so excited to see you when she wakes up."

Auntie? My nephew! My nephew is here.

I call out into the darkness again, "Where are you guys?" I feel around me. There's absolutely nothing here.

"Can I have a moment alone, please?" A familiar voice breaks through.

"Of course, Mrs. Wong. Take as long as you need," Thorne sounds calm, speaking to her. "The little guy and I will head down to the cafeteria and grab some snacks. What do you think about that?"

Maverick giggles in response.

For a moment, I'm surrounded by so much silence that I assume I'm alone again.

The voices come, and the voices go.

"Hey, Rosie." Mrs. Wong breaks through again.

I can't explain it, but I want to cry. She's been like a mom to me ever since my biological mother died, and right now is one of those "I need my mom" moments.

"You need to come back now." She's direct as always, but there's a hint of emotion I hadn't quite heard before.

"I'm trying." I sniffle. "I'm trying."

"We've all lost so much."

I hadn't heard Mrs. Wong cry since four days after my mom's funeral, and I recognize the sound immediately.

"We can't lose you too, Rose. We can't."

Her words sink in, but no matter how hard I try, I can't remember what happened.

"I never told you how proud I have always been of you girls. Now I fear I've missed my chances to..." Her voice trails off.

My heart is breaking.

"Nobody blames you for anything, Rosie. What happened..." She is silent for a moment. "It wasn't your fault. We all need you to come back. Especially your husband. He's not doing well without you."

For the first time, from the endless darkness, I feel someone touch my hand. Mrs. Wong is reaching for me, pulling me out. But when I try to hold her, she's gone.

I use everything I have to reach out in the darkness. It's working. There's a crack of light breaking up the blackness that has surrounded me for who knows how long.

When I open my eyes, I'm blinded by the overhead hospital lights, but they are blocked almost immediately by a man's face.

"Oh my God, you're awake!" He runs into the hall, disappearing from sight. "She's awake! Nurses, please. She's awake!"

People grab me, touch me, and stab me with needles.

I'm being transported in and out of different rooms, loaded and unloaded into a variety of machines. I can't remember how I got here.

My heart races until I'm settled back into a room by myself.

After a while, the man from before and a woman wearing scrubs enter the room.

"How's she doing?" the man asks.

"Please sit," the woman offers, directing him to the chair in the corner. "As you know, she slipped into a comatose state approximately sixty-three hours ago after experiencing a severe seizure. Now that she has awakened, she is exhibiting signs of full-body paralysis and seems completely unable to communicate at this point."

"Is this just a temporary side effect from having such a difficult seizure?" he asks.

"The paralysis does appear to be a result of the seizure; however, her brain is showing signs of injury to her hippocampus. Meaning her recovery may be slowed. I still hold out a positive prognosis in the long term despite these results."

"This injury..." He pauses. "To the hippo—-"

"Hippocampus," she steps in. "That's the area of the brain that converts our short-term memories into long-term memories. While monitoring your wife's brain activity, we found decreased activation and evidence of shearing injuries in the white matter tracts connecting the hippocampus to the prefrontal cortex, which we believe may be resulting in some retrograde amnesia. We plan to keep a close eye on her brain activity during her healing process. But I must advise you that we may see her memory recall get worse before it gets better."

"Amnesia?" He sounds like the wind has been knocked out of his lungs. "But... you said before that she would know who I am, who her family is."

"That was before she went comatose."

I hear a sense of guilt.

"But we aren't without hope. At the seventy-two-hour mark, we performed another MRI, which showed a significant reduction in brain edema, especially around the brain stem. Now that the swelling has reduced, we can find no signs of permanent ischemic injury or diffuse axonal injury, which would have greatly worsened her situation."

"That's good, right?" A small hope returns. "If it's not permanent, that means she'll get better—"

She cuts him off before his hopes get too high. "The current outlook for substantial recovery is favorable. With intensive rehabilitation therapies, she may experience a gradual recovery of motor functions. In the long-term, full recovery of mobility and speech functions are not guaranteed but does remain plausible, given her early signs of improvement and brain healing."

"Ok..." He hesitates. "Let's start rehab right away. The sooner she's back to herself, the better."

"I understand your desire, I do," she says calmly. "But it's important to have realistic expectations of her progress. The retrograde amnesia adds a complicated layer to an already difficult diagnosis. While most patients are able to experience initial gains in hand and facial movements rather quickly, she may not be able to replicate the same results."

"I don't understand."

"Rehabilitation results rely heavily on a level of trust and cooperation with caregivers, therapists, and even immediate family members. I—" She hesitates, collecting herself. "In the past few hours, Rose's memory recall has seen a significant decline. When she was first admitted, she attempted to communicate and cooperate with her care team. However, during her recent tests, we had to take several breaks. Her fear and distrust of the doctors were causing her heart rate to spike to dangerous levels. We can't allow her heart to stay elevated. She is at an extremely high risk for blood clots. Honestly, I don't think her brain can handle another injury. She has already been through so much. We will have to work on her terms to protect her overall health best."

"Which means…" He trails off. "If her memory doesn't improve, she may never cooperate with her therapies."

The doctor nods. "She's a fighter. All she's been through, and she still hasn't given up. We can't give up on her first. You have a long road ahead of you both, but in my professional opinion, I believe the worst is already behind us."

"So what do we do now?"

"For the next twenty-four to forty-eight hours, we want her to get as much rest as possible. Her brain needs time to heal. After that, we will complete some more scans. At that point, we should be able to start her rehabilitation. As soon as she's stable, we will do everything we can to get her ready to go home."

The man nods.

"I'm going to check on some of my other patients and will return in a couple hours to check her vitals. In the meantime, keep talking to her. It's important for patients with amnesia to be surrounded by familiar family and friends. That's why we want to try to get her stable enough to return home. Being in the comfort of her normal surroundings should help her brain to start putting the pieces of the puzzle back together."

"Ok." He sighs. "Thank you, doctor. For everything."

51

Chapter Fifty-One

*N*o. No. No.

I need to go back! Something terrible has happened, and everything I love is slipping away from me. I feel numb inside. I'm an empty shell where hope used to live.

Charlie enters the room, his presence more calming than being surrounded by hospital staff.

He looks... worse than I've ever seen him. His hair is unkempt, his beard wild and overgrown. He is pale, and his green eyes are buried in dark circles.

Charlie's eyes meet mine, and there's a flicker of something. Recognition? Relief? Despair? I can't tell.

"You're awake." His words fall flat, but he does attempt to smile. "You've been... gone for four days," he says quietly, not meeting my gaze. "I thought I lost you this time."

This time. The words ring in my ears. *This time?*

I try to process it, but the exhaustion from my real life's recent events weighs heavy on me, clouding my mind.

Charlie's hands tremble as he adjusts my equipment. His eyes are red and puffy, as if he's been crying for the entire four days.

"I thought this was it," he says. "I thought you were never coming back this time. I don't know what I would've done if you..."

He explains everything. How long I've been out, how hard it's been for him. But there's something more. I can tell he's on the verge of a mental breakdown.

"I thought..." He trails off. "I thought that if you didn't come back this time, that"—he wipes his eyes on the sleeve of his flannel shirt— "if you didn't come back, it meant I could finally move on with my life. That I wouldn't be stuck here, doing this." He gestures dramatically toward all of the medical equipment to me.

"But I was wrong." Charlie looks me dead in the eyes now. "You slipped into another coma, and instead of viewing the time in the hospital as a break, I sat beside your bed for four days, crying my eyes out, praying that you wake up."

He sounds almost agitated, and I can't tell if he's upset with me or the situation.

"I had four days to do whatever I wanted, to live my life!" He softens. "But I couldn't leave you alone. The thought of not being there when you woke up... I couldn't do that to you. Despite you always looking at me like I'm some terrifying stranger, I couldn't give up the hope that you'd wake up and finally recognize me."

Charlie paces the room now, running his fingers through his hair. He's practically rambling like a madman, but I'm lost in my own confusion. How could I have been in the hospital here and in my real life? I can't tell what's real anymore.

"What does that make me?" He yells, but not out of anger. Frustration, maybe. "A glutton for punishment? I can't go a single day without my wife, but she can go months without ever recognizing my face."

He throws a trinket from the TV stand against the wall. It shatters into a million little pieces. "I didn't mean that," he says regretfully. "I know it's not your fault."

Charlie comes close to me, so close I can feel his breath on my skin. "Do you remember me, Junie? Do you recognize me at all?"

I stare at his face, trying hard not to blink. If I say no now, I have no idea how he'll react.

Just then, the unknown cat leaps onto my hospital bed, and I'm struck by the familiarity of its face. It looks just like Dolly—older, fatter, but unmistakably my cat.

"Let me guess," he says. "You suddenly remember Dolly?"

Blink.

That's my cat.

My recognition of that fact destroys the last bit of emotional fortitude Charlie has left. He crumbles into the chair beside the bed.

"I shouldn't be surprised, I guess. The doctor says you're progressing really well now," he admits, wiping away a tear that escapes down his cheek. "She said you should start remembering bits and pieces of your life. Part of me just hoped that it'd be me, ya know?"

Charlie is silent for a minute. "I just... I thought I'd have you back by now."

For a long while, he just sits there quietly, his head in his hands.

"Mei had it wrong, you know?" He looks at me with the saddest green eyes I've ever seen. "That day we met, and you told her about me. Remember?"

My brain frantically runs through memories. How does he know Mei? When did Charlie and I meet? I told Mei about him?

"She told you 'Every Rose has it's Thorne." He sighs, his voice heavy with longing. "She was wrong, though. This Thorne needs his Rose more than anything in the world. I would give anything just to have you remember me, even for just a moment."

Charlie's head falls onto my arm, soaking me with tears. "Please come back to me, Rose. I can't do this without you."

At his words, the world around me blurs, and the room trembles with the weight of what he's saying.

My mind races, waves of understanding crashing down on me. Charlie is Thorne. I am Rose. I am his Junebug.

"It is my greatest pleasure to introduce the newly married Mr. and Mrs. Charlie and Rose Thorne." I hear Cam's voice in my head clear as day.

The memories come flooding back.

I can't believe I didn't see it before.

I glance around the room—it's not just a sterile hospital space; it's home. This is the same apartment where we spent our first night together. I can almost hear our laughter echoing off the walls.

Tears threaten to spill as I look at him. How can I let him know it's really me?

I blink—once, twice, three times, my heart pounding with urgency.

Finally, Charlie's eyes lock onto mine, searching for a flicker of recognition.

I blink slowly, deliberately, until I muster the strength to communicate.

.- .-.. .-- .- -.-- ... / -.-- --- ..- .-. / .-. --- ... .

His expression shifts, eyes wide with fear and hope. "Did you say something?"

I move my eyes up and down in a nodding motion, internally begging him to pay attention.

.- .-.. .-- .- -.-- ... / -.-- --- ..- .-. / .-. --- ... . (ALWAYS YOUR ROSE).

I blink once more, my emotions welling inside me.

.. / .-.. --- ...- . / -.-- --- ..- (I LOVE YOU).

"I love you more, Junebug," he whispers, collapsing onto me.

Thorne's embrace wraps around my broken pieces, slowly stitching them together.

"I knew you'd come back. I knew it."

When he finally gathers himself, he looks deeply into my eyes, and I hear his grief. "I'm so happy to see you."

.-. . .- .-.. / .-.. .. ..-. . ..-..

(REAL LIFE)? I manage to blink out.

His answer hangs in the air, heavy with sorrow. "Yeah, baby. I'm sorry. This is real life."

I blink again. .-- .... .- - / .... .- .--. .--. . -.. -.. ..-.. (WHAT HAPPENED)?

"You still don't remember?"

I move my eyes from side to side, the confusion thickening like fog.

"You were hit by a drunk driver. You, Violet, and Mei."

The words strike like a physical blow.

"You had a brain injury that caused a lot of swelling. You ended up in a coma, and when you woke up, the doctors said you had Locked-In Syndrome. But the long-term prognosis was good; they expected a complete or mostly complete recovery." He hesitates, and my heart races. "But... the problem was that you were also suffering from amnesia. At first, you were sleeping a lot. You panicked during therapy, causing your heart rate to spike. Because you were at high risk for blood clots, they had to give you medicines that kept you asleep to not risk another TBI. I hated doing that to you," he confesses.

The pain in his voice pierces me.

As the memories flood back, I see flashes of my life—the accident, the chaos, the blurred faces. I remember lying on the side of the road, my sister's bloody face.

...- .. --- .-... . - ..--.. (VIOLET)? I blink rapidly, panic coursing through me as I stare at Charlie.

His head drops, and I watch helplessly as his shoulders shake. "I'm so sorry, Junie," he chokes out.

My heart shatters at the sound of his sobs. I killed my sister. The realization settles like a stone in my chest. I was the one driving.

-- . ... (MEI)?

I blink again, desperation clawing at me.

He wipes his nose on his sleeve. "Mei... was on life support for a very long time. Mrs. Wong wanted you to be able to say goodbye. She even came to see you, hoping that having family near would bring you back. But the weeks turned into months, and you weren't responding to the memory treatments as quickly as expected. The doctors recommended surrounding you with things you'd recognize from your life before. I tried. I really tried. But Mrs. Wong made the decision after three months to take Mei off life support. I'm sorry you weren't there, Junie."

My heart plummets, the weight of his words suffocating me. I killed my two favorite people in the world. I didn't get to say goodbye. I didn't even get to go to their funerals. Why? Because my mind was lost in this make-believe nightmare? I was so busy convincing myself that I was fine that I couldn't be there for the people who needed me the most.

I blink, a resolve is forming within me. .... . .-... .--. / -- .

(HELP ME).

I've been avoiding the truth. The grief. The pain of losing Violet, losing Mei, and losing myself for too long. But now that I'm awake, I know there's no escaping it. I have to face it head-on.

I close my eyes again, but this time, not to drift away. This time, I'm diving inward. I accept my current situation for what it is.

Tears slip down my cheeks as the painful truths creep in.

Violet and Mei are gone. I'll never hear Violet's laughter again, never see her smile light up a room. I'll never have another movie marathon with my sisters. I'll never receive another piece of Mei's sage advice.

The steady calm and clarity she always brought to my life is gone forever. My life will never be the same.

They are gone, and no matter how much I try to scream or how much I beg God to bring them back to me, I will never see them again.

I want to reach out and pull them back, but my hands are empty. Everything I ever knew, everything I ever loved, has slipped through my fingers.

I'm drowning in it, the grief, the unbearable ache of knowing that I will never feel whole again. I sob until I can't breathe anymore. The pain in my chest is so sharp I fear it might kill me. And maybe it should. Because how am I supposed to keep going in a world without them? How am I supposed to wake up every day knowing that they won't be there? That I will never see their faces, never hear their voices, never feel their love again?

It's a hollow, endless ache that sits in my bones, in my blood, in every breath I take. I am broken and irreparably shattered. And no amount of time, no amount of healing, will ever make this okay. They are gone, and so is a part of me I'll never get back. It's like ripping off a bandage to find the wound is still raw, and it hurts more than I ever thought possible. But I can't run from it anymore. Not now. Not after everything.

If I could, I would trade places with them in a heartbeat. Maverick St. Wren deserves to know his mother, and Violet should be with her son. And Mei... Mei was a better person than I could ever hope to be.

Despite my regrets, I know my sisters would not want me to think this way. If they were here, they'd tell me to live my life to the fullest, to live for them. And that's exactly what I'm going to do.

52

CHAPTER FIFTY-TWO

"Take your time," Charlie whispers, brushing a strand of hair from my forehead. His hands, steady and gentle, ground me in the moment.

I'm really awake this time. No more dreams. No more nightmares.

"I know you can do this," he urges.

My legs tremble as I try to take the first step after months of physical therapy. My calves ache as I slowly place my weight on one foot in front of the other. I'm doing it.

I give everything I have and more. I push through the exhaustion, and I refuse to give in. I have to keep going. I have to get better. For them.

The physical therapy has been brutal. Every movement feels like a monumental effort, and some days, I just want to collapse and cry. But I push through.

With each session, I feel myself growing stronger. The first time I regained control of my hands, it was like something inside me unlocked. I'm finally able to sign again. Slowly, shakily, but it's there. My voice may still be lost, but I can communicate in the way Violet taught me. I think if she were here, she'd be proud of me.

My husband has been there for every step. And I mean every literal step. He's patient. Kind. He takes care of me, and I finally realize just how much he's sacrificed, how much he's done for me while I was lost in that dream world.

One night, after a particularly grueling day, I look at him and sign, "Thank you."

He smiles softly, eyes shining. "You don't have to thank me, Rose. If I had the option to go back, I wouldn't even consider another choice."

But I shake my head. I want him to know how much it means to me. He's been my anchor, my lifeline. If I hadn't had him by my side, I think I would've given up a long time ago.

When I think of my memories from "The Room," I can't help but feel a twinge of guilt. For six months, I treated the man I love like my enemy. Even when I was unconscious for days at a time, he never mistreated me.

He's since told me how hard it was not to touch me, to kiss me, to love me like we had before the accident. He once told me through tears of guilt how terrible he felt for the day he almost took advantage of me.

Charlie broke down thinking about how terrified I must've been of him in those moments.

I told him honestly that there were many times I felt absolute terror but that it wasn't his fault. He was learning to cope, just like I was.

Mainly, I feel bad for all the awful thoughts I had about him during those times.

We still laugh when we talk about how I thought that version of Charlie was a murderer, a rapist, a kidnapper, etc. The brain does un-explainable things when it's dealing with overwhelming trauma.

Despite everything, I think our relationship has grown for the better. Our romance has blossomed again, but it's different this time. Deeper. More real. He understands me in ways no one else ever could, and I trust him more than anyone could understand.

I wish I could have the six months I lost with him back. I wish I could go back and figure out how to wake up earlier. But I can't. I, we, can only move forward. Together.

With my regained mobility, we decide it is time to reopen the restaurant fully, and this time, I'll be by his side.

We honor Violet by displaying her art throughout the space. There's something healing about it, like she's still with us, watching over everything. I can almost feel her with me every time I enter the restaurant.

Together, Thorne and I create a photo wall around the hostess stand. A corner of the restaurant to remind us of all the people who have loved us into being who we are.

We hang a photo of the five greatest friends ever to be seen in human history. A polaroid of my mother, Joy Wiese-Piper, with Violet and I as small niblets. A selfie of Sam and Thorne proudly holding up Dolly on the surprise adoption day. A caricature drawing of Charlie, Georgie, and I from our trip to Six Flags. By the time we have hung all our memories, we are surrounded from floor to ceiling.

I stare at all the images, and tears come to my eyes. In all of space and time, I had the privilege of having these people as my chosen family, even if it was only for a little while. How could I have been so lucky?

I stare closer at the image of my mother. All ability to maintain composure flies out the window. **"Thanks, Mom,"** I sign as I gently press my fingertips to her face. **"You had my back even when I lost my mind."**

I wipe the tears from my eyes. **"I miss you."**

I glance up and down the entire gallery. **"I miss you all."**

Charlie comes up behind me and places a lingering kiss on the back of my shoulder. "I miss them too," he says.

He wraps his arms around my midsection and tucks my head under his chin. "They would be so proud of you and all the progress you've made."

"You think?" I sniffle, tilting my head up to look at him.

"I know so," he whispers, planting a kiss on my forehead. "Come help me put the finishing touches on the dining room," he suggests as he pulls me behind him.

Our grand opening is this Saturday, but tonight, the restaurant is open by invitation only: a family dinner in Violet and Mei's honor.

Cam and Maverick Wren arrive first, then Mr. and Mrs. Wong. Every person here has experienced the most painful loss of all time, and there is a level of understanding and love among these people. We are bonded by the ones no longer with us.

After dinner, we go around the table, each of us sharing our favorite memories of the beautiful women who had been taken from us far too soon.

Wren looks up at me with tears in his eyes. "What was mommy's favoritest thing in the whole world?"

I caress his face and look into his eyes, the big green eyes that he got from my sister. It is such an easy answer, but it takes every bit of strength I have to respond.

For the first time in fifteen months, I open my mouth, my throat sore, my voice hoarse. "You."

53

CHAPTER FIFTY-THREE

With my husband's assistance, I walk into Sam's coffee shop. The entire barista staff cheers.

Sam approaches me and plants a friendly kiss on my cheek. "Welcome back, Rose. The cafe hasn't been the same without you."

"It's good to be back," I squeak.

The coffee shop is the same, but I feel so different.

We sit in our usual spot, the corner booth by the window, where we shared more memories than I had originally remembered. Charlie's hand rests on mine, and I glance at him with a smile.

Within just a matter of minutes, Sam delivers my usual order. I pull the cup to my face and take a long inhale of that sweet aroma. **"Hello, old friend,"** I sign to my cup.

Charlie chuckles at me.

"Do you remember that I would bring your latte home and set it beside the hospital bed while you were still recovering?"

"Really?" I say, surprised.

"Yeah." He seems... embarrassed. "I was desperate, okay? I was trying anything even remotely familiar to try to bring you back to me."

"Well, I'm back now, and I'm never leaving again." I reach up to his face, and he leans forward and kisses me long and hard.

"So," he says. "What's next?"

I look out the window, watching the world move on. For the first time in what feels like forever, I don't feel like I'm stuck. I no longer feel trapped in a dream I can't wake up from. I'm here. I'm alive. And though the grief still lingers, though the loss of Violet and Mei still weighs on my heart, I know I'll be okay. I have Thorne. I have my memories. And most importantly, I have myself.

I look back at Thorne, squeezing his hand gently. **"Whatever comes next,"** I say, signing with a quiet confidence. **"I'm ready."**

And for the first time, I believe it.

54

SURVIVING THE IMPOSSIBLE

MY JOURNEY WITH LOCKED-IN SYNDROME

BY ROSE THORNE, STAFF WRITER AT THE MANHATTAN BEACON

One man's reckless choice set off a chain reaction that shattered lives, mine included. In an instant, everything I knew was gone. This is the story of how one moment changed everything—how I was forced to rebuild, face my grief, and find hope in the wreckage.

Eighteen months ago, a man decided to get behind the wheel of his truck even though he was extremely intoxicated. That man's actions stole the two most important people in my world away from me and left me with injuries so severe that I became trapped inside my own body.

On October 21st, 2022, that same man was sentenced to fifty-five years in prison for two counts of Aggravated Vehicular Homicide and one count of Assault in the Second Degree.

For days following the accident, the news swirled with stories of this man's life prior to getting behind that wheel with a blood alcohol level of 0.24%.

The press ran stories including details such as a man driving 85 MPH in a 40 MPH zone had run multiple red lights ending in a deadly crash, the lifesaving efforts of two fire stations, the police response on sight only three minutes after the first 911 call, and the EMTs who did their best with what they had.

Not one story spoke for the side of the victims. Yes, "a woman was pronounced DOA," but that woman was my beautiful sister, Violet. There was no mention of the "Brooklyn Art Academy for the Deaf and Blind" that she co-founded in 2021.

No one explained the blood-curdling cries of the three-year-old who was just told his mommy wouldn't be coming home. Or the loneliness that her husband Cameron had to deal with each night going to bed alone.

Yes, "a woman was taken off life support after being in a vegetative state for 3 months." That was my best friend, Mei. No one mentioned how her parents sat beside her hospital bed every single day for those three months while their restaurant suffered and threatened to close.

There were no comments about how she learned to administer COVID-19 vaccines on the frontlines in Wuhan during the worst pandemic in recent history or how Mei risked her life every day for the greater good just to be killed by a drunk, reckless driver just hours after arriving back in her home country.

And, yes. There was "a sole surviving victim of the accident." Me.

In the first six months after the accident, my brain created a false reality to protect me from the magnitude of loss that I wasn't ready to face. I wasn't surviving or coping with my new circumstances; I was hiding.

My mind splintered, forming a world where I could remain unaware of the devastating truth. For months, I couldn't even recognize the man who was caring for me—my husband, Charlie Thorne. In my confusion and pain, I believed him to be a captor, a villain. But in reality, he was my greatest protector, standing by me every single day, nursing me with a love I was too broken to recognize.

The path back to reality was grueling. When I finally woke up and realized all that had happened, the grief was nearly too much to bear. My mental health threatened to shatter once again. My sisters were gone, and I would never get a chance to say goodbye, never feel their warmth, or share another memory with them. Every moment was filled with the weight of that loss.

I wasn't just waging a war for my body. I was in a battle to save my soul. Through the haze of grief, a part of me fought to survive.

I learned firsthand the amount of trauma a nervous system can handle before it starts to break. I was constantly confronted by the frustration of not being able to communicate or express even the simplest of thoughts. I almost didn't make it out alive.

There were days I wish I hadn't. But over time, with therapy and support, the impossible became possible. Small movements in my fingers became a lifeline, proof that I couldn't give up yet.

For months, I poured every ounce of my energy into my recovery. I spent hours each day learning to control my body again, relearning how to move and how to speak.

Functional electrical stimulation (FES), robotic therapies, and intensive speech therapy helped bring me back to life. And slowly, piece by piece, I reclaimed myself.

The physical recovery was only part of the journey. The emotional healing has been just as hard, if not harder. Accepting that Violet and Mei are gone is a pain I can never describe. I will never see their faces again, never hear Violet's laugh or share a secret with Mei.

There are days when that grief still consumes me, but I've learned that healing doesn't mean forgetting. My love for them will always be with me, and I honor their memory by continuing to live for them.

Today, I've regained almost full motor function. I walk, I talk, I work. I've picked up painting in honor of my sister, something I thought I'd never be able to do again. It's a tribute to the love we shared and the strength I've gained. I even help teach classes at her art school so that her dreams can live on.

Through it all, I've learned that recovery is not just about regaining what was lost but finding the strength to live with what's left. My journey with LIS has been the hardest war of my life, but it's also shown me the incredible resilience of the human spirit.

Locked-In syndrome is a rare and devastating condition, affecting roughly 1 to 5 in every 1 million people globally. With the help of modern technology, medical care, and emotional support, many LIS patients regain some form of communication, and some even experience partial recovery of motor functions. Quality of life for these individuals can improve over time, and survival rates are significantly better with appropriate care.

I treat every single day as a blessing, fully aware that the odds for a full recovery were not in my favor. My hope for the future is that all patients struggling with LIS can have the same hopeful prognosis I was given.

I've started a charity called The Daisy Chain in honor of Violet and Mei, dedicated to supporting LIS research and offering resources to families affected by this devastating condition. I want to be a beacon of hope, to show that even when you're locked in, there is a way out. One small step at a time.

If you or someone you love is facing LIS, please know that you're not alone. The journey is long, but recovery may be possible. Keep fighting. We are stronger than we think.

—Rose Thorne

55

AUTHOR'S NOTE

Thank you so much for reading The Daisy Chain Reaction. I hope you fell in love with the characters and felt the emotions of their journey. Want to see Rose's story from her loved ones' point of view? Make sure you read The Daisy Chain Collapse, available on 01/01/2026.

As an indie author, it absolutely makes my day to hear feedback, comments, and receive character art. If you have anything you like to share, feel free to reach out to me at atasignl@gmail.com and you'll get a response from me!

Indie authors are nothing without our reviews. So if you'd be willing to leave a review on Goodreads and Amazon, it would mean the world to me. https://www.goodreads.com

If you make a video review on TikTok or Instagram, please tag me in it and I'll help boost your video.

https://www.tiktok.com/@acnightingale

Thank you for your support!

MORSE CODE PUZZLE

SOLVE THE CLUES FOR A SNEAK PEAK OF BOOK 2

Alphabet | Numbers

A · —
B — · · ·
C — · — ·
D — · ·
E ·
F · · — ·
G — — ·
H · · · ·
I · ·
J · — — —
K — · —
L · — · ·
M — —
N — ·
O — — —
P · — — ·
Q — — · —

S · · ·
T —
U · · —
V · · · —
W · — —
X — · · —
Y — · — —
Z — — · ·

1 · — — — —
2 · · — — —
3 · · · — —
4 · · · · —
5 · · · · ·
6 — · · · ·
7 — — · · ·
8 — — — · ·
9 — — — — ·
0 — — — — —

R · — ·

Section 1: Decode the Message

... . - .... / - .... . / ..-. ..- - ..- .-.

. / -.- .. .-.. .-.. . .-.

____

-- .- -..- / .- -. -.. / --. . --- .-. --.

.. . / --. . - / -- .- .-. .-. .. . -..

____

-- --- -- -- -.-- / -. --- / -- --- .-. . /

.... .. -.. . / .- -. -.. / ... . . -.-

____

Section 2: Encode the Message

The Daisy Chain Collapse

__________/________________/

________________/________________

Stay With Me

______________/__________________/____________

Create Your Own Code

Write a message for another reader — or for one of your favorite characters.

Plain text:

Your Morse code: